I0728888

Dysfunctional

ANN MOREAN

Zeta Publishing, Inc
P.O. Box 953
Silver Springs, FL 34489
www.zetapublishing.com

This is a work of fiction. All of the characters, names, incidents, organizations, and dialogue in this novel are either the products of the author's imagination or are used fictitiously.

Ordering Information:
Quantity sales. Special discounts are available on quantity purchases by corporations, associations, and others. For details, contact the publisher at the address above.
Orders by U.S. trade bookstores and wholesalers. Please contact Zeta Publishing: Tel: (352) 694-2553; Fax: (352) 694-1791 or visit www.zetapublishing.com

First published by AuthorHouse in 2014

Rev. Date: 9/5/18

ISBN: 978-1-947191-97-6 (sc)
ISBN: 978-1-947191-98-3 (e)

Library of Congress: 2018954800
Printed in the United States of America

CHAPTER

1

THE OLD FASHIONED WOODEN SWING was swaying back and forth, giving Millie a hypnotic sense of drifting aimlessly in a Netherworld somewhere. Her thoughts drifted back to the past, then to the present. She thought, *I should go to bed; this thinking about the past and dreams of the future is a waste of time.* She was living in the present, which was neither pleasant nor unpleasant, it was like being in limbo. She tried in her mind to separate the reality of her life and the fantasy that would creep into her thoughts when she was alone and sitting quietly.

Of course, she told herself. I would love to live my life differently, but this is the one I'm living and there was no going back and changing anything. I'm a single mother with a daughter and a surrogate mother to my niece and nephew. At least until my sister comes back into their lives and assumes responsibility for them.

So I dream about what life could be.
Doesn't take anything from anyone, doesn't hurt anybody and it doesn't cost anything.—Her dream man was just over average height. He had dark, slightly curly hair that he wears

longer down the collar of his shirt. He has dark—brown eyes that can make a woman feel like she is being softly caressed. His wide mouth and sensuous smile could make a woman's toes curl up in her shoes, but he's not built like the heroes in the romance novels she frequently read. Her dream man is just a tad on the stocky side, with solid, robust, broad shoulders and strong long muscular legs; his hands are big with long, slender fingers. She could close her eyes and visualize him anytime she wanted to. Total recall any time that she chose to daydream. Not that looks were all that important, she also fantasied about his character. He possessed a good sense of humor, he was quick tempered, but the flare ups were short lived. He was loyal, true and made her feel loved and protected. She wouldn't go there with fantasies of having sex with him, that was unsafe and unpredictable. Millie wasn't too sure about that aspect of her dream man.

Hey, I'm good at this dream business. I've practically got it down to a science, she thought, as she got up from the porch swing and went inside, then locked the door. She took a quick shower and donned her skimpy nightie, then checked on her niece Melody and her nephew Paul before she crawled into her bed with her daughter, Terry. She tried to concentrate on nothing, so her mind could go blank and she could fall to sleep.

Millie awakened in the morning to the sound of her alarm clock going off. She took a moment and stretched out languorously. The real motivation that got her to get out of bed was; it was finally Friday. The last day of the work week and payday. She made a mad dash out of bed and swiftly dressed in cut-off Levis and a tee shirt. She quickly ran a brush through her short, dark curly hair, brushed her teeth and splashed cold water on her face, put some lipstick on, then headed for the kitchen. She grabbed the paper sack from the fridge that contained her lunch, just as she heard the horn beeping out in front of her home. Totally in sync, her neighbor, Barb, who was her baby sitter and one of her best friends came out of her apartment next door. Barb, always got Paul and Terry off to school every morning, then dressed Melody and took her to her home for the rest of the day. Rain or shine, this was the daily routine, Monday through Friday, not unless it was mandatory overtime on Saturday.

Sally sat patiently in her car and waited until Millie jumped into the passenger seat. Every morning they had the same conversation. "Did anything new or exciting happen to you, Millie?"

Millie laughed. "Same-o same-o, the usual. Tomorrow is Melody's birthday. I finished that dress I was making for her, even pressed and wrapped it. I wish I could get her something else, but the rent is due this week."

"She'll be happy. Piece of cake making a three-year-old happy. Wait until she is a teenager, that's when the fun begins." Her friend sagely informed her.

"Well then, I really do have something to look forward to, don't I?" Sally pulled into her usual parking spot and they both went into the plant, and headed for the break room area where another friend, Tess always brought a large thermos of coffee to share. Millie and Sally walked to where Tess was sitting. She poured them each a cup of coffee. Millie glanced at the clock, right on schedule, ten minutes until the whistle blew and they'd have to go work.

Tess laughed and greeted them, "It's TGIF day. Am I getting old or are the weeks getting longer?" Sally just glared at Tess. They'd both worked for this company for thirty years. They'd both long ago given up the fantasy of having someone like Richard Gere come into the plant and sweep them up in his arms and carry them out of there like in the movie, 'Officer and a gentleman.' They both expected to continue working and get a gold watch in just over ten more years.

The ten minutes flew by and when the whistle blew; they all headed for their designated work stations. Millie pulled her chair out and sat down at her sewing machine. She flicked the power switch on, took her shears, and cut the tie string on a bundle of blouse parts. For the last four years of the nine years she'd worked here, she'd joined shoulder seams. A boring, repetitious task, but one that Millie was skilled at. None of the other girls on that job could match her speed, thus she was able to make a lot of extra money on piecework. The extra twenty—five dollars she made every week helped to feed her kids. She was always striving to increase her speed, her productivity. Often when the end of the day came her hands were trembling. She'd turn off the machine, shut her eyes and try to regain her normal composure. Satisfied that she'd done the best she could—if only she'd been able to finish school, or was able to attend night school. Maybe she could when Melody was old enough to go to school, she hoped. Another thing she could do expertly, besides sew was to dream.

Saturday evening after their supper was over, Millie cleared the dirty dishes from the table and placed a birthday cake in the center of the table. Terry, Millie's ten year old daughter set three candles on it, while her mother got the small plates out of the cupboard. Just then Sally and Tess walked unexpectedly into the kitchen. Millie's kitchen was like a second home to whomever she knew; no one ever knocked, just walked in and always received a sympathetic shoulder to cry on or attentive ears that listened to the triumph of their lives. Terry lit the wicks on the three candles and they all sang happy birthday to a beaming, happy, little auburn-haired girl. Melody blew out the candles and Sally got in the fridge for the ice cream, while Millie cut the cake; Melody's favorite, chocolate with creamy chocolate peanut butter icing. When they were finished eating Tess cleared the table, took a wash cloth and cleaned off Melody's chocolate smeared face. Then she handed the little girl a gift-wrapped present, then Sally gave her one. Terry got the gifts from her family and gave them to her. Melody squealed with delight every time she opened a gift. When the presents were all opened, Terry said to her little cousin, "Melody, bring them all in the living room and we can all look them over again. Did you see the coloring book and crayons that Tess gave you? Wow! May I color one of the pages, please, pretty please with sugar on it?" Melody giggled with glee.

The three women watched and listened to the children, then

Millie commented, "she was really surprised and she's happy, isn't she?" Millie breathed a sigh of relief.

"Your birthday is next Saturday and you've got a surprise coming to you, girl." Sally blurted out. Millie raised her eye brows, the scepticism showed on her face. As much as she liked her two old friends, Millie knew she had plenty of reasons to be leery of their machinations.

"What are you two up to now? If it's another blind date, you know I won't go, you've tried this before." Millie chided her old friends, that were always trying to get her hooked up with a man.

Tess laughed. "No, we know better than that now, after ten times standing 'your date' up, and Sally and I catching the devil from them because you never showed up. We won't attempt that again."

"We're taking you out. It's time you were introduced to the wild side of life. We're taking you to the club with us next Saturday night." Sally gave her a stern look with a message that commanded respect and brooked no resistance.

Millie laughed and knew better than to argue. "You know I don't have the right clothes to wear and I can't afford to pay a babysitter."

Sally handed her a large shopping bag, and Millie pulled the contents out. A black dress, black high—heeled shoes, and sheer black nylons. Millie had never been able to buy anything like this in her life. She ran her hand over the silky fabric of the dress. "No excuses now. Tess and I paid for the outfit and my daughter, Marty is babysitting for you. It's going to cost me two pizzas a week for a month, but it's worth it. It's time you got out and at least try to meet someone, you're too young and beautiful to live like a nun, it's time you got some romance in your life."

Millie just shook her head, according to her old work pals, all your problems could be solved in bed, a cure all for everything. "Hey, you two are still looking. What makes you think I'll get lucky?"

Tess and Sally roared with laughter. Sally, barely able to speak, sputtered out, "Honey, getting lucky is getting laid; we're hoping for more for you; meet Mr. Right and have a happy good life. We're rooting for you. You are one gorgeous girl, if you aim high, you'll have men falling at your feet."

"In your dreams." No, maybe in her dreams, she'd never be able to tell them about her secret dream man, the one that rode into her life on a white horse every night; they'd razz her constantly. "Okay, just once, I'll go out with you two, then maybe you'll leave me in peace."

Tess and Sally whooped with joy, they'd been trying to get her out socially for years. They had a plan, and it was going to be better than the fourth of July fireworks. The two matchmakers helped Millie with the dishes and left the house happy that their plan was gaining momentum.

Every day the following week, Millie got up a little earlier and fixed her hair differently each time. The girls at work voted on her new hairdos, and they'd all agreed Thursdays' hair style looked the best. Millie was beginning to actually look forward to going out. The girls at the plant gave her well-meaning advice and warnings all week. What did they think she was? Just because she'd never been on a date before did not necessarily mean she didn't know what to do or how to act. Or did she? Well, going out once would satisfy her old friends and then maybe they would leave her alone. Let her live her lonely, frustrated life in peace.

Saturday night Millie stood before her full-length mirror and couldn't believe her eyes. She thought she looked amazing in her black dress with her creamy shoulders exposed and a decent amount of cleavage showing at the top of the bodice. There was a slit up the side, revealing a shapely leg. She used more makeup than she usually did, and she'd practiced all week learning to walk in the high heels. Thank God, they weren't stilettos. She'd mastered walking properly, but she was told at work by the girls that they were torture on the feet. One girl recommended sponge insoles, which did help, a little.

She wondered why women chose to torture themselves like that, but when she looked at her image in the full length mirror on the back of the bathroom door, she got her answer. She'd never looked better.

Later that evening, when they walked into the nightclub, Millie strained to see in the large room. It was dimly lit and the cigarette smoke was so thick, she couldn't see two feet in front of her. She thought, gee whiz, I could have worn anything with that. The strobe lights over the dance floor provided nearly all the light and Millie's eyes were having trouble adjusting to their constant flickering. The live music was extremely loud, although it didn't sound too bad. But you wouldn't be able to hear yourself think in here, let alone hear what anyone said to you. She followed Tess and Sally to an unoccupied table, then tried to ignore the open stares from the men congregated at the bar. She didn't have time to lay her purse on the table because a tall swarthy looking man approached her for a dance. She didn't want to dance, she wanted to get acclimated to her surroundings before she left her seat. She shook her head and waved him off. Before the waitress brought their drinks, two more men were hanging all over her and asking to dance.

Was this called fun? She gave Sally and Tess a dirty look. She took a sip of her Tom Collins and puckered her face up, wishing it was sweeter. Both Tess and Sally got up to dance, leaving Millie alone at the table. Lord, she felt self-conscious, so out of place here. An older gentleman came up to the table, smiled gallantly at her, and whispered in her ear; "Will you dance with me, beautiful Lady? You'll be safe with me, little one." She believed him, but soon found out that his intentions weren't fatherly as he kept pulling her closer, laying his hand too low on her back. She broke away from him and returned to her table. He laughed and walked away. She refused to dance again, and after awhile the men had pegged her as a snob, and perhaps thought she was too good for them. They griped to each other. "Why had she come here, if she didn't want to dance or mingle with the men?"

The men asked Sally and Tess about her and complained.

Sally and Tess felt Millie didn't need to win a popularity contest, just meet the right man tonight. They wondered where he was, he was usually here. They watched the doorway for his appearance. It was close to midnight when he walked in. Sally and Tess breathed a long sigh of relief, they'd accomplished what they'd set out to do.

Millie looked up and noticed the two men that appeared in the doorway, and were casually looking around. The one walked toward the bar, obviously they weren't together. She just glanced at them, then her eyes returned to the first man. He looked familiar. A little over average height, build thick and solid, broad shoulders and dark slightly curly hair down to his collar. Even from a distance she knew his eyes were dark. She actually giggled when she realized he looked like her own dream man. What was he doing in this nightclub? He looked her way, never taking his eyes from her and started walking towards her. Millie felt panicky. What could she possibly say to him? She had to get out of there, so she got up quickly and headed for the ladies' room.

He intercepted her, when they were both near the dance floor. Not giving her a choice, he deftly took her into his arms, and swung her out on the dance floor. Her feet no longer hurt as she felt like they'd been dancing together forever. "You weren't trying to run away, were you, doll?" His dark eyes gazed into her face, the corners of his eyes crinkled. His smile was devastating, just as she'd always imagined it, just as she'd dreamed it. If there had been room in her high-heeled shoes, maybe her toes would have curled up.

Millie blushed like a frustrated, hormonal teenager. He laughed and whispered in her ear, and she could smell his woodsy cologne and the mint on his breath. "You're shy and beautiful, what a wonderful combination. You obviously don't get out socially very often, do you? Relax, beautiful, I haven't bitten anyone in a long time." He laughingly teased as he nibbled at her ear with his teeth, sending shivers through Millie.

They kept dancing, he still held her when two songs ended

and the band started another. When that song ended, they started playing a Texas two step number. She pulled away from him. "I don't know how to dance to this music." She started walking away, but he pulled her back.

"As light as you are on your feet, you can do it. I'll show you the basic steps, nothing to it." Millie tried to follow his steps and she quickly caught on. She liked this dance; she'd often tried to do this in the middle of her living room floor when this snappy music played on the radio. She threw her head back and laughed. He was mesmerized. Her laugh was gay and melodious, not the forced laughter he heard every day from polite society. When the song ended, she asked to go back to her table.

"I don't suppose you know how to dance to a waltz or the rumba?" He asked as they were walking to her table.

Millie laughed. "Heavens no, the last time I danced was at a high school dance, and we would have considered those dances just for old fogies. Ballroom dancing wasn't our speed. I need a break, that's a vigorous dance and I never did it before." They walked back to her table. He wondered about the last words of that last sentence and wondered if that remark could be taken literally.

He was surprised to see she was with Tess and Sally, his old boozing buddies. Although, Sally had called and told him, they would have a surprise waiting for him tonight at the club. They'd tried this before. The women they tried to fix him up with were just a little on the coarse side for him, all right for an evening of amusement and whatever, nothing more. "Tess and Sally, glad to see you, buddies." He hugged them both and then he waved to the waitress for service.

"J.B., we want you to meet our little friend. J.B., this is Millie Nobles and Millie, meet J.B. Cornell, an old friend." Tess happily made the introductions.

J.B. took Millie's hand. "Tess, Millie and I are already good friends. I taught her how to do the Texas two-step. I'd be happy to teach her anything she wants to learn." He teased, his husky voice sexy with suggestive, sexual innuendo.

Millie's face turned scarlet. She put her hands up to her face. She was so embarrassed by his insinuation and she knew he was just teasing. She knew men and women bantered like that.

J.B. laughed and pulled her to her feet. "I'm sorry, love, I'll try not to embarrass you anymore, let's dance again; I like this song, don't you?" When they resumed dancing, Millie buried her face in his neck, trying to regain her composure, which wasn't going to be easy as he drew her closer, her body nestled into his. She felt her body quiver.

Tess and Sally were right, she thought, I'm so naive and inexperienced with the opposite sex, it is downright pathetic. A woman my age should be able to tease and flirt right back, not blush and flutter like a school kid. Millie wondered if she'd ever become accustomed to a hard, masculine body pressed against hers and not trembling like she was now.

J.B. danced her to the furthest corner, it was secluded and darker there. She raised her face to say something and he dropped his face down and kissed her, pressed her butt to his hard erection and with the other hand caressed her body. His hand roved over her breasts, her hips, her bare shoulders. He broke the kiss off because he was losing control, and he'd laughed at her. He knew one thing for sure; he was going to get to know this woman a lot better, a whole lot better. He reluctantly separated from her. They just stood quietly and talked. She looked so vulnerable, he wondered if she was innocent. He couldn't believe Tess and Sally would try to hook him up with a virgin, for gripes sake. They were going to get a piece of his mind, when he got them alone. When J.B. gained back his control and when he was more presentable, they slowly walked back to the table, hand and hand. J.B. chided himself, he never lost control like this. Hell, she was just another beautiful woman, nothing spectacular about her.

Tess laughed. "Now you have to admit, J.B., we'd make good matchmakers. I've thought you two would hit it off. Millie isn't like Sally and me. She's a lady, born to it, I guess. All she needs is some romance in her life; she's too young and beautiful to live without it, and Sally and I knew you were the right one to supply that to her." She took a swig from her bottle of beer and laughed again.

This time when Millie's face got red, it wasn't from embarrassment, she was angry. "Tess, I can't believe you. I thought you knew me better than that. You know I've always lived respectably. This is definitely the last time I'm coming here ever and I'd like to go home, now."

"Chill out kid, the night is young and I'm not finished drinking. Besides, J.B. is a decent man too. Don't be so damn quick to judge. Lighten up and get off your high horse; it's time you knew how adult men and women reacted to each other. Hiding away and never going out socially is a cowardly way of life."

Sally returned to the table. "Is she giving you a hard time, Millie. Tell her to kiss your ass, don't take any of her crap." Sally muttered sarcastically.

Much as she liked Tess and Sally, she hoped she wasn't being judged by the company she was keeping. She shouldn't have been thrust into a situation like she had been tonight. They should have known she wasn't prepared for this kind of socializing. Maybe this was what kept getting her sister, Susan into trouble. She thoughtfully mused.

J.B. leaned close to her so she'd hear what he said, "Millie, I'm leaving shortly, I have an early meeting in the morning, so I'll have to get up early. I'd be glad to drop you off at your home; no problem." J.B. looked sincerely at her, surely her 'dream man' wouldn't turn into a monster when she was alone with him. Besides, hadn't she just been telling herself she should learn how to handle bad situations? Good God, she was twenty-six-years old today, not a flustered teenager.

"Thank you J.B., I would appreciate it." She stood, then turned to talk to Sally and Tess, "I'm sorry Tess and Sally, I really do have a beastly headache, I think it's the smoke in here." J.B. and Millie walked out of the club together.

Tess and Sally nearly cracked up laughing. Finally Tess was able to talk. "She left with him, you know she's going to get laid. If I know J.B. Millie doesn't stand a tinkers' chance in hell against him." They signaled the waitress for another round of beer. The night was young and they'd accomplished their mission. They got their two favorite people together, now they could just stand back and watch the sparks fly.

J.B.'s car was parked nearby. Millie was surprised when she noticed it was a BMW. He opened her door and she slid across the smooth leather seat. When J.B. walked around the car, Millie admired the lush interior of the car. He got in the drivers side and expertly pulled the car away from the curb, then wheeled out on to the thruway. She told him the area where she lived, and he took the exit ramp near her home. "I live on Wilson street. I'll tell you when we are nearing my home." They rode in silence for several blocks. "Slow up now, J.B. How lucky for you, I see there is a parking spot right in front of the house."

J.B. pulled close to the curb and turned off the engine. He hoped she'd linger for a while and talk, instead of running inside her house like a scared rabbit. She surprised him, when she invited him into her home for a cup of coffee. Usually for him that was an open invitation, but he wasn't sure with this woman. He followed her up the steps and she paused to open the door with her key, then they both stepped inside. Millie walked over to a young woman sleeping on the sofa. "Marty, I'm home, you wanted me to waken you, but I wish you would stay here until morning, it's very late." Millie didn't want her walking the three blocks to her own home. She thought that had been understood when she arrived earlier. Millie had no idea what time it was.

Marty blinked a few times before she could open her eyes. She grinned at Millie, wondering how she made out. She sat up, stretched, then yawned. "That's all right, Millie. I have two tests on Monday, and I need to do some serious studying. I only have to walk three blocks from here, and I'll be careful." Then she noticed the man standing in the doorway. "Millie, you shouldn't have invited a man into your apartment. Don't pay any attention to what Mom and Tess say. You aren't like them. I'm not leaving until he does." The young girl glared defensively at J.B.

J.B. laughed and threw his hands up in the air. "What! I have a sign on me; beware of the big bad wolf? I came in because Millie invited me in for coffee, and I'm sure that was all she was offering."

Marty instantly liked him. "Okay, I'll leave, but you mind your manners, or I'll tell Mom and Tess and they'll skin you alive."

J.B. laughed and agreed. If this was Sally's kid; she'd grown up decent. Maybe the old gals weren't as tough and hard as they let on. Millie seemed to like them.

J.B. smiled when Millie kicked off her shoes and breathed a sigh of relief. "You have no idea." She smiled and walked into the kitchen, flicked the light on and started making coffee. J.B. followed her and pulled out one of the mismatched chairs and sat down at the table. He could smell freshly washed laundry, and noticed the scent of lemony furniture polish and that the kitchen floor was spotless. What was the real story behind this beautiful woman who lived in poverty and was so naive and innocent. He meant to find out. She obviously had children to have a babysitter here, so he could forget about her being a virgin, but for sure she was, well not quite innocent. He knew when he kissed her, she'd never been kissed like that before. He wondered about her being friends with women like Sally and Tess. They didn't have a very good reputation, and they both went through boyfriends like a Kansas tornado. This woman seemed reserved, intelligent and refined. What was their connection? What the hell, he'd ask.

"Millie, how do you know Sally and Tess?"

"We work together at the mill, and I've known them for nine years. I know they are a couple of characters, but then I'm not very judgmental. They're very good to me. They help me a lot with the kids and everyday Sally picks me up and takes me to work in her car."

Then they aren't social companions. Tonight must have been some kind of lark. J.B. got that question answered when Millie said, "Today is my birthday and Sally and Tess wanted to do something special for me."

"Happy Birthday, Millie."

Millie grinned and poured them each a cup of coffee. "Thank you."

J.B. gave her a meg-a-watt smile. Millie was lost to his sensual assault. She closed her eyes briefly, then blinked a couple of times as if to clear her head. He smiled to himself. With the right kind of persuasion he could score so easy with this woman, but something held him back.

CHAPTER

2

J.B. COULDN'T TAKE HIS EYES off Millie. He'd thought she was a very pretty girl back at the dimly lit club, but here under the bright kitchen light, he disagreed with his first impression. She was beautiful, but unaware of it. He wished her hair was longer, but he liked the short bouncy curls. He looked deeply into her hazel eyes, were they green, blue, or a tawny color or all three? Her thick dark lashes fluttered up and down. They weren't false. She was real, so was her spontaneous laughter, frown when she was angry at Tess, and her real concern for Marty. Her face didn't keep secrets well, it mirrored her every thought, but her smile was what cut through him. And he knew every time she smiled, his mouth gaped open in wonder. He'd already taken stock of her figure, between five six and five seven inches tall. Shapely legs, slim waist and curvaceous hips. And her breasts! His eyes dropped to them; the dress exposed just a teasing glimpse of them. He wondered what it would be like to lay his face there, he'd already felt them with his hand. J.B. picked his cup up and drank. He'd just look at her face from here on out, as he felt himself getting hard again. It had been a long time since any woman affected him like this. He prided himself on his self-control and restraint. He'd wanted Millie since he'd first laid eyes on her in the club, the desire just kept intensifying the longer he was with her.

"Millie, you have children, how many?" A change of thoughts and conversation was a must.

"I actually have one daughter, she's almost ten years old, but I'm raising my little nephew and niece, so yeah, I have quite a family." Millie told him, the love shining in her eyes.

"You look too young to be a mother of a child ten years old. How old were you when she was born?"

"Fifteen."

J.B. pulled his head back in disbelief. A child having a child. They were never ready for that kind of responsibility. "Tell me about it, Millie and why aren't you living at home?" He drew his brows together and asked, "tell me why are you raising your sister's kids? Where is she?"

"As Tess would say, are you writing a book or something? But I'll humor you and answer your questions. Are you ready for another cup of coffee? This is going to take a while." She rose, stepped back and J.B.'s eyes greedily roved down her body all the way down to her slender feet in the black nylons. He raised his eyes and stared into Millie's smiling eyes.

"You're lovely, Millie, forgive me for staring." He wanted to stand, take her into his arms and kiss every inch of her body after he unzipped that black, figure clinging dress. He wanted to show her another purpose for a kitchen floor, or lay her across the kitchen table, but he restrained himself. He wanted to hear her story.

After Millie refilled their cups, she returned the coffee pot to the stove. This time he watched her cute, rounded derriere, and he nearly moaned out loud.

Millie began talking: "I've never been on a date in my life, but when I was fifteen I was allowed to go to the high school dances. I had kind of a crush on Ruddy Walters, and I mostly danced with him. One night, he coaxed me to go to one of the empty classrooms. We started kissing, then we got to experimenting. Well, you know, one thing led to another and we ended up having sex right there on the floor of Mr. Hathaway's science lab. I got pregnant, and I'd just celebrated my fifteenth birthday." Millie paused, took a sip of coffee and watched for a reaction on J.B.'s face. She closed her eyes and continued talking. "My parents were irate, to say the least. They literally washed their hands of me. They legally emancipated themselves from me, but my father did pay the rent on an apartment, and moved my belongings. He never even said goodbye to me, just stared at me like I was an insidious insect as he walked out the door for the last time. I haven't seen either of them since."

"What about the boy, this Ruddy kid, did he help you?"

"No, as soon as he learned I was going to have a baby, his family moved away. I hoped for a long time that when he got older and more responsible, he would come to Terry and me, but he never did."

"How did you live? What money did you have?"

"I received public welfare and finished out my school term. I would have been a senior the next year. When Terry was two months old, I got a job in a garment factory; it was that or waiting on tables, and with that job, I would have been away from my baby too much. I checked on going to night school, but there was no way I could pay a babysitter while I attended. I hoped to do that when Terry started school full time, but then my sister came to me for help. She hadn't paid her rent and she'd been evicted. They were on the streets when she finally came to me. She stayed three days then one morning I woke up to find a note on the kitchen table, she left the kids, said she'd be back for them when she got her life straightened out; that was almost two years ago. I haven't seen nor heard from her since."

Telling it was so easy, how could anyone explain the fear, the uncertainty, when she knew she was the sole responsibility of three children. The times she spent worrying and the frequent times when they were sick. She didn't have the money to take them to a doctor, so she read about home remedies from the medical book she'd gotten at the library; she prayed she was doing the right thing. She could write a cookbook, on how far you could stretch a pound of hamburg.

J.B. was an attorney, and he often did charitable work for single mothers. It really pissed him off when the fathers or mothers neglected to pay their child support payments and shirked their responsibility. He wanted to go off on an angry tirade, instead he said, "Millie, you aren't legally responsible for your sister's children, you should be getting compensated for taking care of them."

"So I've been told by the girls at work, but I'm afraid they will take them away from me. I'm all they have, and they are the only family I have."

"Do you at least get food stamps?"

"No, I'd have to go to the welfare office and apply for them. I told you I'm afraid they'd bust up my family."

"Millie, did the people at the welfare office treat you that you and the children are entitled to the help that is available."

"I don't ever want anybody looking down their nose at me again. I didn't have any choice when I was pregnant, now I'm independent. I can take care of my kids without having someone make me feel degraded and stupid."

J.B. had often heard this sad tale. He'd been responsible for getting several social service employees fired for their hauteur attitudes. He knew the system was corrupt, but it was all they had. "Millie, I'm an attorney, and I can get you help and believe me, you won't be humiliated again; I personally guarantee that. Let me be your friend and attorney."

"I can't afford a lawyer, not on my pay." She looked directly into his eyes, then blinked, her long lashes scooped down her checks. She would have to make him understand that she didn't take charity from anyone.

J.B. laughed when her face got indignant and proud. "Believe me, sweetheart, I work cheap, you can afford me."

Millie looked at him disbelieving his last remark. "Why are you willing to help me J.B.?"

"This isn't the fifties and sixties anymore. We've got excellent programs to help you mothers get on your feet and become more self sufficient."

Millie got quiet; she seemed to be pondering something, then she finally spoke. "Do they have any kind of program to help me get more schooling? If I could get a better job, I wouldn't need any help from anyone" J.B. had already thought about it. He drained the coffee cup. He hadn't realized it was cold, so he shuttered with the unpleasant taste.

He stood up, then stared down at Millie. Her lipstick was gone, she looked fatigued, but he'd never saw a more desirable woman; her eyes shone with hope and something else, like she was star struck or something. He still wanted to take this beautiful woman in his arms, pick her up and carry her to her bed. He'd just met her this evening, but he knew for certain that he'd never wanted a woman like he wanted her. He stood there gazing into her eyes and knew too, that he wanted more than just her body, more then carnal satisfaction. He wanted to make her happy, and watch her beautiful eyes fill with delight. He wanted to kiss her tears and her problems away. He wanted to love and protect her. These strange feelings overwhelmed him were foreign to him. She was not his usual one-night-stand-woman; and not this beautiful woman looking adoringly into his eyes. He was now her mentor, and his behavior was going to be proper. He'd get her life squared away before he'd even think about anything personal between them. He hoped he could keep his distance from her and resist the temptation to make love to her until they both became senseless.

How in hell was that going to be possible? As he exchanged the dazed stare in her eyes? "My hero, my very own dream—man is here in person." She softly spoke, then stretched up and kissed him on the mouth. A sweet grateful gesture, but it started a fire in them both. J.B.'s hands clenched her shoulders. Millie got a confused look on her face, innocent of the passion that wafted over them like a tidal wave. She was no longer a teenager full of curiosity. She was a woman with a woman's desires, but not fully aware of them yet. No one ever accused J.B. of being anyone's hero before. J.B. used every ounce of will power to step back, smiled at her, and headed for the front door.

"Millie, as soon as I've found out what can be done, I'll be in touch. But I promise you, that something will be done, you're not going to be raising your kids all alone anymore, darling." He stepped forward, their eyes locked. Millie thought he was going to kiss her. Instead he hastily stepped back and walked away and out the front door.

Millie brought her hand to her mouth and wondered why this man was having this effect on her. Granted she didn't date, but there were men at work that she talked and joked with. Her landlord was friendly, the good-looking checkout man who that worked in the Jiffy market and flirted openly with her. Not one of them ever affected her this way. She smiled as she locked the door, turned the light off, and headed into her bedroom. J.B was her dream man in human form. She was convinced of that. He'd finally come into her life.

J.B was glad the evening air was cooler, when the fresh air hit his face, he started breathing again. He sat in his car and watched Millie in the house before the lights went out. She was going to bed. He tried his darnest not to visualize her stripping off that black dress, standing naked, before she slipped her nightgown on, or perhaps she slept nude.

After J.B. was home and in bed, he was wide awake. He couldn't stop thinking about Millie. God, he'd never wanted a woman like he wanted her. When when he touched her on the dance floor, the feel of her was overwhelming. It had only whetted his appetite.

He recalled her story. She'd only experienced sex once and that was with an amateur fifteen-year-old randy kid. She'd never been made love to; she was the closest thing to a virgin he'd find in this day and age. The things he could teach her about lovemaking aroused him again as he headed to the bathroom for another cold shower. This time he stayed under the frigid water until, he was shivering uncontrollably. Sleep was a long time coming. Finally he drifted off to sleep and she was in his dreams. He woke up in a cold sweat, moaning her name. He looked at the bedside clock, it was only four o'clock.

Damn, damn, he uttered as he headed for the bathroom again. This time when he got in bed, he mentally made a list of the different organizations he needed to contact. He purposely kept his mind on her problems and what he could do to change her life. Then he finally fell into a restful asleep.

*   *   *

Millie lay stretched out on her bed in the room she shared with her daughter. Enough light was coming through the window for her to make out objects in the room. She stared at the black dress hanging on the closet door, then in her mind, she started recalling everything that happened that night: Her initial disappointment with the atmosphere of the club, her old friend's scheme for her to meet J.B.; the way she felt when she was in his arms dancing; the kisses and caresses in the secluded corner of the dance floor; the feeling of his hand roving over her body and later alone with him in her kitchen. She quivered, just recalling the unfamiliar feelings that had rushed over her.

She'd actually told him more about her life than she'd ever told anyone. Could he help her change her life? She thought about all of it for a while. She was attracted to him, but that was because of her stupid dreams. It was just a coincidence that J.B. looked like her dream man, that's what confused her. She'd wanted him to kiss her before he left last night, but he didn't. Was it because he didn't want to get involved with a single mother, or in the bright light of her kitchen, he hadn't found her that attractive? She rolled over on her side, fluffed the pillow, and closed her eyes tight. She could still see the twinkle in his eyes and his grin, when he said something foxy to her. Okay, she told herself, after she'd lain awake for an hour, think of something else, get your mind off him, he's an illusion. He's just a figment of your imagination. You'll probably never see him again anyway.

She concentrated on what to do about her sister, Susan, who was only two years older than she was. She'd been with, drunks and drug addicts, but she still kept right at it, when time after time, she'd been disappointed in men. With every new guy, her eyes shone with such hope and happiness. It never lasted, then she'd be shattered and start drinking heavily again. It was a never-ending vicious cycle.

Her mind went back to J.B. His expensive clothes, his car. She wasn't from his world. He was a lawyer, probably associated with beautiful sophisticated women. He just came to the club to slum, pick up a one night stand and then go back to his own world. No way was she going to follow in her sister's footsteps. Any association with J.B. was a losing situation. She'd probably never hear from him again anyway, since she'd stymied his intent to make out with her, or did she? She remembered how she wanted him to kiss her before he left. She finally acknowledged, she didn't understand any of it, drifted off to sleep.

Millie awoke in the morning with a headache. She didn't drink that much last night, only two drinks all evening, so she contributed her headache to the smoke-filled room. When she went into the kitchen and saw the dirty cereal bowls, she knew that Terry and the other kids had already eaten breakfast. They must have made toast too; the crumbs were still on the table. She made a pot of coffee, turned the gas on under it, sat down and waited for the old coffee pot to start perking.

Her mind went to last evening; her instant attraction to J.B. and how she'd wanted him to kiss her. She remembered the feel of his hands roving over her body on the dance floor, but with her newly formed convictions firmly in place, she dismissed the last lingering thought of him. One good thing came from her conversation at her kitchen table with J.B.; she intended to make some changes in her life and one of the first things she was going to look into was going to school. She fully intended to try to locate her sister and get her back in their lives so she could take care of her own children.

Not that she didn't love them, but J.B. was right about that much. Paul and Melody, as much as she loved them, weren't her responsibility, not when their own mother was alive and wasting her life away. Then maybe she could fulfill her own dream of finishing school and improving Terry's and her own lives.

She poured a cup of coffee, added milk to it and slowly began feeling like a human being again. She made two slices of toast, savored them with peanut butter and jelly, then got the roasting chicken out of the fridge, cleaned it and added stuffing to it. After putting it in a roaster, she put the pan in the oven and turned it to 250 degrees. She peeled potatoes, adding cold water to them, and sat them on the stove. Dinner was started. Now it was time to get the kids ready for church.

Millie always enjoyed going to church and the kids were happy about it too. They chatted all the way home, telling her what they did in the little church. She hoped she was instilling the path for a better life for them. Walking home from church, they were nearly in front of their apartment house, when Millie noticed the shiny silver BMW pulling. She was shocked when J.B. got out, wearing worn jeans and a bright blue pullover shirt. In broad daylight, she thought he looked even more handsome. He took her breath away. Then she remembered her convictions.

"Morning." J.B. smiled at her. His eyes roved over her quickly, she looked young and innocent today wearing a yellow sun dress and white sandals. She was a completely different looking girl than the beautiful, tantalizing woman in the black dress last evening.

Millie was trying in vain to restore her recent convictions she'd made last night. She never expected to see him again, especially in the bright light of day. She was finding out how good he looked in casual clothes. She smiled at him as she walked up to the side of the car.

"Good morning. I'm a little surprised to see you." J.B. laughed at her bewildered face.

"I'm full of surprises." He was looking at the kids with a quizzical look on his face, and they were staring at him with more than just curiosity. "Hi, you must be Terry. You're the biggest, and you look like your mother, and you must be Paul, and you, little one, must be the birthday girl, Melody." He flashed them a smile.

The kids grinned back at him and looked adoringly up into his face. Millie wondered if anyone could resist this man. When he turned the charm on. She was keeping her mind in order, now if she could control her heart rate and stop the tingling in her body, she'd be just fine. On a sudden impulse, she asked, "J.B., would you care to have dinner with us?"

Millie gazed into his smiling face, noticed how his eyes crinkled up at the corners. "I'd be honored, but I really stopped around to take you all out for lunch."

"I already have the meal started, so we'll take a rain check on that invitation." She wondered where she suddenly acquired this flippant, bold new lingo. Maybe Tess and Sally were rubbing off on her.

"Sounds like a plan, need some help cooking?" He grinned at her. His eyes twinkling.

"Ever mash potatoes?"

"No problem." He followed them into the small apartment. Millie rushed into the kitchen and opened the oven door, the aroma of roasted chicken penetrated J.B.'s nostrils.

"I was hoping it didn't burn, the preacher was a little long winded today, but it is okay," she flipped the gas on under the potatoes, and after tying an apron around her waist went to the sink and started washing vegetables.

"Want me to set the table?" J.B. offered. She nodded and he reached into the cupboard for the mismatched plates and dishes, then the different-patterned silverware. He shrugged and thought, so what? They work, don't they? He knew people lived like this, but he'd never witnessed it. He watched as Millie used an old-fashioned cabbage shredder to make coleslaw. When she finished with that, she stuck a fork into the boiling potatoes, then took the pan to the sink to drain them. She handed J.B. a metal potato masher. His mother hung one of these old relics on the wall for a decoration. He thrust it into the potatoes, smashed them, then started whirling it around.

If his ancestors could do this, he could too. Millie added a big dollop of butter to the pan of potatoes. His cholesterol was going to love this meal.

Later, when they were eating, and J.B was going back for seconds, he remarked, "Millie, I haven't eaten a meal like this since my grandmother passed away, you're a wonderful cook." He turned to the kids and asked, "isn't she kids?"

Paul answered. "The best, and tomorrow night. We'll have waffles with the left over chicken and gravy. It's to die for." He rolled his eyes, then he crammed another large bite of mashed potatoes in his mouth. When they were finished eating the meal, Terry removed the plates Millie served coconut cream pie and poured coffee for the two of them.

"I take it all back, this is better than my grandmothers." He savored the delicious pie. He wondered what planet this woman came from. Women didn't cook like this anymore. If it wasn't out of a box or frozen, they didn't cook. Definitely he'd never dated a woman that could make a pie. "I think I love you." He closed his eyes, still savoring the delicious pie.

"My grandmother always said the way to a man's heart was through his stomach. I always thought that was an old wife's tale." She threw back her head and laughed. J.B.'s heart lurched in his chest.

After J.B., Millie and Terry washed the dishes and tidied up the kitchen. J.B. suggested going to an amusement park. The suggestion was greeted by hurrahs from the kids. After squeezing them all in his compact car, he took them to a popular local park. This was a very special treat for them. After they arrived at the park, he approached the ticket booth and bought a big string of tickets and told the kids to enjoy themselves. Millie and he watched the children scoot off to get on the rides. He led Millie to a garden, as they walked the path, Millie was silently admiring and gazing at the many varieties of flowers planted in beds. She muttered wistfully, "someday I'd like to have a house with a yard, so I can plant flowers, that's on my someday list."

J.B. thought about his parents' two acre property with

the lavish garden in the rear, that he paid a gardener to take care of. He showed no interest in it at all except to admire it occasionally. Millie would be happy with just a small patch to nurture with pride and love. This woman had more facets than a prism. They found a cement bench under a shady tree J.B. and Millie sat down. J.B. put his arm on the back of Millie's shoulder, and almost immediately felt her body quiver.

"I have to work on that. I'm not used to an attractive male touching me. It's going to take some time to get accustomed to it." She murmured almost to herself.

J.B. laughed, leaned over and nuzzled her neck. "Don't ever change, Millie. I like you just as you are." He placed her hand over his heart. She raised her eye brows in surprise when she felt his thudding heart. He gazed into her eyes. She knew he was going to kiss her; she parted her lips in anticipation. When his mouth came down on hers, his tongue licked the inside of her lips, and touched her tongue. She leaned into him and his arms tightened around her waist. She tried to remember what the minister said that morning about resisting temptation as she put her arms around his neck and nestled her fingers in his hair. After several kisses, J.B. pulled away from her, then pulled her up off the bench. He was losing control. This was neither the time nor the place. Her face looked dazed, then she looked at him with a puzzling expression. God, she looked so beautiful aroused from his kisses.

"J.B., if you are only playing with me with nothing serious in mind, please stop it. My future plans don't include a man, and if they did, I'd want marriage, not just a love affair. I vowed to myself that I wouldn't screw up again. I'm begging you, if you aren't serious, don't mess me up." Her beautiful misty eyes gazed sincerely into his.

J.B. stared at her. Talk about putting your cards on the table. Millie couldn't have been more specific with her simple request. Marriage, that was the last thing he had in mind with her. He anticipated the sexual conquest and he desperately wanted to make love to her. She wanted him, too. It was taking all of his self-control to wear her resistance down and make love to her until he got her out of his system. He intended to help her get her life straightened out, but marriage?

Never.

Not in this lifetime.

They walked into the park and found the kids, looking tired but happy. Terry was clutching a teddy bear she'd won. J.B.'s eyes misted when the happy little girl wrapped her arms around his waist and hugged him. "Thanks, J.B. for bringing us here and treating us to the rides and my teddy bear. I'll keep it always."

He dropped them off in front of their house, accepting everyone's grateful thank you, grinned and winked at Millie and drove off.

Millie watched until he was then out of sight, knowing she'd probably never see him again. But what a memory she had now to fantasize about her dream man. In her dreams, she'd never been able to conjure up the emotions that he'd aroused in her. Now she had enough memories to last a long, long time. She had no regrets about the brief interlude. She'd made memories. Maybe someday when the children were raised, she could meet someone like J.B. again and have a life of her own. One filled with love and passion.

CHAPTER

3

J.B. WAS PLEASANT AND CONGENIAL when he dropped Millie and the kids off in front of their home. He'd talked and joked with the children, but silently withdrew from Millie. They thanked him for a wonderful treat and he drove off. He waved at them as he pulled away from the curb.

Millie was hurt by his cold withdrawal, but she realized that if she hadn't spoken up, she'd be hurt a lot more later. Better to end it before she became further involved with him. She'd have to go back to the drawing board with her fantasies of her dream man. It wasn't supposed to end like this. What happened to her fantasy of him riding in on a white stallion, scooping her up, taking her to Paradise?

She had no problem getting the kids to go to bed. They were exhausted.

The next morning when she got into Sally's car to go to work, the first question was. "Well, Millie, did you get laid, and how is he? Never can tell about these good looking charming men."

Millie cringed at the crudeness of the remark. "No, I didn't get laid. That was yours and Tess's idea, not mine. I had a pleasant weekend, but now it's over." Millie's chin came up.

"How in hell did you blow it, kid, he was primed when you

left the club?" Tess and Sally both believed sex was a cure-all for everything.

"I mentioned marriage."

Sally laughed. "I would've loved to have seen his face. I forgot to mention to you that he isn't exactly the marrying kind."

Millie's big night out went through the shop like wild fire. She had several girls pat her on the back. One older woman said to her. "You did the right thing, Millie, stick to your guns if that is what you want, but marriage doesn't mean happiness. I've on my third marriage, and it's lousy. I only keep it together for the kids' sake." Millie thought about that brief conversation the rest of the day. Life didn't give any guarantees and for sure marriage was not always the answer. What was?

*   *   *

J.B was shot down like he'd never been before. He respected Millie for it, but not enough to marry her. Hell, he'd handled enough divorce cases to have learned a happy marriage was rare. His parents' relationship was living proof of that. He could have strung her along. He'd had to do that with women more times than he cared to admit to just to get on the good side of them. But he couldn't do that to Millie. She was too sincere, too honest. He didn't want to be the one that disillusioned her about the modern day romances. The casual regard for love and sex.

J.B. kept thinking about Millie, the kisses, the happy time he had with her and the kids. The delicious meal, they'd shared. Especially that delicious pie. He would help her with her life, but he personally was not going to pursue her, there were plenty of fish in the sea. He didn't have to get married and he sure as hell wasn't going to feed her a big line just for favors. There were too many women that were eager to have him for a lover. He just wouldn't think about her anymore.

It was simple.

It would be easy. No problem.

Monday morning J.B. explained the situation concerning Millie and the three children to his secretary, then handed her the list of organizations that needed to be contacted. He asked her if she could arrange phone calls, rather than personal interviews, and that he'd appreciate it. He went on with his own work load, and put Millie from his mind for the rest of the day.

By the end of the day, his secretary had performed miracles, all of the organizations she contacted agreed to telephone appointments and one such call was in half an hour. He picked up his phone and punched in the numbers his secretary had given him and asked for the designated person he needed to speak to. While waiting for the call to connect, J.B. leaned back in his chair and crossed his long legs. This was for Millie and just the thought of her made his blood rush again. Maybe when all was accomplished, he could put her out of his mind once and for all. This call should get the ball rolling. The woman he was going to speak to was head of the social services in the county. "Mrs. Montgomery, this is J.B. Cornell. I'm grateful that we can talk via the phone."

"J.B, your reputation precedes you. I can handle everything for you, and I'll work with the other organizations. We all know how much you advocate for single mothers' rights and help them. What can I do for you?" She'd dug out Millie's record, and noted that Millie hadn't asked for any type of assistance since right after her child was born, nearly ten years ago.

J.B. explained Millie's situation and the reason she hadn't requested help. She started to protest, but J.B overrode her. "You know you have some case workers that give these women a hard time. That is why it's going to be done through me, I'll handle all that I can personally."

"Miss Prentiss, your secretary was quite informative. I have the complete picture. I'll start the application process moving. I've already called about schooling, if the girl has the ability and her highschool records warrant it, she'll be given an opportunity to go further in school. Nothing pleases me more as when one of the women in dire circumstances like Millie Nobles makes an earnest attempt to get self sufficient. You'll have my full cooperation, J.B."

"Thank you, Mrs. Montgomery. Please keep me posted on the progress of the case." Pleased that he had the personal attention of Mrs. Montgomery, he started to relax. He couldn't do any more until Millie's record was checked and she filled out the applications. He worked later than usual, then grabbed a light meal at his favorite Chinese restaurant and headed home.

After he showered and was dressed in a robe, he got comfortable in his favorite chair, then he started to leaf through a current magazine. The phone rang. J.B. answered and was startled when he realized the caller was Sally, his old drinking buddy from the club. "Sally, this is unusual for you to call me. Have you changed your mind about running away with me to the Bahamas for a wild and exciting holiday?"

Sally laughed; in her dreams, not with this handsome hunk, "Sorry, I can't make it, you'll have to get in line." She laughed heartily, loving her old joke.—"J.B., I called Tess and I were wondering what really happened with you and Millie? Did she turn virtuous on you or what?"

"Something like that. She's a wonderful girl. Too bad I just can't go along with her game plan." Sally was more his type of woman. If she were a little younger, he wouldn't mind going for a round or two with her for a no strings attached relationship.

"That's what we thought. Tess and I didn't know how she would react to a proposition; she's straight and narrow. We thought we were doing her a favor, and we're sorry to have involved you; hope you aren't mad at Tess and me."

"Nope, you know better than that. I'll see you Saturday at the club, we're overdue to tie one on together. You take care. Sally, and thanks for calling." He hung the phone up and wondered if Millie would be at the club again. He tried to remember something his grandfather told him once. "It takes one to forget one." He'd just follow his grandfathers' sage advice. He picked up his little black book and leafed through it. There wasn't a damn woman listed there that turned him on at the moment. None of them had those beautiful different colored eyes or short dark curly hair and none of them ever looked at him like he could walk on water. That was it. As soon as he'd properly disillusioned her, and she no longer gave him those adoring, calf-eye looks, he'd probably never give her a second thought. He was just flattered being her hero. A male macho thing. It was strictly the proverbial ego trip.

Once the papers were all filed and Millie was getting the help, she really deserved, she would be just a passing fancy. He had to admit that his feelings for her went a little deeper than a sexual escapade. She was beautiful, talented, warm, and loving. And her person and her mouth, that kissable mouth of hers, and those lush full breasts, that he'd never tasted. He felt an erection coming on. He went to the bar and poured out a good stiff drink. Now he knew why men became alcoholics. Oblivion was better than remembering. He didn't want this in his life. He didn't need it.

Within two weeks after the applications were filed and processed, Millie was getting food stamps, and was put on the list for a better, bigger subsidized home. Her high school records were released, and she found out that she did have the potential to go to school. She was to be tested at the University for courses that would best suit her. The rest would have to wait until she completed the test.

Mrs. Montgomery called J.B. personally when the results of the test at the college came in. She told him Millie's test scores were phenomenal. High school subjects weren't required, she was to be entered on a collegiate level, even eliminating a few of the elemental courses. "J.B., Millie told the instructors that she has studied from books from the library about history, world maps, politics, and science. She knew every country in the world and their capitals. She is a real whiz kid, just how did you meet this girl?

"It seems both her parents are professors, so obviously she has good genes. She told them her next door neighbors' son is a high school student, and he taught her math. In return she did his essays and helped him with English, which he was failing. I wanted to tell you too, J.B., that a vacancy for a house is available; she'll be moving into it within a week. She is a delight, such a wonderful girl. And so enthusiastic about going back to school." J.B. tried to absorb all this new information concerning Millie as quickly as Mrs Montgomery was telling him Millie's parents were both professors! It didn't surprise him at all that she excelled on the pre-admission testing for college entrance. His mind followed Mrs. Montgomery's explanation.

"Where is the house? Will it be near the college?" J.B.'s mind went to full alert, remembering the odds and ends of used furniture Millie owned.

"It's about twelve blocks, we're arranging for the youngest child, Melody, to go to the day care at the college. Oh! I see what you're getting at, we'll have to put in for a car for her. She'll need transportation. Can you think about anything else? How about a cash advance for clothing and some better home furnishings? She has been struggling for so long all by herself; we surely owe her all the help that is available for her. She deserves all we can give her."

"I'll take care of the furniture. Do appliances come with the house?"

"Yes, stove, refrigerator, dishwasher, washing machine and a dryer are included." Mrs Montgomery wasn't surprised to hear that J.B. was going to come through again. He'd always helped the needy women with certain needs. No one ever questioned his generosity, just gladly accepted it.

"Great, Mrs. Montgomery, keep me posted." J.B. sat quietly when he hung up the phone. After over three weeks, he found out that it didn't help to get drunk. He couldn't work enough hours, or get physically exhausted to rid her from his mind, from his dreams. He picked the phone up and dialed a good friend's number that owned a furniture warehouse. He remembered the mismatched kitchen chairs, the odd dishes and silverware, and the worn, sagging furniture in the living room. Millie cleverly disguised the worn furniture with slip covers, but now she was going to get all new sets. It would give him satisfaction to know Millie would be sleeping in a bed that he'd purchased especially for her. A king size bed made up with satin sheets and a down comforter. Blue to match her eyes, or were they green? They were still a mystery.

*　　*　　*

Millie's mind was whirling with thoughts about the way her humdrum life was changing. She was going to college; she was moving to a much better home. She'd been sorting through her household furnishings.

When she thought about all the possibilities she could do and after deciding to make new drapes, she was on her way to the new house to measure the windows and the color scheme. She rode the bus to the housing development and walked the short distance to her new house, enjoying the nice weather and the tree-lined street. This was going to be wonderful living here. She used the key that Mrs. Montgomery had given her and entered the house. What she saw startled her. This couldn't be the right house; it was completely furnished. She stepped back out onto the small porch and checked the house number. No, she'd been right. This was her new home; the house number was right and the key fit. She entered the house again and starting looking around. Her mouth hung open. Where did all this beautiful furniture come from?

She'd been told that the appliances would be installed, but nothing was ever said about new furniture. She walked from room to room, gasping at the decor; it looked like an expensive Interior Decorator had cleverly arranged the brand new household furnishings. She ran her hand over the matching sofa and living room chairs, new high end matching lamps and a coffee table with an attractive floral arrangement on it. Coordinating drapes and art were already hung. She walked into the kitchen and instantly loved the large table with six matching padded chairs. She pulled one out and dropped into it. Her eyes glanced around at a Bunn coffee maker, a four slice toaster, a new microwave, a blender, and an electric mixer that hung from it's bracket beneath the cabinet. She got up and opened the cabinet door. To find white with tiny blue flowered

Corelle dishes, serving bowls, cups, saucers and dessert dishes and plates to match. She kept flinging open the cabinets. Pie plates, measuring cups, etc. She opened the bottom cabinets and found stainless steel pots and pans. Piece by piece she pulled them out of the cupboard and admired them, she wondered who made the selection? This was like a dream coming true, she thought as she held the stainless steel double boiler in her hands—something she'd often wished she owned and often needed. There was everything she could possibly need to cook anything.

Millie dropped back to the kitchen chair and tried to remember having a conversation with Mrs. Montgomery about household furnishings. She didn't recall one. There had been so much going on lately, that she was getting confused.

She walked into the bedrooms. Paul's was a typical boy's room. The furniture, a single bed and a tall chest of drawers. The bedspread and drapes with rocket ships on them. The desk and chair for him to do his homework at. Two book shelves, filled with adventure stories, including all the Harry Potter books.

Oh my God! This is perfect, she thought, as she walked into Terry and Melody's bedroom.

Terry and Melody were going to share a room. As she entered their room, she immediately noticed the identical twin beds with white dust ruffles, pink comforters, and matching drapes. A vanity with a mirror. A double bureau. A book case and desk combination with a computer and a printer sitting there waiting for Terry, who would be so thrilled. Millie was planning on looking for a used one for Christmas. Millie sat down on one of the beds and closed her eyes. Whoever had designed this room, certainly knew little girls and what they liked, especially Terry.

She walked into her own bedroom, then she sat down on the bed and wept. This was just too much. When she dried her eyes and could focus them again, she looked around. The comforter on the king size bed was multi colored green, blue and a golden brown. The drapes matched. There was a double dresser with a mirror and shelves and small drawers for make—up, and personal belongings. The two lamps had ruffled shades that matched the comforter and drapes. Someone had paid close attention to every detail.

She just had to be dreaming, either that or a big mistake had surely been made. Maybe all this had accidently been delivered to the wrong address.

She went over to the adjoining house and rang the bell, hoping her neighbor knew something about this. A petite red-haired woman answered the door. She carried a small child on her hip. "Ma'am, I'm Millie Nobles, your new next door neighbor and I wonder if you saw who delivered the furnishings to my home?"

The girl told Millie her name and welcomed her to the neighborhood. "I saw the delivery truck and watched what they brought, in. I couldn't help myself, everything was absolutely beautiful. You're so lucky, my furniture is falling apart. The name on the truck was Waltman's Warehouse. The woman that oversaw the men, drove a Cadillac and was dressed to the nines. I tried not to miss a thing, and I'm usually not that nosey. Not much to see in this neighborhood. Maybe you will invite me over some day and show me the way they set it up. The furnishings looked awesome."

"Thanks, Peggy, I haven't time today but you've got a private tour coming to you." Millie grinned at the little tot that looked just like her mom and left. At least, now she had a name. Waltman's warehouse sounded familiar.

She went back into her home and called Mrs. Montgomery first. "Mrs. Montgomery, this is Millie Nobles, I have a question."

"What is it Millie? How can I help you?"

"Could you tell me where all this new furniture came from? My house is completely furnished. Everything is new, and it's absolutely beautiful. I thought at first I was in the wrong house."

"It was donated, Millie. It seems you have a good friend that is extremely interested in your welfare and your future." It wasn't up to her to divulge who was helping her.

"Who? I don't understand, Mrs. Montgomery, maybe all these furnishings were delivered to the wrong address and when the company finds out their mistake, they'll come and take it all away or I'll be billed for it."

Mrs Montgomery laughed. "You know the old adage, never look a gift horse in the mouth. I'm sure you will figure out where it all came from, just enjoy it, Millie. I have to go and good luck to you and your family." Millie kept the phone to her ear until she heard the operator telling her to either hang up or make a call.

She looked in the phone book and found the number of the Waltman's Warehouse. When a woman answered, Millie gave her the address and asked her who this account was billed to. The woman explained it might take her a while to find it. Millie gave her the date that it was delivered. The woman answered. "Now, that helps, I'll just look through yesterday's delivery invoices.—Aw, here it is. Miss, the entire order was picked out and paid for by J.B. Cornell with the help of the owner here at the warehouse, Miriam Waltman. Miss, is there a problem? Everything is under warranty."

"No problem, thank you." She knew that J.B. was responsible for all the good things that were happening in her life, but this was beyond what Millie could accept. This was downright charity, and her pride wouldn't allow it. She didn't take hand-outs. She'd finally conceded to graciously accepting help from the state. She'd already shallowed her pride. Mrs. Montgomery had told her not to look a gift horse in the mouth. This wasn't a mere gift, it probably cost a fortune, and as much as she loved everything in the house, she was going to return it to the store and move her old furnishings into the house.

Then she thought how thrilled the children would be. Terry would cry tears of joy about the computer. Maybe she could call the warehouse back and find out exactly what the bill was and she'd repay J.B. back. Maybe, she should just forget about her pride and accept his generous gift to her and the children. She would love to make the kids really happy for once in their lives. She decided to sleep on it. Tomorrow she'd make a decision.

The next day Tess's friend brought his truck and Sally brought her car to move Millie and the kids to their new home. When they'd made their last inspection and got everything they wanted out of the house, Tess was running the sweeper and Millie was dusting the furniture. They were surprised when a young pregnant woman and a small toddler by her side knocked on the door. She told Millie that the landlord said she could look at the apartment, to see if she wanted to rent it.

After showing the young woman through the apartment Millie told her. "I'm leaving all this old stuff here, if you don't want it, I'll call the mission to come get it."

"You don't want anything?" The girls' eyes shone in disbelief and surprise. "All of it, even the crib, I can have. I was figuring on sleeping on the floor until I could gather up some furniture, I never dreamed I could get so lucky. Thank you, thank you." The girl rushed over to Millie and hugged her with tears of gratitude running down her face. Millie was glad, she'd made the decision to keep the new belongings, and to think she'd made this young woman happy with her old stuff. Things she'd struggled to buy on time one piece at a time, and that she too had been grateful for.

Soon the movers arrived at the new house and started to unload the boxes full of clothes and their personal belongings. The kids were yelling and squealing with delight as they ran from one room to another. Terry literally wept for joy when she saw the computer. "Mom, how did you do this? As soon as I can, I'll make some money babysitting and help pay off the bill. Are you sure you can handle it Mom? Oh Mom, I'm so happy. I never thought I'd ever have such a beautiful bedroom."

"Terry, I'm getting a deferred payment, I'll pay this back when I'm through school and have a good paying job. We have J.B. to thank for all this." Millie believed in being honest with her daughter. She hated liars.

Terry looked at her mother with a troubled face. This wasn't like her mother to accept help like this. What was going on? All of a sudden, there were so many changes happening in their lives. Terry didn't understand what happened that made her mother suddenly reverse her policy about accepting help.

A week after they were settled in their new home, a young man knocked at her door. When Millie answered, he grinned and asked. "Are you Millie Nobles?"

"Yes, I am. What can I do for you?"

The nineteen-year old scanned her curvaceous body and silently told her what she could do for him. "Ma'am, I need for you to sign these forms. I was supposed to deliver your car to you."

"What! I haven't bought or ordered a car, where did it come from?"

"From the welfare office, Mrs. Montgomery signed the voucher. It just says, a car was required because of the distance to the college and transporting a young child back and forth. Just sign on the dotted line, Ma'am, you'll have to ask Mrs. Montgomery about the details, I just deliver them." He smiled roguishly at her.

Millie signed the paper, and he handed her the receipt and the car keys. The young man jumped into the other car that followed him and got in the front with a driver behind the wheel. Millie walked out to the car. She didn't even know how to drive, let alone have a license. Her neighbor, Peggy came out and a small crowd was gathering around looking the car over.

Peggy walked up to Millie, leaned over, and spoke quietly. "Millie, this is a Chevy Mimi van. It's a Caravan, and I think it's only a couple years old, if that much. How did you rate? They usually only get something for a thousand dollars, that's the max they spend. Girl! You really have an in with the department. You sleeping with the boss, or what?" She laughed and poked Millie in her rib.

Instantly, Millie knew it was J.B. again. Why was he doing this? She didn't want to call him and confront him. She didn't trust herself to even talk to him on the phone; she'd just find out the fair market price and add that amount to what she already owed him.

Peggy took the key from her and unlocked the doors, then

she climbed in behind the drivers' seat and started up the car. She looked at some papers on the front seat. This was last year's model; it had been used as a demo. She glanced at the mileage: there was less than three thousand miles on it. It even smelled new. She grinned at Millie. "Let's load the kids up and take a spin, and I'll give you your first driving lesson."

"I'll have to get my permit before I try to drive. This is scary. I've never even thought of ever owning a car." She ran her hand over the light blue exterior and then counted the seats and looked at the space inside. She then felt the soft dark blue upholstery. Peggy turned the radio down. The kid that had driven it here, obviously had been jamming; it was playing on a rock and roll station and the volume had been up all the way.

The women loaded the kids in the car after locking their house. Peggy was a good driver. "My dad taught me how to drive when I was sixteen. I bought my first car from the junk yard, then I helped Dad restore it. After we filled in holes and sanded it, we had it painted a bright red with a white lightening symbol on each side; it was really cool. I even lost my cherry in that car." She laughed.

They rode out of the city and onto a secondary road. Peggy pulled over to the side of the road and told Millie to slide over into the driver's seat. She went around the car and got in the passengers' side. Millie was going to get her first lesson. Peggy explained to her what the pedals on the floor were for and told her to never slam her foot on them. Then she told her about the controls on the steering column. She knew Millie wouldn't be able to absorb everything at once, so she'd have to drill it into her. She'd receive two permits, before her dad took her for her test, then she failed...twice.

"Peggy, go over everything just once more time, please. What was this little handle for? She pointed to the turn signals. Again, Peggy patiently explained everything, she even added the emergency brake lever this time. Millie started up the car, strapped her seat belt on, looked in her side mirror, glanced over her shoulder to see if a car was coming, then expertly pulled out onto the road.

"Millie, you are doing fantastic."

"I've never driven, but I've watched Sally for years. I might have some trouble parking; she always does." Millie laughed.

Peggy was stunned at how quickly Millie picked up driving skills. After she got her permit, they went out every day. Millie did have some problems backing up and parking, but after about four attempts, she succeeded at parallel parking. Once when she was trying to maneuver into a parallel parking spot, Millie put the control handle into the park position, got out, and walked around the car. "I wasn't just too sure how much room I had over there. I'll have to learn to judge my distances better." She remembered how Peggy told her that the driver was supposed to know where her car was. She pulled in and out five times, each time getting better. Passerbyes applauded when she aced parking. She laughed and gave them a vee symbol with her fingers.

She passed her test the next Saturday and showed her new driver's license to everyone. She felt every new accomplishment was going to make life better.

Her life wasn't in limbo anymore, she thought as she pulled into the college parking lot, and deposited Melody into the day care, then headed for her first class. She felt good. She had watched the girls going and coming at the school for several weeks, and she studied what they wore, then made a wardrobe that was in sync with theirs. The first day she wore her greenish blue blazer and a plaid skirt with a lot of matching blue in it. She'd been letting her hair grow longer, and the curls were touching her shoulders. She grinned as she got admiring looks from the boys. These kids were only eighteen or so, and that made her feel good. She was going to fit in with the young crowd.

All was well with Millie's life, except for her secret, hungry longing for J.B. She was very busy, and she didn't have time to day dream. Just when she was starting to get J.B. out of her mind, she would remember him while alone in bed and hunger for his kisses and strong embrace. She cried every night into her pillow and wished to God that she'd never met him. Ignorance was bliss. He'd awakened the woman in her, and now she yearned for him. She missed his smile, his jovial manner, and the way his eyes crinkled up when he laughed. She missed him, loved him, wanted him.

For over four months. J.B. stayed away from her. Sometimes Sally or Tess would mention his name, but Millie heard nor saw anything of him. The longing and the heartache wouldn't abate. She often crawled into bed exhausted after taking care of the children, cleaning the house, washing the laundry, and going to school. She'd go to sleep instantly, but would be awakened by vivid lifelike dreams. Whispering his name; she would turn on the bedside lamp to make sure that J.B. wasn't in her room, that she'd only dreamed of his mouth on her, and his naked body clinging to hers. She could only imagine what making love with him would be like.

Millie decided to listen to her heart. This was a modern world she lived in. The sexual revolution allowed people to enjoy a healthy sex-life without the stigma. Society accepted this, but she knew deep down in her heart that it was morally wrong and not condoned by the church. She told Sally and Tess she wanted to go with them to the club again Saturday night. Neither woman asked her why. They had looked at Millie's sad eyes and brave smiles for weeks now and on Saturday nights, they listened to J.B. cry in his beer, although he never mentioned Millie. These too fools were pathetic. Sally called J.B. to make sure he was going to be there. This time, they'd stay out of it.

Didn't Millie and J.B. realize that they'd fallen in love with each other?

Saturday night, Millie dressed again in the only decent dressy outfit she owned. The black one that Sally and Tess gave her for her birthday. For once she was hoping Sally and Tess connived and called J.B. and told him that she'd be at the club. Millie could have called him, but if she ran into him accidentally, then maybe he wouldn't think she was running after him.

This time when Millie entered the club; she wasn't frightened by the unfamiliar scene. She knew what to expect. They'd just gotten settled at their table and ordered drinks, when a pleasant looking young man came up to Millie and asked her to dance. She smiled and walked out on the dance floor. J.B. had just arrived. The first person he noticed was Millie. His heart lurched in his chest. God, she looked beautiful, her dark wavy hair was almost down to her shoulders, better, much better. She was dancing with some young punk. He wanted to walk over to them and flatten him as he watched the man put his arms around Millie's waist and draw her closer. He was tired of denying his feelings for her. Hell, if that was what she wanted, if that was what it took, he'd marry her, but not having her was becoming unbearable. He'd never met a woman before that haunted him like Millie did and he'd only kissed her. He watched the couple dance for a short time, he couldn't help it, he felt like he was going to blow his stack as he walked out on the dance floor and tapped the guy none too gently on the shoulder. "She's my girl." He muttered and glared at the startled man. The young man saw the fury in J.B.'s eyes and quickly dropped his arms around from Millie, turned around, and left the dance floor. J.B. hoped his dance steps were correct. His mind was in a blur, but his body responded to this beautiful woman's body instantly.

The music stopped. J.B. gazed into Millie's eyes, what he saw there, instantly diminished his anger. He saw surrender, love, and desire. J.B.'s heart thumped in his chest. The band started playing another song, the same one they'd danced to before, months ago, a slow romantic melody; one they both loved. J.B. pulled her into his arms. They danced as one person. Millie laid her face against his neck; her hair brushed against his chin. She smelled his woodsy cologne and felt the slight stubble of his beard, and warm breath wafting over her face. It had been just over four months, since she'd seen him, but it had felt like eons. Just to be in each other's arms was delicious. A feast to end their torment. As the song ended, J.B. whispered in her ear. "Sweetheart, let's get to hell out of here."

He didn't get any argument from Millie, just a smile that

warmed him clear through to his soul. She winked at Sally and Tess as she picked up her purse, took J.B.'s arm, and they left the club.

This time when they watched Millie and J.B. leave the club together, Tess and Sally were somber. "That's what they should have done the first weekend they met; they'd saved themselves a lot of misery." Sally contemplated. She truly did have her doubts about the success of Millie and J.B.'s relationship. They were from two different worlds, but nevertheless it was going to play out. Just maybe they were going to be one of the lucky couples that loved forever and made it work. Sally picked her beer bottle up and lifted it for a toast. Tess did the same. "I sure hope they make it, it would be nice for a change to have a happy ending." Sally philosophized.

J.B. was hesitant of where he should go. He couldn't take her to her home, the baby-sitter would be there. He could drive to a motel like he'd done hundreds of times, but Millie wasn't that kind of girl. He wouldn't, couldn't cheapen what he felt for her. J.B. drove to his home. Tonight he wanted Millie all to himself. Sally's daughter was with the kids and he'd take her back to her home when he could part with her, maybe in five years or so. He unlocked his front door, after they stepped in, he turned and locked it behind him. He switched on a light. He thought, I should offer her a drink, a cup of coffee, a glass of wine, but his manners had gone AWOL. He picked her up and carried her up the spiral stairwell, just like Clark Gable, carried Scarlett O'Hara in the movie, 'Gone with the wind.'

He released her when they were in his bedroom. They gazed at each other, like they were starved for the others' look, touch and heat. Millie swayed toward him, then her arms went up and around his neck, her fingers wove through his hair. J.B. savored the moment as he read the desire in her eyes. He lowered his mouth to hers, and he was swept away as Millie's mouth returned his ardor. He silently reminded himself to go slow, but the raging passion that rose between them was in total command.

Millie was unbuttoning his shirt, when she succeeded in removing it, her hands ran over his naked chest then moved across his broad shoulders. He was kissing her mouth, her neck and down toward her breasts as he deftly unzipped her dress, unhooked her bra and with one smooth movement removed most of her clothing. All that remained was the black panty hose and black panties. He pushed the sheer hose down her legs, when he stood back up again, she was naked before him. He gasped as his hands reached for her bountiful breasts. The nipples protruded out stiff and ripe. His mind commanded him to lay her on his bed, but he was enthralled with her breasts, as he caressed them with both hands, using his thumbs to pluck at the hardened nipples. He felt Millie unbuckling his belt, pulling the zipper down. He released her long enough to untie his shoes and rid himself of his trousers, underwear and socks. He reached into his night stand drawer and found a foil package, then he sheathed himself. Only the light from the hallway shone into the room. Together they squirmed and wriggled to the bed. J.B. shoved the comforter and sheet aside and he lowered Millie down, still kissing her, his big hand still caressing her breast. From a faraway distance he heard Millie's voice, "J.B., I can't wait, I want you now, please don't make me wait." She moaned into his ear. Another time he would give her all the pleasures a man can give a woman, but now their bodies demanded copulation. He gently pushed her legs apart and started to enter her, she was wet, tight, small. He heard Millie moan, then she thrust her hips and made the union between them complete, her muscles drawing him in further and tightening around his engorged manhood. He pushed into her the full extent. He stopped moving to regain control, and give Millie time for her body to accustom to his size. J.B. starting moving slowly at first, then with total abandonment, Millie met his every thrust and they both convulsed with ecstasy, shattering all awareness of consciousness. Their bodies, still connected writhed with quivering shudders. Millie still drew him closer, nearer to her core, draining him.

They laid quiet, trying to come down from the height of the

universe. Millie was the first to stir. "That was beautiful, I had no idea that it was like that." Still encased in J.B.'s strong arms, she snuggled closer to him, nestled her face in his neck. Millie thought momentarily, 'this is the reason I was born.'

J.B. aroused slightly. "It was beautiful, more than that, it was incredible. Millie, you were born for me, we belong together." He started to become aroused again, wanting to make love to her again, but sleep lulled him, so as he dozed off, still holding her tightly to his body. Millie relaxed and felt the gentle serenity sweep over her sated body and she too, fell into a blissful dreamless sleep. She hadn't known making love could be like this. Better than any fantasy, she'd ever had.

Sunlight was streaming through the large bay window as Millie and J.B. both roused from a deep dreamless sleep. J.B.'s first thought was, Millie is here in my bed. She is really naked and in my arms. His mind went back to last night. He thought he was a real macho man, completely experienced and no longer anticipated anything new in the love making department. It was never like last night was. Millie was right, it was beautiful, earth shattering ecstasy. It reached right down into his soul, they were as one person, completely joined. The second time they'd made love was not so frantic. They took their time and explored and enjoyed one another's bodies. Their simultaneous climax nearly brought tears to J.B.'s eyes. He was gazing into her lovely face. The long eyelashes sweeping down her cheeks. They fluttered, then opened.

This morning, her eyes were more green, he drowned in their depth. Realization and awareness appeared in them. She smiled at him, and love and tenderness washed over him, as he lowered his mouth to hers. The kiss was tender, gentle; drawing them both into another plateau of awareness. Into another dimension.

This time when they made love, J.B. took his time, gave her pleasure; glorified in his power as a man when she writhed beneath him. He muted her moans with his mouth as he made love to her entire body.

Later they showered together, then Millie put on her

wrinkled dress. J.B. put fresh clothes on. She watched as he shaved, mesmerized with his daily ritual. This was the first time, she'd ever watched a man shave. His face lathered with shaving cream, he glanced in the mirror and realized she was watching him. He kissed her upturned lips, she giggled as she wiped the white cream from her face.

Together they walked down the spiral staircase. Millie hadn't looked around last night when they came in, now she strolled through his home, and admired the beauty of the old, beautifully restored Victorian mansion. Whoever decorated this house must have exquisite taste, she thought as she gazed into each room with J.B.'s arm around her waist. This house was as beautiful as her parents's home.

Millie was surprised when they walked into the kitchen, where an older woman was standing at the stove cooking. "Good morning, J.B. I'm cooking up a storm, figured you would be starved this morning. You never touched the casserole I made for your dinner last night." The housekeeper knew J.B. was entertaining a female last night, when she walked in the front door and saw the high heeled shoes and the purse on the floor. This was the first time he'd ever brought a woman to his home in the night to her knowledge. This one must be special she thought to herself; it's about time too. She'd been praying for this to happen for a long time.

"Mary, I want you to meet my girl, this is Millie Nobles. Millie, my housekeeper and self appointed priest, Mary Anders."

Mary turned away from the stove and for the first time looked at Millie. Her natural beauty transcended with the rapturous look on her face, and took Mary's breath away. She watched as Millie's eyes fluttered with surprise and confusion. Was she embarrassed at finding she and J.B. weren't alone in the house?

"I can't tell you how happy it makes me to meet you, Millie. I hope you and J.B. are hungry; I made enough food to feed the homeless." She smiled warmly at Millie.

Then Millie smiled. "It smells delicious, and I am famished."

She glanced at J.B. and blushed as he watched her with thoroughly acquainted, knowledgeable eyes. They roved over her body. She felt a shiver run the entire length of her.

Mary turned and grinned as she started to dish up the food. Beautiful, modest and enthralled with her boss, nothing could have made her happier. J.B. was actually glowing, if that was the right description of her ruggedly, handsome employer.

Her Irish blood blessed the saints that sent this woman to J.B. She prayed nightly for him to meet a special lady and end the years of loneliness she knew he endured. It was surely a good sign that he'd brought this one to his home.

Mary went into the adjoined laundry room and gave them privacy, but she could hear their laughing and could feel the happiness radiating from this couple.

Mary watched from the front window when J.B. and his lovely girlfriend left the house. J.B. opened the passenger car door for her, but instead of allowing her to get in the car, he pulled her into an embrace and kissed her. Mary witnessed the love and passion emitting from the radiantly happy couple. She felt like an intruder, a voyeur watching their tender lovemaking. Just as Mary started to walk away, Millie pulled away from him and got in the car.

After J.B. started up the engine, he turned to Millie and again pulled her into his arms. "I'm sorry, sweetheart, I can't get enough of you. When am I going to see you again? Tonight? Tomorrow morning? For lunch? Tomorrow night, for sure."

Millie laughed. "Now I know why they invented honeymoons, just so the happy couple could stay together until they'd reached their satiation point. Darling, I have school, children, housework and in my spare time, I study. As much as I'd like not to. I have to leave you, but please make it soon. I couldn't bear to live without you now. You may have created a hungry, greedy monster last night." She pretended to growl as she bit at J.B.'s neck.

J.B. laughed as he untangled himself from her arms and started up the car. Now he knew why he couldn't get Millie from his mind. Work, women, booze, nothing even faded the memory he had of her etched in his heart. He was in love with this woman. For the first time in his life, he'd fallen in love.

But he also knew it would take some time to convince her of his sincerity. Besides Millie needed to get on her own feet; she had to prove to herself she was worthy of a better life. But for sure, he'd see her often, even if he had to park on her door step.

on the list. Why aren't they on the invoice? And I know these prices are not right. I'm aware of what these items cost." She glared suspiciously at him.

"Hank sold everything to me at his cost, less than fifty percent of the retail price and the items that aren't listed; Hank's wife, Miriam contributed. She was the one that picked everything out and coordinated the colors. The extra things were her special donation to you and the children. If you want to appear ungracious, confront her with it. I had nothing to do with that." He was cross with her and couldn't understand why she just didn't accept his help graciously and go on with living. Why did she have to be so different from the many women he'd helped before? Darn stubborn woman. She'd had no rest until he got a copy of the invoice from Hank Waltman who owned the warehouse.

Millie was getting better at swallowing her pride, she told herself it was for the children, they deserved more than she could give them for now. "I'm sorry J.B. You know how I get my hackles up sometimes. She did a wonderful job, selecting and coordinating everything. I'm thrilled every time I walk in the front door. It's awesome and I truly do appreciate everything you and Mrs Waltman did for me, but it just goes against my grain to accept that expensive of a gift. I'm sorry, that's the way I am and I can't help it."

J.B. just grinned at her, then hugged her close. Didn't this woman of his realize he'd give her the moon if she asked him for it? She already had his heart and his body was her captive slave to do with what she wanted. Spending money on her just gave him more pleasure.

Millie made a special effort to go to the warehouse when Miriam was going to be there and personally thanked her for her generous gift. When Millie pulled into the parking lot and went inside, she glimpsed around at how cleverly the warehouse was arranged. They'd partitioned part of the gigantic building and made it look like rooms displayed with furniture as though it were a home. Clever idea, she thought. It would really let you see just what a room would look like, before purchasing. A tall, slender, older woman came up and greeted her. Millie told her who she was and thanked her for her generous gifts. "You have exquisite taste, I love what you did in my home. Thank you so much." She told her how happy her gifts made her and the children, and just how grateful she was. Miriam was delighted by her thank you. Miriam's instant impression of Millie was a credit to J.B.'s taste in women. She told J.B. later, that he'd found a real gem and to mind his P's and Q's and not screw up with her.

That weekend, J.B. invited Millie and the children to his home for dinner. Millie was surprised by the invitation. Many times Millie had been there, but only to go to bed with J.B., or spend intimate weekends with him. Millie just assumed that was the only relationship, they were going to have, since he'd made his feelings quite clear in the beginning, that he had no intentions of ever getting married. J.B. professed to loving her and she was happy with that. Millie had three children to raise and her life was filled with them, that and completing college. She had her own dreams of bettering their lives when she graduated and got a better job.

Millie and the children arrived at J.B.'s home on Saturday evening as per instructed. As she parked her car behind his in the driveway, she wondered what the occasion was. She'd had him over for meals at her home several times, but this was a first for him to reciprocate. Of course many times he took them out for fast food or a family buffet. J.B. had been more than good to them. Millie wasn't nervous, just curious. J.B. answered the door when Millie rang the buzzer. He'd told her it was casual, so she wasn't surprised to see him in a pair of dark slacks and a blue dress shirt unbuttoned at the neck.

J.B. smiled and welcomed everyone in. Of course Millie was already familiar with the house, having been there so many times, but the children were awe-struck as they roamed through the downstairs rooms. Terry ran her hand over the Chippendale table that gleamed with the Tiffany lamp on it and smiled with admiration.

Paul stood in front of the fireplace, stooped over and looked up into the flue. He grinned as he told Melody that he bet Santa Claus could get down this chimney. It was a concern Melody always had because they didn't have a fireplace. Millie had told them she always left the back door open so he could get into their home. It was just too much for Melody. She crawled up on J.B.'s lap stared earnestly into his face, and asked him. "Does Santa Claus come down that chimney?"

J.B., looked at Millie; he didn't want to say the wrong thing and disillusion the little tot. Millie took her cue and answered, "Nobody ever sees Santa, Melody, but I'd say it's a very good possibility that this is how he gets into this house." She winked at J.B. who looked relieved when Millie came to his rescue.

Mary, J,B,'s housekeeper, stood in the doorway and quietly observed the small scenario and smiled at J.B.'s discomfort. She then announced that dinner was ready. The children stared at the dining table that could seat twenty people and the gleaming crystal chandelier overhead table. The place settings were all down at one end. A booster seat was on one of the chairs, and Melody hopped up on it with her big brothers' assistance. J,B. set at the head of the table with Terry and Millie on each side of him. Knowing the children would be uncomfortable with a formal course meal, Mary served the food family style. The children relaxed and enjoyed the good food that Mary had prepared.

After they were finished with the meal, Terry innocently volunteered to help Mary with the clean-up. Mary looked at J.B. and smiled, then answered the little girl, "Thank you, darling, but I have a helper tonight. But I appreciate your offer, however I think J.B. just expects you to be his guest." Millie remembered, from her own childhood, the snobby, arrogant servants that worked for her parents, and realized that Mary had used a kind and loving diplomacy to deal with Terry. Millie silently chided herself for not explaining to Terry better social behavior. Long ago Millie willingly accepted and became comfortable with the middle class lifestyle.

Millie and the children didn't stay too long after the meal, because it was getting close to Melody's bedtime. They all thanked J.B. and went home. Millie contemplated they'd gotten the invitation. What was J.B. up to? Did he want to point out subtly, the difference in their social status? Was he trying to tell her something? Why? She hadn't demanded anything from him.

J.B. asked Millie to marry him two weeks later after Millie had finished her first semester and was on a short break. They were in a small quaint restaurant, and an elderly man was playing a violin, while they savored the delicious Italian food. J.B. drew her left hand closer to him and slipped a diamond ring on her finger. "Millie, will you marry me, please say you'll be my wife. I love you, baby."

Millie gazed into J.B.'s eyes and then stared at the ring. Millie couldn't forget nor forgive the separation they endured just because she mentioned marriage to J.B that first weekend, nor the uncomfortable feeling she had when she'd taken the children to his home for dinner. It just wasn't going to happen. She believed he felt obligated to ask her now. He knew her religious beliefs, that she didn't approve of singles fornicating, but their desire for each other overrode that belief. Still, he knew Millie anguished over it. She'd told him she wanted to set a good example for the children. She adamantly refused his marriage proposal, but after a lot of coaxing, she did accept the diamond ring he offered her. Being engaged was enough until she was through school and was independent. Maybe by then, she would be assured that J.B. was sincere and this wasn't just a sexual fling on his part. There were still too many unanswered questions in her mind to accept him and his life completely.

Millie went to the police station and asked for their help in locating her sister, Susan. She was told they couldn't really list her sister as missing, because obviously she abandoned her family and chose to disappear and shirk her responsibilities. They would investigate, but gave Millie little hope. She was told, these people often change their names, even their looks to avoid being found. She told J.B. about her visit to the police station and their lack of encouragement one evening when he was at her home. He'd brought pizza for their dinner and later the kids were in their rooms, either doing homework or playing games on the now, family computer. "J.B., I went to the police station and asked them to help find Susan, they seemed to think that it would be impossible. They're going to look through criminal records and traffic violations, but they didn't give me much hope." She looked so discouraged, it nearly broke J.B.'s heart. He knew how much she cared for her sister and worried about her.

"She doesn't want to be found, Millie. She ran out on her kids. My God, sweetheart, Melody wasn't even a year old yet. How could she do that? How could she desert her children?"

"Melody, of course has no memory of her, but Paul does. Can't you see how sad he looks sometimes?

I know how it made me feel when my parents excluded me from their lives, it's a hurt you never get over. I still can't believe Susan left her children like she did."

"I'm sorry Millie. You are more emotionally involved in this than I am, but I think Paul is very well adjusted. He's a good kid. Are you sure you want to stir up a hornet's nest, by trying to bring her back into yours and the kids' life? You said she was a heavy drinker, perhaps she has a drug problem also."

"Yes, my sister and I were very close growing up; we only had each other. We were physically provided for, but any love or family connection; we found in each other. I just feel deep down inside me, that Susan needs me, that she's crying out for me. But she's too ashamed to come back home. She's in trouble, J.B., she needs me and her children need her."

J.B. smiled at her. This was so typical of the woman he loved. She was a wonderful caring human being, and he'd do what he could. He wouldn't tell her of his plan, but already one was forming in his mind. He had all the resources necessary at his finger tips to find her sister and the willingness to do so. The police were indifferent about runaways. For one thing, there were too many of them and it would take too much manpower and money to even attempt to find them. They'd just check to see if the person missing had a record of some kind. They even checked the national register for serious traffic violations. He wondered what her sister was like, was she like Millie or was she cold and indifferent? He was going to find out, if at all possible. Maybe her sister wasn't even alive.

Two months later, the private detective that J.B. hired found where Susan Nobles was located, Millie's gut feeling was right. She'd sunk to the lowest level of humanity. He chose not to tell Millie of the circumstances under which they'd found Susan, or to even tell her she'd been found. He asked the private detective to pick her up. She was placed in a rehabilitation facility, to get detoxed and cleaned up, if she was willing to receive the help offered her. Often they weren't able to break the drug or alcohol habit.

J.B. was going to take a plane to where she was; he wasn't dragging Susan's butt home to Millie and the kids, if she was going to be trouble. They didn't need it, nor would it help Susan. He'd deal with it. If and when Millie's sister was prepared to enter society again, he was going to make damn certain she was sincere. Millie and those kids had been hurt enough because of her.

J.B. had taken his laptop with him on the flight to Trenton, New Jersey and conducted business as usual. When his rental car pulled into the parking lot of the rehabilitation center, J.B. pulled into a visitors parking spot and entered the building. He hadn't known what to expect, but he got the shock of his life when he was directed to Susan's room. He raised his eye brows when he saw her and thought, she looks just like his beloved Millie and Terry, but years of abuse had taken its toll. Her entire body had a dissipated look, her skin was gray and shallow, her hair limp and lifeless and she was skin and bones. He could hardly believe that this relic of a human being was Millie's sister, and Paul and Melody's mother. His heart went out to her as he pulled a chair up. He watched her long lashes lift over her sunken eyes and he stared into eyes like her sisters. He only read hopelessness, despair and something akin to death. "Susan, my name is J.B. Cornell, I'm your sister Millie's fiancé. I would like to help you. Your sister and children want and need you back in their lives. Will you accept my help?"

She looked like she was trying to concentrate, as if she were trying to recall her sister and her children. He watched her face as the memory returned. She moaned, it sounded like an injured animal, not a human sound. "They don't want me back. They'd be better off forgetting they ever knew me. I'm worse than trash. What I've done is beyond what a decent human being can possibly fathom." She closed her eyes, the long lashes sweeping down her cheek. J.B. noticed a tear slide down her face. She was right about that, which is why J.B. chose not to tell Millie the way they'd found her and where. They'd found her in a filthy brothel. She was supplied with drugs and alcohol for services rendered. If Susan recovered and J.B. took her home, her secret was safe with him. He watched as her eyes opened wide. "Hell, my own parents didn't want me."

Now, J.B. knew how to reach her. Evidently Millie was made of stronger stuff, she'd accepted her parents' rejection and went on with her life, well not quite unscathed, but able to function as near to normally as she possibly could. She didn't even harbor any hate for them; it was more like she pitied them. Susan had been destroyed by their rejection. She'd never been able to cope with life since. He would talk to her psychiatrist, fill him in. Maybe she could be reached. He'd felt little hope when he first entered Susan's room, now he felt there was a chance and Susan was going to get it. He stood and patted Susan's bowed, dejected head. "I'll be back in to see you, you're going to be all right, Susan, just hang in there."

"Millie's lucky to have you in her corner, I was never so lucky." Susan's eyes were changing, for the first time, he saw hope in them. She attempted to smile, but it was like her facial muscles forgot how. It was a pathetic sight.

J.B. didn't have to wait long to see Susan's doctor. They discussed Susan's case, and J.B. filled him in on what he knew. The doctor confided in J.B. that Susan always refused to open up to him. Now he'd obtained information to work with, he could get to the root of her lack of self esteem and work on her emotions for her two children and her sister who was making such a sacrifice raising them. "Mr. Cornell, thank you for coming here to the clinic. My heart aches when I can't reach them and they pull back. If Susan was released now, she'd go right back to that life; she doesn't have any self worth. She feels she deserves nothing—How long are you staying, Mr. Cornell?"

"My flight home is tomorrow evening, and if I can help you any more, just give me a call at the hotel I'm staying at." J.B. gave him the numbers.

Early the next afternoon, J.B. received a call from the clinic. He was asked to come immediately. He feared the worse, as he drove his rental car through the unfamiliar streets. He was thinking maybe Susan had attempted to take her life. Perhaps she did! He rushed into the hospital and was told by the receptionist to go directly to Doctor Simpson's office.

He saw was Susan crumpled up in a chair wailing. J.B. crouched down in front of her chair, then gathered her frail body in his arms and sat down in the overstuffed chair holding Susan's frail body close to him. "Come on, Susan, talk to me. What can I do to help you?"

Sniffling, and using the back of her hand to wipe away the tears, she answered him. "The Doc has been talking to me, trying to tell me that my parents' rejection was not my fault. Well, maybe that is true, but my behavior the last twelve years is my responsibility, I don't deserve a family anymore. So many men, the booze, the drugs. I don't even deserve to live."

She remained huddled in his arms. "Susan, listen to your doctor, you couldn't cope with the rejection. Millie accepted it and so has Paul."

"What do you mean, Paul has accepted it?" The statement registered into her drug damaged brain. "Does he think I rejected him, for God's sake?"

"What would you call it? You ditched him. You left him with a loving aunt, but you rejected him."

Susan's face registered denial.
Then slowly acceptance won out. "How's he taking it?"
"He's sad sometimes. Millie knows he's thinking of you, but

he prays for you and still loves you. He told Millie that when he is grown up, he is going to find you and take care of you. He's a wonderful boy; you can be proud of him."

"Do you think the kids and Millie could forgive me and take me back in spite of all the terrible things I've done?"

"In a heartbeat. Susan. Love never dies and they love you, they are family. I have no idea what sort of human beings yours and Millie's parents are. I know they are intelligent people, both hold down responsible positions, but some human factor was definitely missing in their personal genetic make-up, that they couldn't love their own children. It surely as the devil, wasn't anything you or Millie said or did. It's their own dysfunction, not yours or Millie's fault."

"In my heart, I never left my sister and my children, I just felt unworthy. I was there for three days and witnessed how capable and strong Millie was, and what a good home she was providing for Terry. I'd never been able to do that. I didn't deserve them. I believed they'd all be better off without me in their lives." J.B. felt Susan's body quiver with self repulsion and the ugliness of what her life was.

"Susan, I'll make a deal with you. If you get your act together and get physically back on your feet again, I'll personally come and get you and take you back to your family." J.B. took his hand and raised her chin so he could see into her eyes, so much like Millie's. "I'll promise you, your past behavior can be our secret, it'll never be known to Millie or your children, not unless you want to tell them. That will be your decision. They won't hear it from me."

"You know the truth about me and yet, you make this offer; where in hell did Millie find you?" J.B. laughed and winked at her.

"I'll confess something to you. I wasn't worth a hill of beans until your sister cleaned my act up. I have my issues too, but after I met your sister and she became part of my life, I've changed my mind on a lot of things; including marriage. If you trust her, she'll get you on the straight and narrow path. She is one strong minded little cookie; one to be reckoned with.

She's an amazing woman." J.B.'s eyes misted over and filled with love when he spoke of Millie. Susan saw this and hope soared through her. She'd never believed that a man could love a woman like J.B. loved her sister. At least she'd never experienced it.

She scrambled off his lap, and stood up. She was a little wiggly, but she managed. She stuck her hand out to him. "You've got a deal, partner." For the first time he saw the familiar resemblance between the two sisters as her eyes flashed. He shook his hand, then patted her gently on the frail, bony shoulder.

"Way to go, Susan." He gave Susan and Doctor Simpson his home, office, and cell phone numbers and told them to call anytime. "Susan, you'll know when you're ready to come home. Your doctor will call me, and I'll come get you and bring you home where you belong."

"J.B., how has Millie been coping with raising the kids alone? I feel so guilty, dumping my two kids on her; she had enough responsibility just raising Terry."

"When I first met Millie, she was working in a sweatshop, a sewing factory, barely able to make ends meet. I called in a few markers and now she is getting the help she was entitled to all along. She is going to college for one thing."

"College!" Shock registered on Susan's face.

"When you're ready, maybe you can do the same thing. We'll look into it when you are well and back home." He hoped that would give her incentive to get better, but he doubted if she was college material anymore. The hard drugs always did a number on the brain cells.

"I probably won't see you again before you catch your plane, J.B. I want to thank you, I never had anyone believe in me before."

"You've got to be kidding, you've got a family waiting for you back home." He hugged her and left, knowing for sure that she was going to make it. J.B. felt good as he boarded the plane that was going to take him back home. Back to Millie. He thought about her on the flight home, while gazing out the window at the earth below whizzing by. He knew Millie had no intention of marrying him. He didn't even know how he'd managed to talk her into taking his diamond ring. She felt undeserving. Maybe if Susan got well and came home, he'd have an ally in her.

Five months later, Doctor Simpson called and told J.B. Susan was able to go home. "Mr. Cornell, the money you've been sending to Susan, she hasn't spent. She felt she didn't really need anything. She has the money to pay for her airfare back home. I just called to let you know when her flight is scheduled to arrive. You'll be surprised when you see her again. It's one of my rare success stories, and I owe a good part of it to you. You seemed to know just the right things to say to her, even gave her incentive. You're in the wrong field; instead of being a lawyer, you'd have made a fantastic psychiatrist. You've got natural talent."

J.B. thought about what the doctor had said to him. If he was so damn smart, why couldn't he convince Millie to trust him and marry him. He loved and wanted her more than anything in the world. Why couldn't he make her believe that?

The day that Susan was to arrive, J.B. planned his day so he could personally pick Susan up at the airport. He still hadn't told Millie about finding her over five months ago. If Susan wasn't what he hoped she'd be, he was going to put her up at a motel, and keep her away from the family until he was sure she was sincere. He wasn't going to allow anyone to wreak havoc on his family. J.B. was pleasantly surprised when a totally different woman from what he'd seen at the hospital walked toward him. He watched as she gracefully and confidently walked across the tarmac.

Her smile was incredible as she recognized J.B. She'd probably gained forty or fifty pounds, showing off a shapely figure. Her hair and skin glowed with good health. She looked great. "J.B., I can't wait to see them. I'm going home."

J.B. picked her bag off the carousal, took Susan's arm, and led her to where his car was parked. "You look great, Susan.

You did it, I'm proud of you."

"I won't let you down J.B. I owe you big time." J.B. could easily accept from Susan, he just wanted more from Millie. So much more.

They drove the forty-five minutes to Millie's home in near silence. Occasionally he glanced at Susan. She was nervous, and she kept clinching and unclinching her hands in her lap. He'd read that if the former addicts were in a stressful situation, they were thirsty. An overpowering thirst: "Susan, reach behind you, there is a small cooler of drinks; you can get me out a soda, if you will." He flashed her a smile.

She handed him his coke and got a fruit juice, and nearly drank the whole thing before she released her lips from the bottle. "God, I was thirsty, Doc said I would be when I was upset. I'm scared, J.B., what if they don't want me?"

"Susan, I haven't told them that I found you and that you are coming home. This is going to be a shock for them. I want you to realize that maybe their first reaction seeing you might be disappointing. Give it some time. It'll be all right after the initial shock wears off.

J.B. pulled up in front of Millie's home. Susan's head scanned the area and smiled, "Is this it? This is really a nice neighborhood. When did Millie move here?" Surprise and pride showed on Susan's face.

"A while ago. Do you see who is walking up the sidewalk, Susan?"

Susan leaned forward and peered through the windshield. "That can't be Paul, he's gotten so big."

Paul spotted J.B.'s car and ran the rest of the way. "J.B., you should see my report card, it isn't as good as Aunt Millie's, but I think it's great." He looked at Susan for the first time, when J.B. opened the passenger door and Susan got out. "Mom, is that really you?" His eyes widened with surprise and shock.

He dropped his back pack and rushed to Susan, nearly knocking her off her feet as he grabbed her and hugged her. "You look wonderful, Mom, just as I remembered. I'm so happy to have you home." He gazed adoringly into his mother's face. Together they walked up the sidewalk to the front door. Susan couldn't stop touching him, amazed at how big and strong he'd gotten. Her son.

J.B. hesitated, maybe he shouldn't go in, perhaps the family needed privacy to get reacquainted, but when Susan turned and pleaded with her eyes, he followed her into the house.

Paul and Susan went in first. J.B. stayed in the back ground, and quietly observed the reunion between the two sisters. They both cried, and couldn't seem to be able to stop hugging one another. This was always J.B.'s reward when a plan came together. The expense or his time was immaterial. This was all the satisfaction he ever needed. "I hate to interrupt, but may I suggest Chinese for dinner tonight? My treat."

Paul responded immediately, "Yeah, that sounds good, count me in, want me to go with you? I can run in the restaurant and carry it out for you?" Paul's eyes were shining with happiness and joy. He kept looking at his mother. "Do you like Chinese food, Mom?"

"It sounds great." Susan was holding Melody on her lap who was nearly four years old now and had she'd been just a baby when she left her with Millie. Paul told her this was their Mom, but Susan didn't think she realized what a Mom was. Aunt Millie was the one who that had always been there. Susan knew it wasn't going to be easy establishing a relationship with them again, but remembered what Doctor Simpson told her, and the promise that J.B. made her. Somehow she was going to make it.

"Terry, J.B. tells me that you have a computer. I took several courses in computer technology. I hate to brag, but I think I'm pretty good. Need any help with anything?" Susan shyly offered.

Terry's eyes brightened, it was so frustrating to try to figure out how to work a computer, when you didn't know anything about it. Terry grabbed her hand and dragged her into her bedroom, Melody tagged along, still puzzled about who this lady was. She looked so much like Aunt Millie and everyone kept saying she was her mom.

Miriam was looking for a assistant at the warehouse. Miriam preferred the designing and decorating work, she hated the office work, just maybe, he could get Susan a job. Miriam and Hank would be good for Susan and wouldn't hold her past against her.

Later when they were eating, Terry couldn't stop talking about all the things Aunt Susan could do on the computer. Susan was happy that she had taken those courses and could teach Terry. It took so little to please Susan and make her happy, just a kind word made her want to cry. "That was just your first lesson, every day I'll show you more. It's almost magical what you can do with it."

"You'll have to show me. I've managed to type a few papers, but knowing how to use it, would really help me in school. A lot of the kids have lap tops, and they've been showing me a few things. Thanks, Aunt Susan." Susan looked like a little kid that just pulled the prize from a cracker jack box. She beamed. For the first time in a long time, she was needed and felt useful.

J.B. thought about getting Susan and her children at their own house, but knew after watching her insecurity, that she would be too frightened to go at it alone. But he would look into a job for her; she needed to be kept busy and involved with interesting projects. Sitting here alone all day while everyone else was going to school, wouldn't be good for her. Maybe Doctor Simpson was right, he did seem to almost feel the needs of these women. He looked at Millie. She was glowing, having her sister here made her happy. That also made the effort and the expense worthwhile, for he was willing to do anything to please the woman he loved.

Millie was wearing a blue sweater and black slacks. He watched the curves of her breasts as she leaned forward, hoping he could get her alone soon. The desire for her rushed over him. She looked up and caught the look of need and desire in his eyes. She smiled and winked. His heart starting pounding. He knew somehow Millie would make time for them.

God, how he wanted this woman. He wanted her in his bed,

in his home, in his life. He wanted her to be his wife. Trying to convince her of that was the problem. Maybe Susan could get through to her; convince Millie that he was sincere. He knew that Millie made his life complete; without her he'd just revert back to dead-end relationships, and his life would be meaningless.

J.B. left them shortly after dinner was finished. The girls had a lot to talk about and intuitively he knew he was one of the subjects. He was almost out the door when Millie grabbed J.B.'s arm and stepped out on the porch with him.

She put her arms around his neck and hugged him close. "J.B., how can I ever thank you enough for finding and bringing my sister home to us, and I've never saw her so together like she is now. You've made a miracle happen somehow. Thank you, my love."

J.B. pressed his mouth to hers, as usual any physical contact affected them both. What was meant to be a tender, sweet kiss escalated into passion between them. J.B. doubted he'd ever get enough of this woman. "Go back in with your family, darling. You have a lot of catching up to do and maybe if you have time, call me." He kissed her again lightly and rushed to get in his car. As he drove off, he saw Millie was still standing on the small porch. A beautiful vision in the moonlight.

CHAPTER

5

M UCH LATER THAT NIGHT, J.B. was home and in bed, still struggling to go to sleep when he heard his doorbell ring. Something must have happened? Nobody would come calling after eleven o'clock. He drew his robe on and flew down the steps in his bare feet. He unlocked the door and opened it. There stood Millie with a silly grin on her face. "Want some company?"

Never had she looked so good to him. He pulled her inside, shut and locked the door. He'd been in the process of tying the belt to his robe, he let the ends fall to his sides, and his robe came apart. He always slept naked. Her eyes filled with desire as she went into his arms and pressed against his naked body. J.B. murmured in her ear, "oh baby, It's been so long. I don't think I can make it upstairs. There is a bearskin rug in Dad's den, you game?"

"Anywhere, darling, it's been forever. They half walked, half ran into the den, before they were midway across the room, J.B.'s robe was off and Millie's sweater and bra were on the floor. J.B. used both hands to rid her body of her black pants and underwear. She kicked them aside and they dropped to the floor. A trail of clothing marked their path. Their lovemaking was filled with a desperate hunger.

Later, when their desires were sated and their breathing was back to normal, J.B. asked, "Do you think the kids are all right with Susan? You know, it's just her first day back."

"Better than all right. Terry is over eleven, nearly twelve years old. She'll be fine, even if she was alone. I think Susan needs to spend time with Paul and Melody without me around. They have to get reacquainted again, especially Melody. They will depend on me more out of habit, and Susan needs to feel needed, loved and wanted. I left a note telling Susan I'd be gone until sometime Sunday. Terry is going to Sally's house later in the morning, so Susan will be alone with the kids." She nuzzled her face into J.B.'s chest, and started caressing his body, almost timidly. The gentle exploration of his body felt like a velvet cloud running over him. He inhaled her scent. He relaxed and enjoyed her feathery fingers gliding over his body. "Do you have any ideas what to do with me for nearly two days?" She huskily murmured in his ear.

J.B. chuckled. "I've been laying here trying to concentrate on that. I can't think of a single thing, you'll probably get bored and go home." He teased.

She giggled as she started kissing his body where her soft hands had already roved. "I've got a few ideas. I read a 'how to book', and there were a few things I'd like to try, just bear with me, I'm a novice." He moaned as her mouth traveled down his abdomen.

Sometime in the night, they managed to get into bed. Millie wondered what Mrs. Andrus would think about the trail of clothes going through the house. She drifted off to sleep in J.B.'s arms. Snug and secure.

Still, Millie was convinced that J.B. would tire of her eventually and seek other companions. What would a handsome, educated, successful man want with her? She'd made up her mind not to dwell on losing him eventually. She was going to enjoy him while he was hers.

Mrs. Andrus saw Millie's car in the driveway upon arriving

for work in the morning, so when she went inside she wasn't really surprised to find clothes strewn across the floor. As she picked up J.B.'s robe and Millie's clothes, and put them in the laundry, she wondered why they didn't get married. She assumed they enjoyed a healthy sex life. She wished she were closer to J.B. and could talk to him. She knew better than anyone why he was still a bachelor at thirty five years old and had no desire or intention to marry.

Much later that morning the pair of lovebirds appeared in the kitchen, both wearing white terry cloth robes. Mary was prepared for them, their hot breakfast was in the warming oven. She was folding towels in the adjoining laundry room. A room that J.B. was responsible for. The room was formerly used as a mud room, and the laundry was in the basement. It was J.B. who transformed the mud room into a laundry room for her so she didn't have so many steps to climb. She'd heard their gay, happy chatter as she worked to finish the laundry.

The conversation was interrupted when the phone rang. J.B. asked Millie to get it, as he was dishing up their food. Millie voice pleasantly rang out, "Hello."

J.B. watched Millie's face register surprise and pleasure as she spoke. "Mrs. Cornell, I'm so happy to finally hear your voice. I'm Millie Nobles, J.B.'s fiancee. I've wanted to become acquainted with you and Mr. Cornell for a long time. Where are you now?" J.B. watched the happy, smiling expression on Millie's beautiful face change to horror as she listened to his mother.

He watched Millie's eyes widen, then a look of shock spread across her beautiful face. J.B. grabbed the phone from her. He listened as he heard his mother vituperatively cutting Millie down, "How dare you presume to think that you are going to marry my son? A common street walker, with a illegitimate child, you certainly have brass, you slut." Millie watched as J.B.'s face changed to a hard, angry scowl.

J.B. broke into his mother's unreasonably cruel tirade. "Good morning, Mother, you certainly sound normal and so

CHAPTER
4

IN THE MONTHS THAT FOLLOWED, J.B. and Millie couldn't have been any happier, and completely in love with each other. Life settled down into a routine. J.B. would go to his office and Millie would go to college. She'd doubled up on her class schedule; her plan was to take the four year course in just a little over two years. No summer breaks for her. When Millie received her scores for the first semester, she was proud to show them to J.B.

"I knew you were smart, but a 4.0! I never received anything close to that in college. Millie, I'm so proud of you." He picked her up and swung her around the room.

In the preceding months, J.B. and Millie got into some disagreements. One was the matter of the household furnishings that mysteriously was delivered to her new home, then Millie discovered who had made all the arrangements and who paid for it. Millie insisted that J.B. give her the invoice; she vowed she would repay him when she was finished with school and held a better paying job. As she read the list of items, several were missing. "J.B., all the items I received aren't listed." She started naming off the deleted items. "The comforters, the drapes, the chaise lounge in her room and many others aren't like yourself this morning. Some things will never change." He slammed the receiver back in the cradle.

J.B. turned to Millie. "I'm sorry Millie, as you guessed that was 'Mother Dearest'. I'm sorry you had to hear that from her. It's a typical reaction you'd expect from her. Thank God my father is normal, or I probably would have ended up being one of those statistic childhood suicides. I can only apologize, sweetheart. I can't change her. That's the way she is: An evil persona. Except when she putting on her false airs and trying to influence people, she's good at that, too."

J.B. watched as the color started coming back into her face; she was staring at J.B. with a vacant stare. Her worse nightmare was coming true. She was just beginning to believe that J.B. really loved her, and now she was finding out that she wouldn't be accepted in his family. Nausea spread through her body; the bitter taste of bile surfaced in her mouth. She knew she was going to be sick, as she rushed into the bathroom.

J.B. stood helplessly in the kitchen. He turned, as he felt a familiar soft hand on his shoulder. "Oh, my darlin' boy, I'm so sorry." J.B. looked into the kind loving face of the housekeeper and wished again for the millionth time, that she'd been his mother. "I couldn't help but overhear, J.B. May I make a suggestion?"

"What, Mary o' mine?" She hadn't heard his boyish nickname for her in a long time.

"Let me talk to Millie, when she comes out of the bathroom. You know I've always been here for you, and I don't mean to interfere, but I don't want you to lose this wonderful girl of yours. I've watched now for several months; she has made you happy." J.B. watched as her kind loving eyes misted over with unshed tears.

J.B. started to say that he could handle it, but when he saw Millie come out of the bathroom, he knew by the determined look on her face that the war was over and he'd lost. He nodded to Mary and left the room.

"Millie, child, sit down here with me, and we'll have a cup of tea. I want to tell you a story."

Millie started to walk away, but then she noticed the tears running down the old woman's face, so she stopped.

"Talking never does much good, Mary. Facing facts square on has always worked for me and I'd never fit into this family; I know that now." Mary admired her determined proud little face.

"That is exactly what J.B. has been praying for, that you wouldn't fit in, as you said."

"What?" So, she was right then. Her inner feelings were correct. Always intuitively she knew something was wrong.

"Sit down, child and I'll explain. Please, for the love of God, please, listen to me. Don't break that boy's heart again."

That heart-felt plea softened Millie's resolve as she sank into the kitchen chair. She watched as Mary placed two cups of water in the microwave and got two tea bags from a small cannister sitting on the counter. Millie's mind was whirling, she was so hopelessly in love with J.B., but she'd always felt deep down that the romance was ill-fated. A no win situation.

Mary placed the steaming cups on the table, dropped the tea bags in each one, and started talking in her soft Irish brogue. "Millie, I've been with this family for thirty years. I was right off the boat from Ireland and anxious to start my new life in America. Then I was hired as a maid here in this house. J.B. was five when I first met him. I've learned about all the secrets of these people during all these years. Craig Cornell had just struck it rich, so to speak. He'd made modest investments with money he'd inherited from his uncle, and the stocks he'd bought sky rocketed. It made him a wealthy man overnight. They bought this house and restored it; then the small family moved in and I was hired. I was frightened, but Marsha Cornell was more frightened. She was ill-prepared for the change in their social status. I liked her then. She was fun-loving and was a bit of a tease. Then she started to change and not for the good.

"Craig was like J.B. He possessed a natural charisma, but Marsha didn't. She wasn't accepted by the elite members of society. Craig is a genius about selling and investing and making business investments and speculation. His good fortune continued until they were one of the wealthiest families living here."

Millie interrupted the fascinating story. "What was Marsha's life before they came into money?"

"They were the poor working class. I believe Marsha worked as a clerk in a dress shop. Craig was a salesman, just regular people living in a rented modest home. When they came into money, they started receiving all kinds of invitations to social affairs. Craig joined the Country Club and took up golfing. That man could fit into any circle. J.B. is so much like him." Millie remembered the first night she'd met J.B. he had looked so comfortable and relaxed in her shabby little kitchen, yet he lived in this impressive home. She brought her attention back to Mary as she continued on with her story.

"Marsha started changing over the months that preceded. A hard, bitter shield appeared almost magically, after she'd been snubbed and poked fun at several times. She was so humiliated. I felt very sorry for her, and Craig didn't help much. He just naturally assumed she'd adapt to their new life-style, but she didn't. She gradually learned how to put on the fake smile, and the indulgent tolerance. It became a role for her. Craig didn't like it, but he loved her and stayed with her. I believe their personal life was happy, but after a while, if the old Marsha existed, it was only in their bedroom. Even with me, she never let down her guard. At first, we were almost like girlfriends, she often wept and confided in me. But that all changed. She became a bitter, mean minded shrew.

"That's why J.B. doesn't introduce me to his friends and include me in his impressive life, he stays in mine, where it is safe but secretly afraid that I'll change like his Mother did." She sat quietly and sipped on her tea, wondering where J.B. was and knowing his heart was aching. Didn't she know all about past issues with parents?

"Millie, knowing the history now; I have a question for you. Can you handle it? Or will you struggle like Marsha did and give in to the mock protocol most wealthy people live by." Millie thought about that for a few seconds. Her life was changed just knowing J.B. She was accepted at college by wealthy young students; they seemed to like her, and she didn't think she'd changed, or had she? Her neighbors were poverty stricken, and enjoyed several good relationships with them. One she was teaching to cook another, she was teaching to sew garments for her three little girls. No, she hadn't changed. Her life was changing, but she wasn't. She was still friendly with Sally and Tess, always would be, regardless of how they misbehaved and where she lived. They'd been good to her and were her friends when she had no one else. But she hadn't really been challenged by the wealthy elite yet. She hadn't invaded their own territory.

She looked honestly into Mary's crystal clear blue eyes and answered. "I don't know that yet, maybe J.B. knows more about that than I do, and that's the reason he never took me into his inner circle. I guess I won't know until I face it, will I?

"I'm going to hunt up J.B., and Mary, thank you; no wonder J.B. loves you so much. I share a mutual affection." Millie grinned at her, and Mary's heart swelled with happiness. This girl was special, J.B. was worrying in vain.

"Go find your man, you silly girl." Millie could tell the openly acknowledged affection embarrassed her. She had the same crusty personality, with a heart of gold beneath just like Sally did.

Millie laughed as she started her search for J.B. For the first time, she was allowing herself to be really happy with her relationship with J.B. She found him sitting quietly in an overstuffed chair in his bedroom. He was going over some papers. She glanced at the twisted sheets on the bed and could smell the musty smell of their passion. He laid the papers on the stand alongside of him, then he stood and advanced toward Millie, eagerly searching her face for some kind of reaction. Was she angry? Hurt? Or had Mary gotten through to her, and made her understand that his mothers' behavior had nothing to do with the way he felt? He didn't realize he was holding his breath until Millie smiled at him. He exhaled and opened his arms. He nearly took her breath away with the fierce hug, he gave her. "I love you J.B. And whatever is in the future for us, we'll handle it together. Whether it's my wayward sister or your disillusioned mother, or even my ever loving dysfunctional parents. Together, I think we can make a pretty good jab at it. It's just you and me, love. Do you think you can handle that?"

Before J.B. kissed her, he muttered, "In a heartbeat, love."

*   *   *

Susan woke up and for an instant wondered where she was. She was back with her family. This was the first day of the rest of her life. She threw the comforter back and wondered where Millie was. She wasn't in the king-size bed they were going to share. She must be an early riser, Susan thought as she stepped into the shower. The children were up already, Susan discovered when she walked into the kitchen and spotted the dirty cereal bowls in the sink, then she noticed the freshly brewed coffee. Terry must have made it for her. She smiled as she thought about someone making an effort for her; it had been so long. She poured a cup and went into the livingroom where the kids were absorbed in Saturday morning cartoons. "Good morning." She greeted them, they were still in their pajamas.

Melody turned around shyly and spoke softly, then smiled sweetly. "Good morning, Momma." All the love a person could ever want was right here in this room, why had she looked elsewhere for it? "Good morning, sweetie. Terry, where is your mother this morning? Did she have a class?"

"No, Aunt Susan, she left a note. It said, she'd be back Sunday morning in time to go to church with us; she's probably spending time with J.B." Terry grinned knowingly. "She doesn't think I know about that kind of thing."

Susan laughed. Not her prim and proper little sister. She didn't blame her for a second. J.B. was something else. She'd never met a man like him, now with her questionable past, never expected to. Millie was so lucky. Fortunately Millie had saved herself for such a man, and her reputation was impeccable, she just had that one episode when she was fifteen and got pregnant. She was worthy of such a fine, educated man like J.B.

"What's the usual routine around here on Saturday, besides watching cartoons?" Susan grinned.

"Mom usually runs the sweeper and dusts, then she does laundry and sometimes she bakes cookies. Either that or she sews something for one of us. Mom is always busy with something. Melody and I have already cleaned our room, changed the sheets, dusted and ran the vacuum in there. That's our job. I don't know about Paul, if he did his or not. Did you Paul?"

Paul was totally absorbed in the adventure cartoon. He looked at Terry and said impatiently. "What did you say, Terry?"

"I just wondered if you cleaned your bedroom yet, and took the recycling to the bins. You know that is your job every Saturday." Terry sounded like a miniature Millie. That made Susan smile.

Paul frowned. "I will, right after this one is over. Geez, it is Saturday, you know, can't a guy have a little relaxation." Susan pictured him grown into a man; he was already getting a man's attitude.

Susan went into the kitchen to get another cup of coffee; Melody followed her. "Can I be your little helper today, Momma?" Susan picked her up and hugged her.

"Sure, I would love for you to be my helper. You can show me where everything is, can't you?" Melody beamed.

Susan's first day with her family went well; she couldn't bake or sew like Millie did, but she was a good cook. She found the ingredients for lasagna, and soon the house was filled with the pleasant aroma of the sauce cooking. Melody tagged along as she ran the sweeper, kept switching loads in the washer to the dryer, then folded the dry ones. She allowed Melody to do the dusting. She watched her little daughter as she meticulously dusted everything. The day flew by, and she wondered what she'd do all week when the rest of the family was in school. She hadn't worked a regular job in years, she thought, her guilty past suddenly eroding her mind. Doctor Simpson told her not to dwell on that. It couldn't be changed, she was told to only concentrate on the future. She quickly put the bad thoughts from her mind; it was like she'd been brain washed by the good doctor.

Sally came to pick up Terry and take her to a soccer game. Sally introduced herself when Terry went into her bedroom to get the soccer ball J.B. had given her. "You must be Susan, good to have you back. Millie has been so worried about you. Everything going all right so far?" Millie had told her about her two crusty friends. "Do you want me to put a word in for you to my boss for a job at the plant?"

Susan smiled warmly, "No, I was kind of hoping I could find something where I could use my skills with a computer. I took a couple courses a few years ago."

"Hey, that's great, better than working in a sweatshop. I never made the effort to learn another skill. Now you know what they say about teaching an old dog new tricks; it's too late now." She left out a boisterous laugh.

"I've been told, it's never too late." Susan shared cautiously. Sally gave her a knowing grin when Susan made that last remark. But before Terry left for the game, she told Paul and Melody to be good and listen to their mother.

After the laundry and the cleaning was finished, Susan cooked the lasagna and layered it with cheese and sauce. "Hmmm, that looks good, now we have two good cooks in the family. Someday I'm going to learn too. I have a lot of things to learn, don't I?" Melody asked innocently.

"Yes, you do, darling and momma will be right here to teach you and help you in anyway that I can."

"I hope so, momma." Melody's round innocent eyes gazed at her Mother.

When Susan lay in bed that night after the children were bathed and had gone to bed, she relished the memory of the compliments she'd received that day. She'd made more good memories today, than she had in the last three years of her wasted life. She felt hope surging through her as she drifted off to sleep. Tomorrow Millie would be back, and although she didn't expect Millie to share in her joy, Susan was happy for her and J.B.

Susan wondered what she'd do with her time when the older kids were in school and she and Melody would be left alone. She could clean, and do the laundry, and have the evening meal ready, so Millie would be free to study, or spend time with J.B, but would that be enough? They'd told her at the clinic to keep busy and not sit and dwell on past mistakes.

But what was she going to do when Millie was finished with school and Melody started school? What if Millie and J.B. got married? The days would stretch out long and empty. What was she going to do? For the first time, her life didn't evolve around a man. She could make her own choices. It wasn't right for her to sponge off Millie. She should try to make a life for herself and her two children, but could she? The old fears of being alone and abandoned came back to her. Doctor Simpson had told her she may still need more counseling when she became involved with just ordinary living again. What would be a normal annoyance for a normal person could become a real dilemma for her. Was Millie the right person for her to confide her problems with, or should she seek professional help?

CHAPTER
6

MILLIE RETURNED HOME SHORTLY AFTER breakfast Sunday morning. Terry and Susan gave each other knowing looks, but said nothing to Millie. After greeting everyone, Millie checked the refrigerator and found a large glass baking dish with leftover lasagna. Sunday dinner was already prepared. She grinned at Susan and went into her bedroom to get ready for church.

She was beginning to feel guilty about her romantic rendevous with J.B., nearly every weekend, then coming home and going to church. She felt like a hypocrite, the worse kind. And she was trying to set a good example for her daughter. She came back out. "I don't think I'll go to church today. I've got a slight headache, and I think I'm coming down with something." Geez, now she was lying to boot.

"Okay if just us kids go? I'm big enough to take care of Melody when she crosses the street and stuff like that." Terry pleaded with her mother. Millie nodded and they went in to get dressed. Millie felt so damn guilty.

"You having a bad day, sis?" Susan looked at her innocently.

"Something like that."

"Well, if you would get married to J.B., then I think your

headache would go away." Susan looked up at Millie.

Millie burst out laughing. "You always could read me like a book, Susan, I never could keep a secret from you."

"Maybe I'm your conscience, Miss Goody Two Shoes." Susan leaned back in the kitchen chair and laughed at the surprised look on Millie's face.

"Do you think Terry suspects anything like that?"

"Yep. Kids aren't that dumb, not like we were. They usually know the score by the time they are eight anymore. Probably Paul knows."

"Oh God, fine example I'm setting for them."

"Millie, relax, you just started going out with J.B. a few short mouths ago, up until then, knowing you, you were probably squeaky clean. So, the kids will connect you with J.B. You're expected to be a human being, you know. It's natural for a woman to search out a man and vice versa."

"I've got something to tell you, but don't get your hopes up yet, J.B. has to ask them."

"What, Millie, don't do that to me, you know I can't stand suspense, what is J.B. going to do? Tell me?"

"Good friends of his own the warehouse, where all these household items in this house came from.

He's going to tell them about your skills with a computer and try to get you a job."

"Wow, I swear Millie, if you don't marry that guy, I'm going to beat you to it. He's absolutely wonderful."

Millie looked dreamy eyed. "Yeah, he is, isn't he."

"Lord, I can't stand being around a love-sick calf. I'm going to church with the kids. You stay here and moon around if you want to."

They both laughed as they went into their bedroom to change clothes for church. Millie would silently ask for understanding and forgiveness today. She hoped the sermon wasn't about adulterous, lecherous behavior. She'd look guilty as sin.

As Millie was getting dressed she asked herself; why don't you marry J.B. now?—She started to make a mental list.

Number one—You have to get your career started after you're through college. Number two—If you got married, you'd lose your welfare check, J.B. would have to support Terry and you. Number three—Susan just got home, she needs more time.' I'll talk to him, she knew he wasn't a pauper, he lived in a mansion, drove an expensive car. She didn't know what a lawyer made, but it was probably more than she could imagine. She thought about what his mother said to her on the phone. If she married J.B., she'd really have to see which list was longer. I love J.B., and I miss him terribly when he's not around. Susan would have this apartment and furnishings for her and the two kids. Terry and her would share J.B.'s life. She could go to church with a clean conscience. She could sleep with J.B. every night.'

Susan's voice broke into her reverie. "Stop your daydreaming, and get dressed." Millie laughed. The no list was longer, but the yes list was surely more appealing. She'd talk frankly and openly to J.B. the next time they were together.

Maybe!

Thanks to J.B., Susan got her job at the warehouse, and luckily another employee lived in the next block, so Susan didn't have to wait around for the buses. The first night, Susan was so excited, that she talked incessantly about it. Millie tolerated it as long as she could, then butted in, "Sis, give it a break, will you? Go make cookies or you can hem this dress for me. Or do you want me to start telling you about my day at school?"

Susan grinned sheepishly. "I can't help it if I can't take things in stride like you do, I get excited."

"I know, Sis, and I'm happy for you." She paused and reflected a moment. "You know isn't it neat to be together again? I really missed you. Just our silly disagreements are fun." Susan gave her a hug, making the kids giggle.

Susan was wondering if Millie was feeling the same way she did. She was home where she belonged, with her sister and the kids, and she loved her job. J.B. was coming over later and Millie planned on talking to him about getting married soon, rather than wait another thirteen months when she graduated from college. They both owed so much to that man. He'd completely turned each one of their lives around.

Millie agreed when J.B. called that he could beep his horn and she'd meet him in the car. So when Millie heard the horn, she waved to them, while throwing butterfly kisses to the kids, and then went out the door smiling.

Susan knew that this was the kind of happiness she'd never know. Once a good man found out about her past, he'd drop her like a hotcake. She could dream though.

After Millie was settled in the front seat of J.B.'s car he smiled at her and said, "You look perky tonight, you must have had a good day at school." J.B. eyes swept over her sweater-clad chest. He thought Millie was so beautiful and now that her dark hair was shoulder length, the waves circled around her face like a puffy black cloud. He couldn't get enough of looking her. "I missed you. We don't see each other often enough."

"I've been thinking about a way to remedy that." J.B. was stopped at a red light, he turned, arched his eye brows and the question was in his eyes. "Yes, we need to talk about getting married sooner."

J.B. pulled into a vacant lot and stopped the car. "Millie, are you serious? Have you changed your mind about waiting?"

"Yeah, first we have to talk though, get a few things straightened out, before we can set a date."

"Shoot, what's your problem?" J.B. wanted to take her in his arms, but this was the first time he'd ever heard Millie talk this way. She never did anything rashly. He intended to hear her out. He couldn't believe this was happening.

"Details, you would call them, but they are important to me. Terry and I would live with you, wouldn't we?"

"Right, with Mary and me. You and Terry already have her wrapped around your fingers, so no problem with that, is there?"

"No, but I'd lose my welfare grant, and you'd have to support us until I am finished with college and am working again. Do you have a problem with that?" He didn't tell her that she wouldn't be funded for college either, but paying her tuition wouldn't be a problem, not if Millie was happy.

He grinned at her. "No problem, sweetheart."

"Susan would keep the house and the furniture, and she loves her job; I think she's going to make it. She said, that she needs month to get stocked up on clothes and such, and she wanted to know if you'd take payments on the furniture you bought?"

"Damn it Millie, I don't want to be repaid for that. It was something I wanted to do, just watching you and the kids enjoying it was all the reward or pay back I ever wanted."

Millie interrupted, "J.B., will you marry me?" He was throwing caution to the wind and going for it.

J.B. took her face in his hands, "We could fly to Las Vegas tonight, and we could be married before midnight, that soon enough? It wouldn't be a problem for me, the sooner, the better."

Millie laughed. "The kids would be so disappointed if they couldn't be there, and I want Susan to be my maid of honor, and Paul to give me away. I'm nearly finished with my gown. I've been working on it for months." He might have known, this girl and her dreams, she would want a perfect wedding day, which was fine with him. He was thinking about his mother and her parents. Not inviting them to his and Millie's wedding wouldn't be right, even he couldn't get away with that and he'd been thumbing his nose at society for years.

"Sounds like a plan, love. Big wedding, tiered cake, flowers galore, a good band at the reception. The works. The whole kit and caboodle. You got it, and after all this big hoopla, you will be my wife, my woman." He gathered her into his arms and kissed her, never wanting to let her go, "I love you, my precious wonderful woman."

"Oh J.B., I love you with all my heart and I'm sorry it's taken me so long to put my trust in you. It's my problem and I'm trying to overcome it. You are the first person in my life that has always come through for me. It's almost like a novelty in my life. I just have to accept it more graciously."

"I know, baby, I understand and I'll never let you down." They sealed their bargain with a tender kiss.

The next few weeks were hectic for everyone. J.B. insisted that he hire a wedding coordinator. The invitations were already designed and were being printed. Millie's gown was finished and she worked on Susan's, Terry's and Melody's. J.B. hesitantly called his parents and informed them of the plan and the date. Maybe his father would take his mother to Siberia and get lost then be unable to attend, but he knew better. His mother would be there and as usual, and do her thing. God, help them. Millie said she had no intentions of notifying her father and mother, and it wasn't a problem.

Susan was proving to be a big success at the warehouse; she was given more responsibility. She was even promoted to office manager and given a hefty raise. Miriam had wanted to back off from the business for years, now she could spend her time, doing charity and volunteer work, the way she wanted to.

That wasn't all! Susan's luck was changing all the way. She thought she was in love with the owner of the trucking firm that handled all the deliveries for the warehouse. He was fourteen years older than Susan, but he was flirting and coming on to her. Millie counseled her before she accepted a date with him. Susan was sure Gus would reject her when she told him the truth about her past.

The first date, they were a pair, both of them tense and nervous. Gus suggested getting a few drinks after their dinner, but Susan refused. "Gus, I'm an alcoholic, I can't touch a drink or I'd be right back into it again. I was also addicted to hard drugs. I want you to know that straight off, before our friendship goes any further. I've done a lot of things I'm not proud of, but I've finally got my life straightened out. I'm on the right tract now, and if you don't want to see me again; I'll understand." She gave it to him without self reproof, no excuses, only honesty. She couldn't do a thing about her past.

Gus didn't speak for a couple of minutes, he was trying to digest what Susan just told him and he wanted to give her the right reply. Hell, he was no saint, he'd made plenty of mistakes in his forty-three years. "Susan, this is a shock. I'm trying to understand. I would never have suspected. You look like an angel, so feminine and beautiful, but from what you've just told me, your life has been rough and self-destructive. I'm glad you finally got help and you're squared away now. That is the most important thing for you; you've overcome it, I'm proud of you. How about a tutti fruity? It's strictly a fruit juice drink and very good." He smiled at her, noticing the pensive look on her face. God, hadn't the girl been hurt enough? He didn't intend to add himself to the list of abusers that had used this woman. She didn't have to give him details of her past life. She had been and told him all that he needed to know.

"Thank you, Gus, I think that would be good. Gus, there's another thing I want to say. Please don't ever ask for specifics or details about my past. Just take my word for it, that it is best left unsaid. Bad enough I have to live with it; No one else needs to know."

Gus smiled at her. "I'll agree to that, only if you accept me for the man I am today. My past life isn't exactly pure and innocent either. I've made more than my share of mistakes and paid for every one of them dearly." He watched as Susan relaxed and took a deep breath. He respected her for telling him the truth. He tried to never dwell on his past mistakes, he wanted a future, and he wanted it with this lovely young woman sitting across the table from him. The days ahead suddenly looked brighter to him; he hoped he didn't disappoint her, and she returned the feelings he was getting for her. "Wanna dance, Sue? I can cut a pretty good rug."

When he put his arms around her on the dance floor, and she fit into his body like she'd been made for him. He knew this was the woman he'd wanted all his life. "I like the way you dance, Gus, you've got good rhythm"

Gus pulled her close and whispered in her ear. "I like the way you feel in my arms, like you belong there." He could feel Susan's body relax into his. He wanted to throw his arms up in the air and shout, "Hallelujah."

*   *   *

Millie's and J.B.'s wedding day was drawing closer, two more weeks and Millie would be Mrs. James Benjamin Cornell. Millie was always curious about the initials J.B. used instead of a formal first name. She asked him one time about it. The mystery was solved when J.B. explained it. He was named for both his grandfathers. The family, not wanting to show favoritism, started calling him J.B. when he was a small baby.

Sally, Tess and Susan wanting to do something special for Millie. They couldn't have a regular bachelorette party; Susan couldn't drink and no one wanted to tempt her. They decided to take her to a fancy restaurant. They all agreed that a special place like the Medallion would be perfect. Expensive, but they all wanted a night for Millie to remember. It ended up being a party of fifteen, some of Millie's fellow students and neighbors wanted to join in. Their table was at the far end of the huge restaurant, but they were in a position to see everyone who came in, yet they were obscure in the corner in an alcove. Drapes were hanging, so if the party in the corner wanted privacy, they merely had to pull the drapes shut. Their dinner over, some of the girls were drinking wine, others were enjoying a cup of coffee or cappuccino. Millie looked up and saw a party of six entering the dining room, then she spotted J.B. He was with a beautiful, blond-haired woman, and she was clinging to J.B., nestling into his body. He was returning the flirtation, all smiles and affectionate, sexual touches to her body. After they were seated, J.B. leaned over and whispered in her ear. She laid her head against his face, then they kissed, their lips lingering, romantically and tenderly. Millie didn't notice when J.B. pushed her away and moved his chair further away from the woman.

Millie froze. Sally also saw it. She muttered. "That sonofabitch, I can't believe this." Millie's face turned a ghastly gray. The hurt and shock on her face assaulted Sally's tender-hearted nature. She said to the other women. "Let's get out of here." Then signaled for the waiter for the check. Sally knew they would have to walk pass the group. J.B. was in the direct path of the exit. It couldn't be avoided.

J.B. looked their way when the procession of women pass. First he caught Sally's eyes, she was glaring at him. If looks could kill, he would be dead. Then he saw Millie's ashen face and literally felt sick to his stomach. Hell, this was just a little flirtation with an old lover, it didn't mean a thing, but to Millie, it was the end. He'd known her trust in him was fragile. He cursed himself as he watched her walk irately out the door. Now his face was turning gray.

One of his partners noticed and asked. "J.B., did you just see a ghost? God, man you look sick." J.B. closed his eyes, no way in hell was Millie ever going through with their marriage plans. He knew as he was sitting there that it was over with them. Millie's trust and faith in him were just too fragile to laugh this off. She would be hurt and take personal offense.

J.B. had to get out of there, before he made a fool of himself. "I'm terribly sorry, but I'm not feeling well, you'll have to excuse me, I have to leave." He stood and walked away from his group who was staring after him, as he hastened to the exit.

He watched as Millie's car and several others left the parking lot. He followed them. Susan was driving Millie's car. He watched when Susan reached their house, she got out of the car, then locked it. She was alone. Where was Millie?

He knew where Sally lived. He drove to her home and parked up the street. Sally's car pulled into her driveway. He watched as Tess, Sally and Millie got out of the car and went inside. He laid his head back on the seat, and wished like hell for the last hour of his life to disappear. But it didn't. He was going to knock on that door, go in there and talk to Millie. He knew their old buddies were consoling her, probably cursing him out. Maybe that was the ringing in his ears. "Oh baby, I'm sorry." He remained in his car, sitting there for hours it seemed, waiting for Millie to come back out. She never did. They hadn't turned the lights off, so J.B. knew they were still up.

After three hours, J.B. mustered up the courage to knock on the door. No one answered, so he tried the doorknob. The door opened, and he walked inside. First he noticed the empty bottle of Jack Daniels on the floor. He couldn't help but smile. The three of them were drunker than skunks. Millie was passed out, but Tess and Sally were still semiconscious.

The two women looked at the hazy projection of J.B. standing in the room. That was close enough to tell him what they thought. Both in intervals both women blasted him with obscenities.

"You dirty rotten low down bastard. You filthy dog." Tess slurred out drunkenly. "You sneaking weasel." J.B. was relieved to hear the words, he'd been calling himself worse for the last three hours.

Sally tried to stand, but fell back unto the sofa. "You skunk, you're the lowest form of man or beast. How could you do this to Millie?"

"Girls, it meant nothing, it was a mistake. We were just flirting, for God's sake. It meant nothing to me. Millie is everything to me."

"Tell it to the Marines, boy, maybe, they will throw you a pity party. We'll not buying any of it." Sally glared at him. "You miserable coyote, you two-timing bastard." He watched as the two women passed out into oblivion. He raised their legs up, and covered them with a blanket that was on the back of the sofa, then he went over to Millie. She reeked of booze, her lovely face was smeared with dried tears, and her mascara streaked on her checks. He knelt down and laid his face in her lap. Then he rose and gathered her into his arms and sat down in the chair. He kissed her swollen face, then her lips. He was startled when she spoke, her words came out slurred and nearly incoherent. "Oh J.B., I gave you all my love, why wasn't it enough?" He closed his eyes when he heard the pain in her voice. He spoke to her, hoping her subconscious mind would remember his words.

"Millie, my love. I love and cherish you more than life itself, and from the bottom of my heart, I ask for forgiveness. That woman means nothing to me. It was just a stupid mistake — one that I'm praying you can understand and forgive me for. I love you, my darling and I will forever. Please, my love, forgive me." He kissed her lax mouth, savoring her taste, hoping it wouldn't be the last time he could hold her in his arms. He could hear the whimpers and feel shudders in her body. She couldn't get enough to ease the pain, he'd caused her. He thought of a few more names that Sally and Tess should have called him, as he tried to make her comfortable in the chair. He gently shoved her hair out of her face, then kissed her again. He left, but before he went out the door he took one last look at his beloved woman scrunched up in the chair, hoping and praying that this wasn't the last time he'd see her.

J.B. got in his car and drove to his home. He took a shower, but he didn't even attempt to try to sleep. He sat down at his desk to finish some work he'd brought home. His brain couldn't function well enough to accomplish anything, so he went over to his bed and laid out with his arms under his head. What could he say to Millie to convince her that he would never be unfaithful to her? How could he convince her of his fidelity? His loyalty. What could he possibly say to her after she'd witnessed him kissing another woman?

He was guilty of the deed, but somehow he had to convince Millie that it was just a minor flirtation, and it meant nothing.

CHAPTER 7

NEEDLESS TO SAY THE THREE women woke up with hangovers. Sally and Tess were more familiar with them, but this was the first one for Millie. She thought she was going to die, and prayed that she would. Tess offered her a concoction made with tomato juice. Millie drank it, but she knew it wouldn't stay down. She was right about that, and rushed to the bathroom. She was surprised when she started feeling more human later in the day. She thought about her dream of J.B. He was holding her, loving her, whispering endearments in her ear. Begging for forgiveness. That was something else she would stop doing. No more dreams. It was going to be strictly reality from here on.

Sally and Tess didn't say anything to her about last night, and she was thankful. She had to think it out, but one thing was for sure, she'd already decided that J.B. was history. She didn't care how much she loved and wanted him; the image of him holding that woman was printed indelibly in her brain like a photo. She'd never forget it. After managing to keep a cup of tea down and a dry piece of toast, Millie asked Sally to take her home.

When Millie was home again, Susan decided not to mention

anything about last night, and the horrendous repercussions of it. Susan's heart ached for Millie. How many times had she been hurt like this? That's why she'd turned to drugs and booze. The pain was more tolerable. She thought about Gus; it was hard not to love him. He was just a big tender-hearted lug that could give her the empathy her soul yearned for. She didn't mind his rough edges because she knew he had a good heart. For the first time in her life she thought she just might find happiness. Now, it was Millie that was suffering the horrid suffering of heartbreak.

"Millie, I have dinner in the oven. I thought we'd take the kids to the park this afternoon, Gus will be here for dinner. I hope you don't mind."

Millie glanced at Susan's face. She'd lost the hard lines on her face. Her face was softer. She looked more like her big sister did before she started down the wrong path, and it accelerated into a tragic life. Maybe, just maybe, Susan had found a good man in Gus. She hoped so. "I'm happy for you Susan. I think Gus will treat you and the kids okay. He reminds me of a big gentle dog, longing for someone to pat him on the head.—Oops, that didn't sound right did it? I don't think he's a dog, just that he shows his tenderness in a million ways to you and the kids. I personally think his big rough exterior hides a heart of pure gold."

"Millie, I'm so glad you said that, I was hoping that I hadn't imaged it. He's a big softie and I think I'm in love with him. He has asked me to marry him, but I'm afraid, what if—

Millie interrupted her. "Don't be afraid, Susan, you deserve the happiness this man will give you. Marry him and don't ever look back." Susan hugged her sister, trying to meditatively reassure her, to move forward with this new phase of life.

Millie didn't go to the park with the family. She studied Gus doing dinner. He was so besotted with Susan. He was pathetic. She wondered if J.B. looked at her that way. Stop that, she cautioned herself, don't even go there. She decided that what you saw in Gus was what you got, no hidden agendas, nothing about him showed any sign of duplicity.

That afternoon, Millie was sitting on a chaise lounge, studying. She looked up and saw J.B. coming around the house. She knew this would happen, there would have to be a confrontation. "How do you feel this afternoon Millie? You were out of it last night, when I saw you at Sally's." Then it hadn't been a dream. J.B. had held her on his lap and begged for forgiveness. She could still feel his fervent kisses on her face. "Darling, I love you, that woman meant nothing to me. My firm just got her off on a vehicular homicide charge. She was grateful, and I guess I did get carried away when she was all over me like wall paper. Christ, I'm only human, Millie. I'm just a man." Maybe that was the problem, Millie thought, she'd put J.B. on some kind of pedestal, and she couldn't bear the thought of him not being perfect.

"J.B., I've got real good eyesight, and if you would have been someplace more private, there would have been more than kissing. I'm not stupid, nor am I as naive as you seem to think I am."

J.B. closed his eyes tightly. What could he say. Maybe she was right, that damn woman always did have more sex appeal than any woman he'd ever known. Their affair had been hot and heavy, until she got bored and moved on to another man. She knew how to push every one of J.B.'s buttons, like she did with so many other men. Still, she couldn't hold a candle to Millie's sweet, ardent lovemaking. With her, it was making love, not indulging into primal, animal behavior, wanton, physical pleasure. Lustful pleasure that never left a lasting memory. Out of sight, out of mind. "I'm sorry Millie, can you forgive me?"

"J.B., I owe you so much. You turned my life completely around, and I have a wonderful future to look forward to now. And Susan, you saved her life, period. She would probably be dead, if you hadn't found her and gotten help for her. I'll love and admire you as long as I live, but I won't delude myself anymore about you and I on a more personal basis. You were a playboy when I met you and you still are. I know you felt guilty because of my guilty conscience, my own personal moral code, and you felt obligated to ask me to marry you."

"Millie, I love you."

Millie laughed softly, "J.B., you love em all." She started to take her diamond off her finger, but J.B. laid his hand over hers preventing her from removing the ring.

"Please don't do this Millie, I beg you. I do love you, more than you'll ever know. I want you to keep that ring, as long as you have it, maybe I can dream to. Don't deny me some hope."

"J.B., no wonder you are a good lawyer, you always know just the right thing to say. I'll keep the ring, It'll remind me of the pitfalls of foolishly giving your heart away. It'll be a good reminder. Thank you." J.B. looked into her fabulous eyes and the glint, the spark was gone, the one he'd put there and then carelessly removed.

"Darling, you have a good life and thanks to you, I will too. I'm not angry and upset. I love you, J.B., maybe part of me always will. I know I'll never forget you." Millie was finished. He could grovel, beg, but it wouldn't change anything. He'd stupidly hurt the only woman he ever loved and ever would love. He pulled her up from the chaise lounge, held her tight and kissed her, never wanting to take his mouth from hers. She pushed him away, and he saw the tears in her eyes. "Goodbye J.B."

She rushed into the house and slammed the door behind her, he heard the click of the lock. He stood quietly for a long time, before he moved dejectedly toward his car.

The next day at college, Millie walked into the student counselors' office. She'd been thinking about her predicament, her future, and it seemed her goal was too far away. Too far out of reach. "What can I do to help you, Millie?" Mrs Rostrum was pleased to see her here. Millie had the reputation of being very self sufficient, needing no ones' help.

"I was wondering if I have sufficient education and training to get a job in the field. I've been taking courses at night, is it possible?"

"Millie, I'm surprised you haven't received such offers already. We are all confident that you will excel, and be offered top-notch positions when you graduate. I'll send out some queries, see what I can do for you. Could you relocate, Millie?"

Millie hadn't thought about that, but suddenly she wanted to. She wanted to get as far away as she could from J.B. and anything that reminded her of him. She couldn't trust her betraying body to concur with her mind. "Yes, the West Coast would be nice, better weather and better opportunities, maybe."

Millie thanked her and left, she had another hour before her next class. She wandered into the library. A couple of the girls were there that attended the dinner with her. She was waved to and she walked over and joined them. "How are you doing, Millie?" Gwen asked her quietly.

Millie smiled at her young friend. She raised her hand, her thumb and fore finger in a circle, gesturing everything was okay. She opened her book for the next class, but J.B.'s face kept appearing before her, damn, she wanted to cry again. Susan told her to hang in there, it would get better, just keep busy. For the first time, she could really empathize with her sister. Sleep or the oblivion that taking drugs caused looked good to her. Reality hurt too much.

Two weeks later, Millie was asked to go to Mrs Rostrum's office. Millie received an offer from a prestigious firm in San Francisco. She'd hoped it would be a better climate, and they were offering her a fantastic deal; one she couldn't refuse. The wages were impressive, a house to live in, and her tuition paid for her to finish college and get her degree.

"Mrs Rostrum, would you get them on the computer and tell them I accept their offer. I haven't mastered the computer completely yet."

"Sure, Millie." It looked so easy when someone else maneuvered the computer. She sent the message and within seconds an instant message came up. They thanked Millie and said they would fax the information she would need. They also added the cost of moving her belongings to California. She would miss Susan and the kids, but she needed to put space between J.B. and her. She had come too close too relenting in

J.B.'s arms that afternoon in her back yard.

Within a week all the arrangements were made. The movers preferred to do the packing. Millie was just to pack the necessities Terry and she would need a week until her belongings reached their home. She was to catch the plane the following day. She'd never even been in a plane. Life from here on out was going to be a big adventure.

After hearing all about Millie's plans to move to the west coast, Gus got courage to ask Susan to marry him. Millie had taken the kids to the park leaving Gus and Susan alone. "Susie, will you marry me and please don't think I'm just being charitable, Millie leaving just gave me some back bone and the nerve to ask you. I know I'm not good enough for you, but I love you and I want to take care of you and the kids; I even want to adopt the children if you'll let me." That was a long speech for the usually quiet man.

Susan climbed into his lap and laid her face against his. "I'd be honored to become your wife, Gus. I love you and I know you love me, I feel it right down in my soul. The answer is Yes, Yes, Yes.

Gus held her tenderly, then hesitantly asked. "Susie, what if I don't satisfy you in bed. I want you to be totally happy. Maybe, I'll disappoint you."

Susan closed her eyes and remembered something she never allowed herself to do. So many men, perfect strangers, she'd had to please, only with Kevin, Melody's father, did she find her own release. She'd responded to him passionately, but he was a rat, a real scoundrel. A long time ago, she'd come to terms with her own sexuality, but could she make Gus happy? She didn't want to live with pretense and Gus deserved a loving woman for his wife.

"Gus, To be fair to both us, maybe we should make love, then if all is well, we can make plans to marry. I don't want you to be unhappy, either."

Gus stiffened. He knew he'd disappoint her. Ever since he'd been told that he'd never be able to father a child, he'd felt like less of a man. His self-confidence as a man, as a lover ebbed to an all time low. He'd hoped selfishly that she would wait until they were married. "Want to go over to my house and satisfy our doubts?"

They did.

The next morning when Susan awoke in Gus's arms, she never felt so loved, so feminine in her life. Gus's love making was closer to worship than passion, but it touched her very soul, laying there in his big strong arms, she never felt so secure, so loved in her whole life. She could live with this, she thought as her hands started roving over his body, causing an instant reaction. She could trust this man with her life, her children's and her very soul. This time when they made love, Gus showed her his passionate side. She was delighted when her body naturally responded. It was going to be good for both of them. No pretending.

Susan and Gus were married two days later by a Justice of Peace. A civil ceremony was agreeable to both of them. As Gus slipped the ring on her finger, and pledged his vows, she'd never felt happier in her life, nor had anything ever felt so right.

They'd already moved the children's and their personal belongings into Gus's house that he'd remodeled himself. He hoped in vain, that maybe someday, he'd find the love of his life. Finding a beautiful woman like Susan and her children were more than he'd ever hoped for. Loving him, just as he was, was a dream come true. A lovely woman like Susan and two wonderful children who wanted him to be their father. A role he'd never expected to portray since the privilege of fatherhood was denied to him because of an old war injury.

It seemed half the city was there to see Millie and Terry off at the airport. Gus and Susan had gotten married the week before and Susan and the children moved into his home. Millie felt confident she could leave Susan and the kids in good hands. Susan was ecstatically happy, even practical minded Gus looked like he was walking on clouds. Tess, and Sally were there; they knew why she was leaving. They knew J.B. He would persist until Millie gave in, he'd weaken her down. They were disappointed that the great love affair didn't end as happily as they had hoped it would. They didn't have much faith in their old drinking buddy anymore, he'd disappointed them.

J.B. was there. He was standing in the back ground. He even knew where she was going and where she was to work, hell, he'd personally recommended her to them. The name of the university she'd attend, and the address of her home. He should know that address. He bought the damn house, the car, even the furnishings in the house. He hadn't gotten her phone number yet, but he would.

When Millie made her request to the student counselor, Mrs Montgomery, head of social services was immediately notified about Millie's request. Mrs Montgomery in turn called J.B. and told him. J.B. made all the arrangements for Millie job her home and the expensive move across the country. If this was what Millie wanted, he'd see to it that she got it, but he was making damn certain that she'd be taken care of. He paved the way in every way possible. One thing he was sure of, if Millie missed him half as much as he missed her, he still had a chance. Right now Millie needed her space, but he intended to see no harm befall her until she realized they were meant to be together. He thought about that for a while, maybe he was obsessive with Millie. What was the name of that old movie? Magnificent Obsession. But damn it all, Millie was his woman, the only woman he'd ever loved or ever could love. No way in hell was he going to lose her. Not when he knew she felt the same way he did.

If only—.

Millie and Terry were pleasantly surprised when they enjoyed the flight. They took turns at the window seat, and marveled at the scenery far below. When they went through the white puffy clouds, Terry giggled. "Mom, you're always telling me to get my head out of the clouds. How am I doing now?" Millie giggled and was looking forward to a closer, better relationship with her daughter. It had been over four years since they'd lived just the two of them together.

Millie hadn't minded the take-off, but she was dreading the descent and the landing. She was sitting by the window when the plane slowly descended. She thought the landscape below looked like a patchwork quilt. Then she spotted the runway, and her stomach tightened up. She was sure that it was going to be bumpy, but the pilot skillfully landed at SFO. Airport. Millie hardly realized they were on the ground, until she saw the men pushing a platform with steps leading down.

A prearranged car was parked at the airport. The car was loaded with their luggage by courteous airport workers and directions to her home were already posted inside the car. They certainly thought of everything. She couldn't believe how easy things were. She'd heard nightmare stories of long delays, waiting lines, and luggage lost. She had been ushered through like she was the Queen of Sheba.

Millie drove the unfamiliar car through the streets and highways of San Francisco. For safety's sake she had to keep her eyes on the road, and her mind on driving, but longed to sit like Terry did and look at the spectacular surroundings. When they left the thruway and entered the streets of the city, scaling one hill after the other was a new driving experience for her, as Ohio was flat as a pancake.

Terry was sitting on the edge of her seat gazing from one side of the street to the other. When she looked down toward the end of the avenue they were traveling and saw the ocean, she let out a shriek. Millie saw a parking spot at the side and skillfully slid into it. Both Terry and Millie got out of the car and gazed at the scene below them. From a distance out to sea, they could see small boats literally flying over the water. The spray of water shooting up in the air. Neither one of them had ever seen an ocean before, and so Millie turned and smiled at her daughter. Going out on a boat and getting acquainted with the sea was on their future agenda. Millie wondered if J.B. knew anything about sailing and if he liked the ocean. She'd catch herself fantasizing about J.B. and wondered how long it would take to put him completely out of her mind.

Reluctantly, they both got back in the car and Millie scanned the directions again, assured that she was on the right street and heading in the right direction. According to the roughly drawn map, they had a ways to go. "Mom, I should be helping you navigate, but I can't keep my eyes from these new scenes. Aren't some of these houses neat? They remind me of olden times. This must be an older section of San Francisco. I thought it burnt down a long time ago.

"From what I've read; the entire city was rebuilt, but greatly improved on architecturally. Before the fire, there were just crude shanties and mostly seedy areas. We'll have to come into town and ride the trolley cars all over the city and explore after we get settled in the house."

Terry turned to look at her mother. She'd been so worried about her. This wanting to move clear across the country was so out of character for her mother, who always seemed to want constancy in her life. Venturing out into the world, and leaving all that was familiar behind her seemed so alien for Terry to comprehend. God, why couldn't her mother forgive J.B. for his indiscretion and marry him as they'd planned, instead of uprooting them and going clear across the country? Terry knew she'd miss her aunt and her cousins, but most of all, she'd miss J,B., who she thought of as her father. Didn't her mother care how she felt? Terry hastily brushed the tears away; her mom was dealing with enough problems, and she didn't need her feeling sorry for herself. Hadn't her mom always come through for her?

Terry and Millie were silent the rest of the way, as they searched for their new home. Millie glanced to the left before turning onto the wide boulevard then saw the Golden Gate bridge and the surging ocean. This made her pull off the road again. She smiled at Terry as they walked to a look out and gazed at the historic scene before. Even though they were both impressed with the awesome scene before them. Millie sensed Terry's mood and had earlier noticed her brushing tears from her face. She put her arm around Terry and drew her close. "Terry, I know this is hard on you, uprooting you from your friends and Aunt Susan and the kids, but this is something I have to do. Call me a coward, if you want to, but I couldn't go though with my wedding plans with J.B. when in my heart, I just don't trust him. Someday when you're a little older, you'll understand." Terry clung to her mother and tried to put her doubts behind her. She was just a kid, and she didn't understand all the adult emotions. Why didn't her mom trust J.B.?

When Millie found the right street and house number, she pulled into the circular driveway of their new home. She was shocked. She'd never expected anything so grand. The house resembled a Spanish hacienda. Even the narrow brick circular driveway added to the charm of the property. When she opened the door with the key, she was astounded as she gazed at the beautiful home. Millie was surprised to see two air mattresses on the floor of the one bedroom. She and Terry went from room to room, oohing and aahing. They especially liked the kitchen with a work center in the center of the room with stools around it so it served a dual purpose for dining. The sliding glass doors lead out to a patio and a built an underground swimming pool. Colorful flowers and beautiful shrubs were tastefully designed in the back yard. Millie couldn't believe she was going to live here. She wondered if they gave her a home like this to live in, what would a vice president of the company's home be like?

Later after she rested and had explored the house from one end to the other, Millie thought about the more practical aspects of setting up housekeeping. She'd need to go to the grocery store soon. She went to the refrigerator to see how much space she would have and gasped when she saw it loaded with a huge variety of different foods. All she would possibly need; the same with the small pantry, fully stocked. This was unreal. She certainly had to thank someone for all these preparations provided.

Millie pulled out a couple cokes from the refrigerator then Terry and she went out on the patio and stretched out on the chaise lounges that were already there with a umbrella table and chairs. "Mom, I think we're going to be all right, I was kinda afraid when you said we were going to relocate way out here, but I'm not now. Whoever made all these arrangements is taking good care of us, aren't they?"

"They surely are, honey."

Millie leaned back, maybe it was the sea air, but she was sleepy. She seemed to feel that way a lot lately, and constantly hungry. She dozed off. Terry sat quietly for a while, then went inside and unpacked their belongings. When she went into the bathroom with the towels that her mother packed in a suitcase, she was surprised to see several blue and green towels and wash cloths already there. It suddenly occurred to her, this was so much like what J.B. did before when they'd moved into the different house in Ohio. Terry had wondered why he seemed to back off and let her mother go. He was still paving the way for them. Her mother would be irate when she learned of this. Her mother thought she was making a clean break with J.B., but he wasn't letting them go.

Terry was going to do a little checking before she said anything to her mother. She'd just learned in social studies how to find a deed through the courthouse. Terry was thinking and would bet odds that J.B. owned this house. She knew he'd bought her mother's car and all the home furnishings. Oh, her mom was going to be mad.

She was also going to check who the major stock holders were in the firm that her mother was working for. Terry wasn't upset, she'd wanted J.B. to become her Dad, and didn't understand what happened, that her mom broke off with him. She'd secretly wished for some brothers and sisters. She missed Paul and Melody. Now she wanted a family of her own, that she wasn't going to get now.

Later when Millie and Terry were eating a sandwich, Terry wanted to say something to her mother, but lacked the maturity for expressing herself tactfully. Still she was going to try. "Mom, if I were you, when you go to work, I wouldn't say anything to anyone about this house, the arrangements for the car, or getting our stuff shipped out here." Millie looked surprised.

"Why do you say such a thing, Terry?"

"Well. I was thinking, you're just a new employee, you never worked anywhere like this, and I don't think this is done for everyone. I think you're getting preferential treatment. Just keep quiet, keep your ears open, and do your job. Besides if this is some kind of special treatment, you don't want your fellow employees jealous of you, do you?"

"I've got myself some smart little kid." She thought about the trip. It was like she was the queen or something. She wasn't a V.I.P. Granted she was straight up in school, G.P.A was a 4.0. She'd take Terry's advice and keep quiet; she didn't want to make waves.

An hour later, Millie was so sleepy even though she'd taken that nap this afternoon, and she was hungry again. Maybe it was the change of climate or time change, she thought as she crawled into sheets at eight thirty, after feasting on ice cream. She told Terry to lock up when she came inside. She couldn't keep her eyes open.

The next day Millie reported for work, and everyone was helpful, and her tasks were thoroughly explained. Nobody asked about her living condition, so she didn't say anything. She confided to her own private secretary late in the afternoon that she was so sleepy, and she couldn't keep her eyes open. Cheryl Anderson laughed. "It's the sea air. I was like that for months, and the time change from the eastern coast doesn't help either. There is a cot in the adjacent room, I'll stand guard, so that you won't be disturbed. Go lay down and take a little nap. That's one of the perks of being the boss." She winked at Millie. Cheryl awakened her in forty-five minutes. "Sorry, but the big boss is coming up here, so hop to it, girl." Millie gave her a grateful look.

Millie freshened up and was working behind her desk when an older grey—haired man entered her office, she looked up in surprise, even though she'd been forewarned. "So you are our new golden girl, and your name is Millicent Nobles and you hail from Toledo, Ohio. Welcome aboard, Millicent. Good to have you with us."

"Please make that Millie, only my teachers in grade

school called me by my full name., that I inherited from my grandmother." She smiled, stood and walked around the desk, hoping that was the proper thing to do. He took her outstretched hand and gently shook it.

"I don't mean this in a personal way, just an observation. You're very beautiful. Now, I fully understand." Millie wondered about that remark, but didn't delve too deeply for an exclamation. "I haven't any experience, but I'll catch on quickly and I appreciate the opportunity the company is giving me." He watched her innocent face; she didn't have a clue. He'd play along with her. Millie continued, "so far, I've figured everything out and my secretary is amazing; she should be in this office, not me." She was right about that too, Cheryl had already paid her dues. This should have been her promotion.

"You'll do just fine, Millie, and don't forget about the board meeting. It's every Monday at four o'clock. See you there." He turned back and looked at her. Beautiful, pleasant speaking, and so naive. J.B. sure found himself a real gem. He liked her instantly.

Millie was so happy that she was welcomed in such a friendly manner, and everyone was so nice to her, especially the men. But hadn't J.B. told her how stunning she looked? She'd taken it as an exaggerated compliment. J.B. said things like that, she didn't think he was ever truly earnest.

Within the next two weeks, Millie was truly efficient in her position. She even starting making memos for changes. Cheryl encouraged and sheltered her every afternoon so she could take a short nap. "Millie, maybe you could get some kind of drug to help this sleepiness you're enduring. I know truck drivers use them all the time. You aren't pregnant are you. I was like that for all three of my kids. All I did was sleep and eat, and I got gigantic."

Millie's periods were always irregular, but she hadn't had a period since she'd broken up with J.B.. That was over two months ago. No, he always protected her. Them. Her eyes widened as she suddenly remembered that last time they'd made love in the shower; they'd taken a chance without protection. Millie tried not to dwell on her memories of J.B., but her mind recalled the entire incident. J.B. was sudsing her body with scented bath wash, his big hand caressing her as he lathered her breasts, rib cage and hips, then both hands gently gripping her buttocks. Millie remembered moaning into his mouth as he snuggled her body tightly to his already sleek body. She'd gasped as he pulled her legs around his hips and he plunged into her body, slowly then he withdrew and repeated the rhythm until she was trembling, her body pleading for release. He squashed her screams and moans with his mouth as she climaxed repeatedly. She remembered the feral guttural noise J.B. made as he reached the height of his passion and found his own release. Could she have conceived a child as they both reached the most incredible orgasm, they'd ever known?

On the way home from the office, she stopped at a drive-thru pharmacy and bought a non-sleep aid and two home pregnancy strips. She had to know immediately if she was actually carrying J.B.'s baby.

* * *

Terry was learning to cook. She searched through her mother's cook books, until she found something she could recreate. Tonight it was Spanish noodles and strawberry shortcake for dessert. They were both going to start school in five more weeks. She was trying to be a good helper for her Mom. Terry knew she was hurting.

Later that day when Millie's car was delivered and the moving van arrived with their belongings, Terry directed the men where to place everything; they even assembled and connected the television and stereo equipment. Terry already knew how to connect her computer up to the internet. Thanks to Aunt Susan. She was anxious to e-mail her and her friends back home. She had so much to tell them. The first plane ride, the awesome sight of San Francisco, and the most beautiful house, she'd ever seen.

Yesterday, Terry had ventured downtown. She found the courthouse and searched for the Register and Recorders Office and searched for the deed to their home. She'd been right. J.B. Cornell owned it. She asked the lady at the courthouse how she could look up who the major stock holders were in a company. She told her to go online. That was the first thing Terry did when the movers left boxes all over. Just as she thought, as James Benjamin Cornell was listed as the biggest stock holder. Heck, he nearly owned the company with 65 percent. She'd decided not to tell her mother, but she intended to e-mail J.B. and let him know she knew what he was up to. The more Terry thought about it, she realized that J.B. was more like a stalker and, his behavior was too munificent. He was buying her mother, and he had been ever since he'd met her. He was so manipulative. She didn't like leaving J.B. and moving so far away from him, but it was her mother's choice.

After Terry was in bed, Millie went in the bathroom to take the pregnancy test. She read the instructions and it suggested that she take it first thing in the morning. She hid the kits behind her make-up and went to bed.

In the morning she nearly forgot about the pregnancy tests strips until she started putting her make-up on. She'd already broken the seal on the package. She sat down on the commode and peed on the designated spot. Within seconds it started to turn blue. Thinking there might be a mistake, she broke the packing plastic of the other one and tested again. It was also blue. She sat there on the commode, stunned. In one way she was happy. She'd have J.B.'s child to love, and in another, she could lose her job if they discriminated against pregnant unmarried women. What should she do? She couldn't talk to her daughter. She was just a child. She'd have to make her own decision alone. Maybe she could confide in Cheryl how she missed her sister, Sally and Tess. Should she call them?

Millie sat down on the side of the bed, her face in her hands. Thoughts were spinning in her head. Should she call J.B. and tell him, he would have to be told. He had a right to know if she had his child. She also knew he would be on the first available flight and insist that they marry for the baby's sake. What about her new life, her job, her home? She would be giving up so much to return with J.B. and his mother that didn't want her, and J.B.'s unconscionable shame of presenting her to his partners and their families. Had he been ashamed of her? She had run away from all that. Did she want to return to it? Did she owe her baby all the heartache that awaited her there?

Millie got dressed for work, pondering the new development in her life. She didn't need this. But then she thought of all the joy Terry had brought into her life and started having second thoughts about having another child.

She put it out of her mind when she arrived at the factory and went into her office. Cheryl was already there and had the coffee made. She raised her eyes when Millie withdrew the no-doze tablets and read the small print on the back of the box. One of the warnings was—don't take if pregnant. She watched as Millie put the box back in her purse. Cheryl immediately surmised Millie was pregnant.

That evening, when Millie got home from work, she was quiet and deep in thought. Lord, she sure didn't need this in her life right now, but in another sense glad that she was having J.B.'s baby, because she'd always have a part of him to love. Maybe it would be a boy and he'd be as handsome as his father.

Later that night Millie slipped her nightgown on and climbed into bed, then she prayed for an answer to her dilemma, and begged God to ease her pain. She also prayed to God to help her make the right decision about their future.

Sleep was a long time coming, and when she finally fell into a fitful sleep, she dreamed of J.B. In her dream they were both pulling on an adorable dark-haired little boy. Their faces showed anger and the little child was screaming in fear. Millie woke up in a cold sweat. Was this a sign of the future? Would J.B. fight to take her child from her? No, he would never hurt a child in anyway. That she was sure of, if nothing else.

The nightmare served as a catalyst that made Millie realize she was not alone in this decision. She knew the way J.B. felt about children. His heart went out to all of them. Besides there was no decision to make. She was pregnant. She was going to have a baby. Millie didn't believe in abortion and having another child was already on her list of dreams and hopes. She also knew J.B. would be a father to this child. Now there were no more doubts. She'd never be able to put the man out of her life, out of her dreams. By sharing a child, and becoming parents together, he'd be part of her life.

If only things were different and they were still together as a couple. All she had to do was close her eyes to see the proud, happy look on his face when she told him he was going to become a father. She agonized over the situation, regretting, the way their seemingly perfect relationship had gone amok. "Oh God, J.B. I miss you and I'll always love you. Why couldn't you have included me in your life? I'd have done my best not to embarrass you or humiliate you in front of your elegant, grand friends. You wouldn't even give me a chance to prove myself at all. Just made your own judgements. Millie laid her head down and wept for the loss of a future with the man she loved.

CHAPTER
8

SOMETHING WAS WRONG IN SAN Francisco. J.B. received his monthly fiscal reports from the company he owned over half of. He'd specifically asked about Millie's progress. At first he received raves from her accomplishments, her natural abilities, then the information stopped. He called the president of the company and talked personally to him. He heard the president of the company tell him, "J.B., I haven't any further information, she's doing a superb job, and I'm happy you recommended her."

"How is Millie? Does she seem happy living there, is she depressed?"

"Millie! Heavens no, she is positively delightful. She's what some of these old fogies working here needed; they're all on their toes now. Competition is real keen. She's a lovely person. She's a real asset to the company. Thank you for recommending her."

"You'll let me know, if there is a problem with Millie, won't you?"

"Of course, J.B." J.B. had been getting e-mails from Terry. She was a smart little cookie, just like her mother. In an indiscreet way, she let him know that if he thought buying her mother would win her over, he had another thought coming. She wasn't for sale. J.B. e-mailed back and asked what she was talking about, that he was only concerned for them. Terry set him straight on the third e-mail. She told J.B. she checked and he owned the house they were living in and she'd found out that he nearly owned the company her Mother worked for. She wrote in the e-mail, "stop pulling strings J.B., it's not going to help your cause. You blew it with Mom." He didn't receive any more e-mails from her. He didn't know what that was all about, but he was sure he'd find out eventually.

So what did he do? What he always did when he had a personal problem he couldn't work out. He called Sally and asked them to meet him at the club on Saturday night. They knew the whole story and they knew Millie even better in some ways than he did.

Saturday night J.B. was waiting for them to arrive at the club, instead of strolling in later in the evening like he usually did. Sally whispered to Tess when they started for the table where J.B. was waiting for them. "He's here already, he must really be in a dither this time, the skunk." They were still mad at him for screwing around on Millie. Or so they thought.

"It's your damn party, J.B. and you're buying. What the hell do you want with us?" Sally greeted him.

"Howya doing, Sally? And you, Tess? I'm glad you missed me."

"Like missing the seven-year itch." Tess grumbled.

"Well, now that we have all the loving sentiments out of the way, have you heard from Millie?"

"Wouldn't tell you if we did, you over-grown son of a Casanova!" Sally sneered. Maybe he'd just drop his money and leave. It wouldn't make her mad.

"Care to hear my side of the story?" He looked pleadingly into their stoic faces.

"Never heard Millie's side, she never said a word, but we both have eyes."

"Looks are deceiving."

"You're living proof of that. You might be good looking, but the buck stops there. You've got the morals of a damn tom cat."

"Aw, come on, girls, gimme a break, so I screwed up. Don't we all?"

"Damn you J.B., you really hurt that girl. Tess and I both love her like a daughter. We feel responsible. After all, we introduced you two."

"I love her, Tess. I'd do anything for that woman. Hell we were all set to get married, and I never thought I'd see the day I would willingly get married."

"So maybe, you set that little scene up with that blond bimbo, so Millie wouldn't marry you. I wouldn't put anything pass you."

"You really do think I'm a bastard, don't you?"

"You've got that damn straight." Sally tipped her bottle up and took a long swig.

J.B. stood up and threw a couple bills on the table. "Sorry I bothered you; I thought we were friends. Sorry about that." He got up and started to walk away thoroughly dejected.

"Sit back down, you dirt bag. We heard from Terry. She e-mails my daughter all the time. She's worried about her mom."

J.B. turned in a flash and sat back down. "What's wrong, for God's sake, talk to me?"

"Terry is on to you. She checked up on some things. She knows you got the job for her mother, you also own the house and set it all up for them. You paid shipped her belongings to California. You're a fool. If you think you could buy Millie Nobles. She's got too much pride to allow that."

Tess stepped into the conversation. "J.B., Millie is real smart, also very beautiful and refined. She could make it on her own. We really appreciate you getting Millie started, getting her back in school, then finding her sister and helping to get her sorry ass straightened out. She was ready for it and so was Millie; all she needed was a helping hand. Not someone controlling every move like she was a damn imbecile." J.B. sat and silently listened.

"But—J.B. started

"No damn buts about it, you're a frigging control freak."

"Remind me to never put your names down for a personal reference."

"There's something else too, J.B., but I don't know if you can handle it."

"After all the kind, loving names you've called me tonight, you think I'm a damn wimp too?"

Sally and Tess laughed. God, it was just J.B., no better, no worse than any other man. They decided to cut him some slack.

"Terry e-mailed Marty that she found two pregnancy test strips in the bathroom waste basket can, and they'd both turned blue."

J.B.'s mouth fell open. He put his hand on his forehead and leaned on the table. "She'd never call me and tell me, would she? She's out there all alone and carrying my baby. My baby." J.B. raised his head. Then looked like he'd just won the lottery. "I'm going to be a father."

"You do know where they come from, don't you J.B.? I thought, you knew enough to be careful." Sally reproached him.

J.B. smiled, remembering that last time in the bathroom, he hadn't gone into the bedroom for another foil package. They'd been so hot; he couldn't bear to leave her that long. Millie conceived his baby. His mind was whirling, spinning out of control. He wondered how fast he could get to California.

"Don't be stupid and rush out there, for sure she wouldn't marry you now. She'd think it was because she was pregnant. J.B., you're stupid, you don't know a damn thing about a woman, and how their minds works."

"Why am I getting the feeling that you are going to tell me?"

Sally never had a son, but if she had, she'd want him to be just like J.B., but she'd never tell him that. "She'd be fine, J.B., she doesn't need you. Besides, you're already doing everything except buying groceries and paying the utilities bills, or are you?"

"I didn't think of that." J.B. quickly replied. Sally snorted.

"J.B., don't be surprised if you get a check in the mail one of these days, for the house, car and furniture you bought for her, even the flight out there and the moving expenses. If a person doesn't have any pride, they are a sorry piece of humanity. And Millie has more than her fair share." J.B. picked up his warm beer and took a drink; this was going to be a long night he feared, and he was just getting the first installment of their wrath. God, he loved these two old dames. They both believed in telling it like it was. It seemed that he'd been doing a lot of things lately that didn't meet with their approval. He set his glass down, straightened back his shoulders, and prepared on the onslaught of criticism that he knew he had coming to him.

*   *   *

After Millie found out that she was pregnant, she needed desperately to talk to someone. She not only talked to her daughter, but her new best fried, Cheryl. She invited Cheryl for dinner, and Millie told her everything, right in front of Terry, who already knew more than her mother did. They talked, cleared away the dishes, then ate ice cream and talked some more. Millie was surprised to learn about the wisdom Terry possessed at her age. Maybe she was doing something right, that girl knew what the score was, about men, life, babies, things that Millie had no idea about. It was a pleasant surprise. Girls should be well informed in this day and age.

Around midnight, they were eating another snack, when they had devised the plan. Terry was to e-mail Marty and tell her about Millie being pregnant. Millie was sure, without even discussing it with them, that Sally and Tess could handle that end. J.B. did have a right to know he was going to be a father. He was already providing amply for them, although Millie didn't know that.

Cheryl knew about J.B. and his scheme to get Millie her job, but she didn't need anyone's 'help'. She was brilliant. She was making suggestions left and right to improve productivity and save money. And there wasn't a person in the plant that didn't like and admire her. That was when Cheryl went into the big boss's office and laid it out to him. She told him everything that Terry had revealed. They devised a plan not to feed J.B. any more information concerning Millie. "Just who in hell does he think he is, goddamn, I might be out looking for a new job, if this gets back to J.B., but I'll not be a part of this kind of control. And furthermore, you tell Millie to find out just how much J.B. has paid to keep Millie in his clutches. I'm going to recommend to the credit union that they bail her out; I'll personally vouch for her loan."

Cheryl laughed. "Go get em, boss."

When Millie asked about getting a loan, Cheryl was prepared for her. She told the plant CEO, and he was willing to back her.

Cheryl and Millie both did some back tracking and came up with the cost of J.B.'s generous gifts to Millie. The total figure was astronomical. Millie took the total bills into the credit union. Millie got her loan with her bosses' signature. It was a twenty-five year loan, but payments that she could afford to meet. God, she felt good when she got a bank draft and sent it to J.B. She felt free and in control of her life again. Even when she worked at the sweat shop, she'd felt good when she paid her own way. She'd swallowed her pride to go to school, but she was forced to accept help if she was going to improve her life. Maybe some day, when she could afford to, she'd pay the state back for their contribution.

She loved J.B., but she wasn't some helpless woman. If he wanted that type of woman, there were plenty of them out there that would love to have a sugar daddy.

When J.B. read his bank statement and saw the huge deposit from California, he knew Sally and Tess knew Millie better than he did. He was being made out as a control freak, a chauvinist pig, a real hard ass. He made one mistake of kissing that stupid blond, and he was getting persecuted for it from everyone. He loved Millie, he really did want to marry her, and he was so happy about the baby. If only he were with her to share this wonderful experience, to feel her growing, hardening abdomen. Just to be able to snuggle up to her, comfort her. Millie, girl, what has happened to our wonderful love? He closed his eyes as many tender loving memories flooding his thoughts.

J.B. went over to the warehouse where Susan worked. Somehow, he just couldn't believe that kissing Verna was to blame for all of this, there was an underlying problem that was being overlooked. When he walked into the office; Hank rushed to greet him. "J.B, old buddy. Good to see you." The two men affectionately hugged. Miriam came out of her office and joined in on the camaraderie.

Miriam put her arms around him, and hugged him affectionately. "J.B., we've heard what is going on, Susan has filled us in. J.B., I'm so sorry. This is all a mistake and if there's anything we can do, just ask."

"Thanks. I'm beginning to feel like a criminal. Good to know I still have friends."

Susan heard the entire conversation from her desk; she didn't know if she had the right to intrude on this private conversation, but when she saw Miriam motion for her to come over, she hastily shut down her computer and walked over to them. J.B opened his arms to her. "Oh, Susie, what am I going to do with this stubborn sister of yours? Can you give me a clue?"

Susan adored J.B. Nothing could sway her from believing he was the next thing to God. "J.B., You're going to be a Poppa. Are you happy about it? I could wring my sister's neck. What is wrong with her?"

"That's why I'm here, Sue. Maybe we can figure something out to do. Please, will you help me?"

Susan hugged J.B. again. She could see the desolation in his eyes, that her own sister had put there. "J.B., Miriam and Hank, one evening I stayed over and compiled a list. I called home to check on the family first. Melody answered and told me Paul and Daddy were grilling hamburgers, and if I wanted one, I'd better hurry home, cause they were hungry. I never have to worry about the kids if Gus is home; he's that kind of Dad. I'm sorry I got off the subject. Anyway, I now have solid evidence to show my sister that you haven't targeted just her with your generosity." She handed J.B. the folded paper. "J.B., is this the only furniture warehouse you buy from?" He was busy scanning the list. Names: One was Mary Wrigley, a crib, set of bunk beds and an automatic washing machine. The list went on and on, when he reached the last entry, a total was compounded. Hell, he'd given over a million and a half to women over the last ten years in household equipment—necessary and important comforts of life. He looked embarrassed, often the gifts were anonymous. And this warehouse wasn't the only place he'd made purchases for needy women and children. He'd keep that information to himself.

"Hell, Susan, you didn't have to make such a big deal of it. It's something I wanted to do, and I can afford to indulge." He tore the paper up.

"What is it, that lawyers say? 'Case closed'. Don't worry, a copy of that is in the mail to my stupid sister and another to Sally. They had no business sticking there nose into your and Millie's personal affairs. Oh, J.B., when I think about the way you helped me, not just with money but the time you held me on your lap and talked to me, so tenderly. It was those wonderful gestures that turned my life around; Doctor Simpson just backed you up. I owe you my life, J.B..

"What's wrong with Millie, Susan? It was the rejection of your parents that caused your problem, but what's Millie's problem?"

"I've thought about it, even put a call into Doctor Simpson. Oh, it's not self destruction as was in my case; it went the other way. I've always admired her pride and ambition, but looking back, she's too independent. It's like an obsession. Millie is a knockout. A gorgeous woman, but for years she has rejected men. I think it was because she didn't want to lose control. She had to do it all alone until you appeared in her life and took over. I bet you had your hands full, getting her to accept help, didn't you? Knowing you though, you probably came on to her like gang busters, and she didn't stand a chance." She stopped talking for a minute, used the pristine white handkerchief J.B. handed her, and wiped the tears away. "She's all alone out in California, having a baby and she's strong enough to tell you to stick your help. I heard she was paying you back for the household furnishings, furniture, the house, the car and even the transportation to California for her and Terry. Doesn't Millie realize what else you've given her besides money? My sister is one stupid mixed-up girl."

J.B. grinned, encouraged by Susan's loyalty to him. "You've got that right."

"Maybe you should go out there, take her to bed, and keep her there. She's helpless when you two are passionate." Susan stopped talking and gave J.B. a devilish look, then continued, "you must be something else in the sack, J.B." She threw her head back and laughed. She looked just like Millie when she did that. His heart wrenched.

J.B. laughed. "I can hold my own." For the first time in a while, he felt like a man again. Instead of all the vicious, vindictive names Sally and Tess called him. "Susan, I realized right from the beginning that Millie was extremely independent. Hell, Susan, I wanted to propose marriage to her almost immediately. I wanted to take her to my home and give her luxuries that she couldn't imagine, but I knew that she had to be independent, that's why I encouraged her to go to school and get a good career. What else could I do? How could I have done anything differently?"

Hank had been listening quietly to Susan and J.B.'s conversation. "The way I see it, go to the root of the problem. Before you can help Millie, you've got to do something about her parents. Make them see the light of day, and realize their mistake.

Susan raised her eyebrows and declared, "I've often thought about going to their home and telling them off, but get real, that wouldn't help what happened in the past. I haven't seen them in years, I can barely remember what they look like. Thanks but no thanks, I don't need to make any fresh bad memories; I have enough old ones to contend with."

"Any reason we can't all go out, have a long lunch, and talk?" J.B. asked

Hank let out a raucous laugh. "Hell, J.B., we can do what we damn please. Girls, go powder your noses or whatever you women do J.B.'s buying."

*   *   *

When Millie opened the large envelope from Susan, she wondered what she was sending her. As she read the information, she groped for a nearby chair and sat down. J.B. had helped hundreds of women over the years. Millie hadn't been singled out by J.B., she was just one of many that he'd helped. She'd turned his generosity into something perverted, unnatural. Terry came out of her bedroom, saw her mother's white face, and picked up the papers that had fallen to the floor. She scanned through it, and her mouth flew open. "Oh Mom, what have we done? J.B. doesn't have any ulterior motives like we thought. He's helped hundreds of women. Look! Susan has even checked off the ones that were helped anonymously.

Terry read the letter that accompanied the information, then she dropped into a chair. Terry, in her young years just learned a valuable lesson, not to be too hasty to cast judgement on other people. She looked at her Mother. J.B. wasn't the problem here; she didn't know what it was, but it sure wasn't J.B. He loved her Mother and he was a good guy.

Terry started to remember, the many genuine offers that her mom and all the kids received, from church members, neighbors, friends at work, and her mother proudly refused their help. Their life would have been a lot easier if her mother hadn't been proud. It was a like a light bulb coming on, but why was her Mom like this? What caused it? She remembered the many offers her Mom always declined from nice guys. Men that would have loved them. It took J.B. to break through the shell around her, but Millie couldn't accept it. She'd been fighting it all the time, and resented his interference with her snug little world. Whoever she was trying to impress probably didn't even care. Terry handed the letter back to her mother. It was definitely going to be a keeper, one that they both should read over anytime they started to get illusions about anything.

Terry went into the kitchen to prepare dinner. She kept

glancing in at her mother. When she saw her weeping, she didn't go in and comfort her. She was just a kid, what could she say or do? She'd been wrong before. She knew that she had to e-mail J.B. and apologize to him for meddling then she was going to call Cheryl and confess her sins. She felt like an evil instigator. Was this all her fault? She felt terrible. What had she done?

Terry stayed true to her new convictions, and she didn't discuss the details with her mother. After they'd eaten dinner, Terry went into her room and closed her door.

Millie got the message loud and clear. Millie sat quietly and analyzed her own mistaken convictions. She had to go back to a long time ago, back to when she was five or six years' old. She remembered her sister, the memory was crystal clear. Susan rebelled, when her parents were unreasonably cold to them. Millie remembered eating dinner with her sister in their shared suite. The housekeeper brought their meals upstairs for them. They never ate with their parents. Susan used to stick her tongue out when their backs were turned and defied them every chance she got. Millie just tried to be a good girl, so they would love her. Later in life, pride was her only strong defense against their coldness. Who needed them anyway? Her behavior was impeccable at home and at school. She prided herself and excelled on any task that was presented to her. Then she got pregnant and was forced from her pedestal.

Her memory flashed to more recent times. The overwhelming love she felt for J.B., she'd felt rejected by him when he never introduced her to his friends, or parents. She'd felt like a mistress; then he insisted they marry. Why? Suddenly she was going to fit into his life. Where was his magic potion? J.B. kissing that blond foozy was just the last straw. But it was as if J.B. got the last word in when she found out she was pregnant with their child. Now she would be tied to him forever, it was a bond between them that could never be severed. They were going to be parents.

She thought about what Susan wrote. Millie still had her

pride and her independence, but what was she going to tell her child? The truth or was she going to make J.B. out to be a cad? She got up, put her sweater on, and went outside and looked into the heavens; was she a Christian hypocrite? Was she judgmental and unforgiving? Why hadn't she demanded J.B. to let her in his private circle? She should have demanded an explanation. She had the right to ask that, instead of pulling back into her shell and avoiding confrontations. She should have been included in the dinner celebration with his partners, their wives, and their exonerated client. Why wasn't she? Why did she have this feeling of inadequacy? Was it the way her parents had treated her? Millie paused and thought about it. Everything she'd ever attempted to do, she'd succeeded, be it cooking, sewing, learning to drive, School, etc. She, by all rights, should be an arrogant, boasting type of person. What were these feelings of inadequacies?

The realization came to her as suddenly as it had for her young daughter. It was her; she was hung up over her childhood, still trying to be that good little girl, never making waves, holding her head up and never letting them see how they hurt her. Oh, J.B., we need to talk, really talk. We owe this to our child.

But first, she was going to mend fences with her daughter that was here, living with her. She'd allowed that child to become embroiled in a situation that she was too young to handle. And she prided herself into believing that she was a perfect mother, she never made mistakes, she wasn't like her parents.

Right! In her own way, she had been worse than them.

What was she going to say to her child? She wasn't even thirteen years old yet and had been subjected to too many hardships. Then J.B. appeared, and every aspect of their lives had been affected. She had to take the responsibility for her own mistakes and, J.B. had to take the blame for his. She knew Terry adored him. He'd been the only father figure she'd ever known, and now she'd been deprived of that. So much for being a perfect parent, she bemoaned as she headed for

Terry's room.

She had to start undoing the damage her stupid pride had caused starting with her daughter. Why hadn't she realized this before?

CHAPTER
9

MILLIE RAPPED ON HER DAUGHTERS' closed bedroom door. "Terry, I need to talk to you, honey."

Millie heard Terry slowly walk across the floor, her mule slippers dragging. Millie laid her head against the door jam and asked God to please give her the wisdom to undo a horrible mistake. The door slowly opened. Terry's precious face was totally blank. My God, she'll grow up just like me. Screwed up, big time.

"What do you want, Mom? I'm busy on the computer."

"May I come in?"

Terry stepped back. "Yeah, I guess, if you want to."

Millie sat down on a small overstuffed chair by the window. "Get comfortable, honey, this conversation is going to take a while."

Terry sprawled out on the bed, clutching the bear that was her constant companion, that she'd won at the amusement park, the day after she'd met J.B. That alone should have told Millie something. Terry was starved for daddy affection. She wanted to have a father. "Terry, I don't know how to begin, but first I want to apologize to you, I should never have confided in you when I discovered I was pregnant and I was so upset.

You're not old enough to be burdened with adult problems, that won't happen again, I promise you."

"Mom, I thought I could help you, I didn't know that I was getting in over my head. I'm so glad Aunt Susan wrote a letter like she did. I won't ever snoop again like that, ever! I feel terrible, like I caused a lot of trouble for everyone." Millie wanted to rush over and comfort her, but Terry had learned a valuable lesson in life.

"I think Aunt Susan's letter has helped us both, we should be grateful for her caring enough to tell us off like that. Terry, I'm going to take a short leave of absence from work; you don't have to go to school for a while yet, so we'll have time."

"Why Mom, and for what?"

"We are going back to Ohio, and getting a few things straightened out. I'm sure Aunt Susan can make room for us for a few days. I don't intend to discuss the reasons for returning home with you. I promised I wouldn't do that to you any more, and I meant it. You just enjoy spending time with your little cousins, Aunt Susan, and your old friends for a while. Okay?"

Terry jumped off the bed into her mother's lap. "Oh Mom, I love you."

"I love you too, baby." Millie caressed her hair. It wouldn't be long until her little girl became a woman, and Terry didn't need any baggage of her childhood. Life alone was enough to deal with.

Millie made the arrangements for her leave of absence from work. She knew they were cutting her a break. She'd only been with them for a little over four months. She didn't have much vacation time coming. Millie didn't know that Terry had called Cheryl and apologized, and told her the truth about J.B.'s generosity and how much he loved her mother. Cheryl and Mr Fredericks were both feeling guilty about jumping to conclusions, based on Millie's paranoia.

Millie called her sister and asked her to meet them at the airport and asked if she minded putting them up for a short time. Susan instantly became angry again. "My God, woman, you need to ask, after you took care of my kids for nearly three years, I ought to slap you for being so damn prim and proper." Susan's flare up was over quickly, then she changed her tone of voice. "Millie, I'm just so glad you are coming home, even if it's only for a few days."

Five days later Millie and Terry stepped off the plane and greeted Susan and Gus with hugs and kisses, and squeals of delight from Terry. J.B. was standing hidden behind a vending machine watching. When Susan told him she was coming home for a couple of days, he couldn't wait to see her, so he just watched from the background and envied Susan and Gus when they embraced her. Lord, she was starting to show; her loose fitting over blouse wrapped around her body, and J.B. could see the roundness of her belly. Their baby was safe and growing. He closed his eyes and sighed with relief. He'd hoped and prayed that Millie hadn't gotten an abortion. It took all his will power to hold himself back from running over to her and smothering her face with kisses.

That night after all the hugs and kisses were equally distributed and Millie and Terry shared their awesome experiences in San Francisco with the family, Millie and Susan ended up in the kitchen alone. Millie was trying out the new tea that Susan found in a specialty shop.

"Isn't that good, and it really mellows you out, I actually become pleasant to be around, don't I, Gus?" Gus had come into the kitchen for a coke.

He grinned at his wife and winked. God, if Susan didn't look all coy and sweet when he did that. So she'd finally found a man that could tame her, and make her content. Maybe there was hope for her.

"Millie, wanna tell me why you came back or do I have to extract it from you?"

"I never did like my dentist, so don't get wise with me, sister. Thank you from the bottom of my heart for the letter and the information about J.B, Susan. God! I nearly messed up my own child with my stupid hang ups."

"You have hang ups, Millie, I thought I was the only one that inherited them?"

"Yeah, I saved myself the price of a shrink by figuring it out by myself, with your help, that is.

Boy, I'll tell you there is nothing worse than finding out that you are delusional. I've finally admitted that I'm more screwed up than you ever were, Susan."

"I don't know about that."

"At least you acted out, loud and clear. I thought I was the perfect one, no problems, had it all together, I could handle everything and I'd just been kidding myself all along. Mom and Dad hurt us, they damaged us, and I thought if I was good and proper, was proud and self sufficient, that I was good. I thought I was showing them how wrong they were about me. I nearly ruined my daughter; I lost J.B. and I'm miserable without him."

Susan giggled. "Well now that we've got it settled that we both screwed up, what are you going to do about it?"

"It's too late, Susan, but at least I can make amends with you, and talk to Sally and Tess about giving J.B. a break. He was a good friend of theirs, and they took sides, shoving J.B. right into a corner. I misconstrued everything he did for me except one thing and that is why I'm here; I should have gotten angry like you do. I should have screamed and yelled and demanded the truth, instead of accepting it like a good little girl. Stay in your shell, girl, then you won't get hurt. That was my motto."

"For years I wanted to be just like you, calm and in control, and now you want to be like me. A loose cannon running about. Let's get real girl, what the hell did J.B. do?" Susan demanded to know.

"He didn't include me in his social life. I never met any of his friends, his business associates, or his parents. I thought I was just his mistress, then when he insisted we get married, I went through a major breakdown; I just couldn't figure out this new attitude or motive of J.B.'s. Evidently, I wasn't his mistress, but why shun me from his world? I came to the conclusion that he was ashamed of me, and my humble existence, but he loved me too much and was going to bite the bullet and go for it anyway."

"Millie, you never talked to him about it, not even hinted at it? You never told him that it hurt, that you felt rejected again? Millie, you should have been with him that night we all saw J.B. kiss that woman. You should have been included in their celebration. After all you were his fiance. Why didn't he ever include you?"

"I know. I never asked. He tried to tell me it was because of the way his mother turned out after she'd been introduced into society. That his partner's wives were snobs. He didn't want me hurt."

"Millie, I noticed that myself, but it wasn't my place to confront him about it, it was your place to do that, and you acted like you didn't even notice. I'd been pissed, but you held it in, like a good little girl."

"Right."

"Millie, you know what we should do? We should march right into our parents nice quiet home and tell them to go straight to hell and stay there and burn. Maybe it would make us both feel better, how about it?"

"Sounds like a plan, best one I've heard in a long time. Let's comb our hair, put on shoes and do it now. I'm in the mood. The bastards, if they didn't want children, why didn't they adopt us out, maybe our new parents would have loved us."

"You're serious, you would really go?"

"I told you I'm not going to be the meek, nice little girl anymore; I've turned over a new leaf. Maybe having J.B.'s baby inside me is giving me the backbone, who knows?" She shrugged her shoulders and slipped into her shoes, "hell, why even bother combing our hair, they don't give a shit."

Laughing, Susan grabbed her purse with her car keys in it. On the way out, she told Gus. "Hold the fort down, Sweetie, we've got a long a overdue date with destiny."

Later, when Susan pulled into the driveway of her parents' impressive house, they noticed the lights on in the living room. They were at home, and no other car was there. Heavens, they wouldn't want us to embarrass them in front of friends. "Are you sure you want to do this, Millie?"

"Don't chicken out on me now. Just what do we have to lose

by coming here and confronting them as adults? And it'll surely feel good tomorrow and thereafter. Think of it as the revenge of the nerds." Millie made a stupid funny face, then she slammed the car door shut and started up the driveway. Susan followed. Susan couldn't believe Millie was repressing this wild, crazy energy all these long years. Wow! Way to go, sis.

When their mother opened the door, she had a sweet, beguiling, totally false smile pasted on her face, that quickly changed to a shocked expression when she saw who was at her front door. "May we come in, Mother?" Millie asked with a sardonic look on her face.

"Of course." Trying to recover from the shock, Carrie Nobles face returned to the fake smile, then she motioned for them to go into the living room. "Carl, look who is here."

Her father's stunned look was worth a fortune in repayment for all the bitter sleepless nights that Millie had tortured herself through. Why didn't they love them? "I never expected to see either one of you again." Her father spoke in a stunned tone of voice. Surprise was written all over his handsome face.

"Your lucky day, I guess. You're both looking well. The years have been kind to you." Millie said, her old cordial voice firmly in place. Susan never said a word. She didn't need to see them. She didn't give a rat's ass, if they were dead or alive. Miserable specimens of human beings. Even alley cats were better parents than they'd been.

"Come sit down, girls, would you care for any refreshments?" Her mother was visibly shaking, but why? Maybe because they weren't little helpless children anymore, they didn't know how to deal with two adult women. What could they possibly give as an explanation for the way they raised their daughters? Susan was beginning to be glad they'd come. Go for it, Millie, she thought. Maybe they would get some questions answered.

Neither one of the girls had changed their clothes, Millie still wore the blue silk blouse and cream colored slacks that complimented her long slender legs. She was also wearing the gold jewelry and diamond ring that J.B. gave her, and her dark hair was partially pinned back in a jeweled encrusted comb that J.B. also bought her. She looked stunning, and Susan still wore her burnt orange suit with a silk blouse in a lighter shade of orange. Her hair was flowing loosely, the dark curls cascading over her shoulders. The girls could almost be made out for twins. Susan's eyes were the same as Millie's, except she had the same jaw line as theirs fathers, and her lips weren't as full as Millie's. Susan looked more determined and stubborn.

Their mother was still staring at them, then her facial expressions changed, and Millie saw tears in her hazel eyes. "You're both beautiful women." She closed her eyes, then slowly opened them wide, she glanced at her husband, and the words starting pouring from her. "Oh my God, I am so sorry for the way I've treated you. I should have been true to my own convictions, but I allowed your Dad to be the main influence. I just went along with everything he wanted. I would give my soul if I could change the past and been the mother to you that I wanted to be, that I longed to be."

Carl Nobles eyes widened with shock. He always knew that he'd been the strong dominant partner in their marriage, but this was ridiculous to blame him now for everything. It was agreed early in their marriage that they didn't want children, but when his father threatened to disinherit him, if they didn't have children, he'd reluctantly agreed to have one. Susan was born, and he learned to tolerate her. He insisted that the nanny care for her in the nursery and stay up in their own suite, sometimes weeks went by before he saw the child. He could abide that. Millie was a mistake, right from conception. He'd wanted Carrie to get an abortion, but she refused. Carrie always seemed to go along with him, never gave him any static, just meekly agreed with him. What the hell was going on now? She was making him out to be the villain. He turned to his wife and snarled at her. "You're telling me after all these years that you actually loved the children we were forced to bring into this world. Why didn't you speak up before? Am I such a controlling monster? Are you afraid of me?" He angrily demanded an exclamation from his wife.

Carrie Nobles merely lowered her eyes after the onslaught,

but she'd been living nearly thirty-three years in fear of her controlling husband. Yes, she was afraid. She turned and looked at her daughters. She didn't know what their lives were like, but neither one of them lowered their eyes in fear when Carl raised his voice and started shouting at her. How did they become so strong? They were able to resist their father and become independent. Watching their faces gave her the courage to lambast her husband. She turned toward him and shouted back at him.

"Yes, you bastard, I've always been afraid of you and when I did work up some courage to defy you, you only had to take me to bed. You know I can't resist you, that's how you've always controlled me, withholding your body from me if I didn't please you. I'm nothing more than a sex slave to you. I hate myself, most of the time, I hate you, except when you make love to me. You have that power over me, always have. I loved my babies, but when I tried to be their mother, you withdrew from me. I prayed when they left here that somehow they would survive. I think being out on the streets was better for them than living in this loveless house."

Carl Nobles glared at his wife. He couldn't deny a thing she'd said. He turned and walked from the room. "Go ahead Carrie, side in with the little bastards, but you'll come crawling back to me, I'm the only one that can please you, you can't live without me. You know what we mean to each other. We'd be lost without the other." He walked from the room, glaring at Millie and Susan.

Millie was stunned. So that was where Susan and her came from. It was no better than sex bondage and white slavery. Millie could commiserate with her mother, J.B. was irresistible to her, that's why she'd tolerated the feelings of inferiority and rejection that she secretly harbored deep in her mind. It was too late for her mother now. She was a stranger to her and her sister. Why make waves now? "Mother, we shouldn't have come here; we didn't mean to upset your life. We only had some questions regarding our parents, and they've been answered quite sufficiently. There is nothing neither of us can do now. It seems that you've made your choice for your life. Susan and I are just fine, whether you know it or not, this visit has been perfect for us. Go make up with your husband and try to be happy with your choices. We'll try not to make the same mistakes in life that you and father have made." Millie put her arms around this strange woman that was her mother. Then she picked up her purse and started for the front door. Susan was right behind her.

Both girls were quiet on the way home, because they were lost in their own thoughts. When they walked in the front door, Gus was still up. He looked closely into Susan's face, and relief flooded over him. He wrapped his arms around her. "Darling, do you feel better? I hope so, there are just some things I can't fix for you."

Millie smiled and thought, Susan is going to be all right; her marriage is right, it's good for both of them. Then she thought of J.B.: the power he held over her, her sexual weakness for him. She obviously was her mothers' child. That was why she'd accepted J.B.'s slight with his friends. Did she want to spend the rest of her life living in his shadow? Or, did she want to be her own woman, and make her own decisions? Did she want a life like her Mothers? Millie admitted to herself that J.B. was not the vindictive, cruel person her father was, but the manipulation was similar. The only difference was J.B.'s personality; his charm got him what he wanted. Millie was always on the fence, so unsure of his true feelings and intentions. She realized that she'd become a victim, just like Susan had become a victim to drugs and alcohol.

"Susan and Gus, I'm beat. I think it's just jet lag, but I have to get some rest. I'll see you both in the morning. Goodnight." They watched her disappear up the steps, her head bowed. Susan had never seen her sister looking so dejected.

Gus stared after her, why was Susan so relaxed while Millie was strung tighter than a drum. "What happened, Sue? Why is Millie so downcast and you look like you just won the jackpot?"

Susan dropped into one of the kitchen chairs, while Gus poured her a cup of coffee. "Gus, I got the right answers tonight from our parents. Millie received a different message. Damn, why did I suggest we go there? It's only going to make it worse for Millie. She'll never call J.B. now. There will no reconciliation between them now."

"Why, Sue, what happened?"

Susan told him exactly what happened, and what was said. "I saw the look on Millie's face. Now she is thinking she has the same weakness for J.B. that our mother has for our father. God, that girl needs to see a psychiatrist on a regular basis." She explained to Gus what had transpired during the short visit to their parents home and why Millie was reacting differently to it.

Gus just shook his head. Then came the solution. "J.B. needs to go there and kidnap that woman and they need to talk all this shit out. Most of it is in Millie's mind anyway. Those two people were meant to be together. They're both miserable without each other. For God's sake, they are going to have a child together. "

Susan wanted to call J.B., but she didn't, couldn't. They'd all intervened in Millie's and J,B,'s relationship too much already. If it was going to happen, those two would have to do it.

Millie and Terry stayed until it was time to board the plane carrying them back to California. She spent time with her friends, but never called J.B, as she had intended to when she came here. Millie now saw the futility of it. She just resigned herself to the loss of her love.

J.B. had asked Susan to call him and let him know what was happening. He thought for sure he and Millie could end their estrangement and be together as a family. Instead she was going back to San Francisco more convinced than ever that her convictions were the only resource she had left. When Millie looked back at the terminal, just before she stepped aboard the plane, she was shocked to see J.B. watching them. Her heart came up into her throat. She just closed her eyes, turned and got aboard the plane, wondering why he was there. He'd proven that he didn't really care. But why was he here seeing her off? It must be the baby she was carrying. After all, having a son was most mens' dream. When Terry and she were settled in their seats, Millie looked out the window and saw that J.B. had moved closer to Susan. They were talking, then she saw Susan put her arms around him in a comforting familiar gesture. Millie laid her head back on the seat and wondered if she was off on the wrong track again. Maybe she should have seen J.B. and talked this through. Was she wrong again?

The plane taxied around the field several times before the pilot got the clearance, for his take-off. Each time the plane circled and she saw J.B. watching the plane she was in, her heart pounded. She knew there would never be another man like J.B. She laid her hand on her stomach and felt her round mound of her son, their son.

Millie was unusually quiet on the flight across the country. Terry slept until the flight hostess announced that they were going to be served their dinner.

Terry ate the hearty baked steak dinner, but kept an anxious eye on her mother picking at the meal. "Mom, remember you are supposed to be eating for two. Eat your food for my little brother, will you please."

Millie looked at her grinning daughter and started eating. Terry wasn't about to tell her mother that she'd spent time with J.B. one evening when she was supposed to be with Marty and Sally. Maybe someday she'd tell her, but not now. J.B. loved them and had begged her to take good care of her mother and see that she took good care of herself.

Spooning a mouthful of dessert into her mouth, she wondered how her their roles had reversed.

CHAPTER 10

ONDAY, TWO DAYS AFTER Millie and Terry returned to California, Susan was outside the warehouse waiting for J.B. to pick her up. She'd already asked Hank to give her extended time for lunch. She explained to him and Miriam that she was having lunch with J.B., hoping she could clear some things up. They'd all been so disappointed when Millie never contacted J.B. when she was home on her short visit. They'd hope for a reconciliation between the two of them. Hank was worried about J.B. He was losing weight and appeared so lethargic.

J.B.'s silver car pulled into the parking area. He reached across the seat and opened the car door for Susan to get in. Susan's eyes widened with shock when she saw J.B. She noticed the dark circles under his eyes, he'd lost weight, and he was starting to look haggard and gaunt. "Where do you want to go, Susan, just name it? It doesn't matter to me."

Susan suggested the local steak house. Maybe she could get a large steak and a buttery baked potato loaded with sour cream into him. He didn't say anything until he pulled into the restaurant parking lot.

When they were waiting for their steaks to come, and Susan

watched J.B. nibble listlessly on his salad. "Susan, what did you mean, about Millie having valid reasons to doubt me, I know I messed up kissing that damn broad, but I thought Millie had forgiven me for that?"

"Millie is convinced that she was more your mistress than your fiancee, she thinks you were either ashamed of her, her humble background, and you didn't care enough about her to meet your friends or your parents. She blames her sexual need for you for keeping the relationship going. She couldn't stay away from you. Ditto, just like our Mother."

J.B. laid his fork down and stared at Susan. "She thinks I only want her body, that I don't love her?" J.B. cursed himself, he knew part of what Susan told him was true, he didn't want to introduce her to his parents and best friends, and business associates, but it sure as hell wasn't because of Millie. It was because his Mother and his partners' wives were such damn snobs. He didn't want Millie hurt; he felt he was protecting her. He'd tried to explain that to her, even Mary talked to her, but Millie refused to believe them. He suddenly realized that he should have had more faith in Millie. He'd sensed that she was like a chameleon. She adapted to people, but still retained her own convictions. Hadn't she been good friends with Sally and Tess, but didn't in anyway follow their ribald way of life? Odds were she could have handled his friends' wives and his own mother and their snooty attitudes, and not taken their rebuffs personally. Christ, his mother had even thrown up to her about having a child out of wedlock. Millie sure as hell wasn't missing anything by not meeting them. He thought he'd gotten through to her that their life was going to be their own to live, and they didn't owe society a damn thing. All these problems they were now having, started when Millie saw him kissing that damn stupid woman, and he'd allowed himself just a moment, before he pushed her away. Was he going to pay for that the rest of his life? And lose the woman he loved, Terry, and his son that was yet to be born?

"Susan, what do you suggest? I just can't let her go. I can't bear this separation. It's killing me. What can I do? I guess made a mistake creating comfort for her. I couldn't stand for Millie to go back to living so poorly, not when I can afford to give her anything. Please believe me, Susan, there wasn't any kind of strings' attached to my gifts to her; it was for my satisfaction mostly. I would give her anything. She can have all I have all of me, but she doesn't want it or me. How could a love so strong and powerful as ours go amok? Doesn't she realize that not everyone finds that soul mate they are searching for? Millie is my life, I can't bear to even think about living the rest of my life without her."

"J.B., Here is my advice, you can take it or leave it. Go to her. Not directly, just move near her and be available and just be there for her. She's so strong and she is the most competent person I've ever known. Would you consider relocating to San Francisco? No past for either of you. A clean slate to start out with. Maybe you could start over like you'd never met before. You could court and woo her, that is if you can keep that thing of yours in your pants. She believes you just wanted a sexual relationship. She feels to blame for it. She says she wants you too much, just like our mother with our father. Only thing, he really is a bastard, and there is no comparison between the two of you"

J.B. thought for a couple minutes. Even though Susan had explained everything, he couldn't accept Millie's attitude. Why did Millie feel that their insatiable appetite for each other was a thing to be ashamed of? Didn't she realize that although the sex between them was the best he'd ever known, it was only part of their relationship? The waitress brought their steak and J.B. dove into it, just airing his feelings to Susan was helping to relax the tight band around his stomach. "Susan, I'd move to the moon if it would mean that Millie and I could be together. I have nothing here, not really. I can manage my business affairs anywhere in the world. Do you think it would work? I've been thinking about changing my career anyway, still in law, but I'd like to be able to do more of the legal work and become an advocate for women's and children's rights. I can afford to work free, and I know my way around the different agencies.

Maybe I could make a difference for more women."

Susan watched as J.B.'s eyes brightened. Maybe a new vocation would give him the incentive to accept that Millie would never want to share his life. "Look at it this way J.B., you have a right to be with her, at least be able to communicate with her. You're sharing a child. You should be there when he is born. She can't stop you from that." Susan hoped that Millie would mellow, when their child was born and see J.B. in another light. Nothing she and Gus could say to her would sway her mistaken opinion of him and their relationship.

*   *   *

When Millie and Terry walked into their home after their trip back to Ohio; Millie felt a sense of relief. She would miss her sister, her family, and her old friends, but she didn't have the stress here. This was going to be her life away from all the turmoil that her relationship with J.B. caused. It would be a new beginning for her, Terry and her soon to be born son. The haunted look on J.B.'s face when she spotted him watching her at the airport, often appeared in her mind's eye. Maybe J.B. did love her, as much as he could love any one woman, but Millie felt it wasn't enough to marry for, then end up another divorce statistic. She didn't want her children to pay for their folly, like Susan and she did.

Getting settled back at work kept her busy the next week, then school started for both Terry and her. Going to night classes was different. She no longer saw all young faces. Many of her fellow students were much older than the students she'd known in college back in Ohio; some even older than she was.

It was her third night at school that Millie met Esther Mantle, another single mom, struggling alone to raise three children. They took their break together. Millie ordered tea when she went through the line at the cafeteria, the woman behind her spoke up. "Hey there, girl-friend, that sounds good, maybe a cup of herbal tea would get me off this caffeine high I'm on. Mind if I join you? I don't know a soul here."

Millie turned and smiled at the woman, she was around thirty years old, looked a little frazzled, much like Millie was feeling. "Sounds like a plan to me, I'm not acquainted with anyone else here, either. I see a small table over in the corner away from the chatter of the kids." Millie laughed, she wasn't that old, but compared to the silly nineteen year olds, she felt ancient.

Esther smiled knowingly. "Aw, to be young, carefree and silly again, those were the good old days." Millie and she giggled as they walked to the small isolated table. Esther stirred in two little containers of cream and three sugars in her tea. Millie thought to herself, talk about a caffeine high, wait until that sugar hits her blood stream. "You don't use cream and sugar?" Esther innocently asked.

"Only in coffee, tea, I prefer plain." Millie picked her cup up and sipped the tea, savoring the flavor. "My name is Millie Nobles, and I'm taking business administration and accounting. What's your goal for the classes?"

"Hi Millie, good to meet you, I'm Esther Mantle, mother of three hellions and I'm taking child Psychology. Hoping to become a better mother and be able to control my kids without belting them, like I'm often tempted to. I also want to start a day care facility, and I need a degree to do that." Millie smiled, wishing she could be so open with her problems and could share them with a total stranger without embarrassment. In one brief sentence, this stranger bared her soul.

"How old are your kids?" A good safe subject should be approached. That was Millie's subtle way, ease in slowly with a new friendship. She might not ever be able to confide her true problems to this blonde, curly haired pleasant woman, who had such an infectious grin, but Millie liked her instantly.

"Jeff is twelve, Evelyn is ten and Darlene is seven. They are really good kids, just rambunctious like I was when I was a kid. My ex doesn't pay any attention to them, and I think that alone causes a lot of their problems. It's hard to be both mother and father to kids."

"Tell me about it. I have a twelve-year-old daughter, Terry.

She's not a problem, her mother is." Millie was surprised when that slipped out, she hadn't meant to say anything personal to this strange woman.

The girls changed their topic of conversation to school and the courses they were taking, then they promised to get together the next night and talk some more. They walked down the hall together until Esther entered her designated class room, waved to Millie, then grinned at her. Both girls secretly hoped a friendship was beginning.

It only took five days for the girls to become intimate friends. Millie invited Esther and her kids over for pizza and a dip in the pool. The kids clicked immediately. Especially Jeff and Terry. Their mutual love of the computer drew them together like magnets. They went to different schools, but knew some mutual kids, mostly sport jocks.

Sitting on the chaise lounges and sipping lemonade, Millie and Esther were keeping a cautious eye on the kids in the pool. "Wow, Millie, I had no idea you lived so classy. I wish I could afford a house as nice as this. We're living in a project, rent subsidized. I'd like to move out of there, but I can't afford the down payment for a house, not yet anyway."

"I have a good job, but I'm just squeaking by, but I'll be able to keep up. As soon as I get my degree, I'll get a substantial raise, then the payments won't be a problem" Thanks to J.B., but she wasn't telling that to Esther. She'd probably think J.B. was her sugar daddy.

"I'm sorry if you think I'm nosy, cause I am, but I can't help noticing the diamond ring you are wearing. Are you engaged, Millie?"

"I was. The wedding was all set, but something happened, and I called the wedding off."

"You're not going to tell me what happened? You'd leave me hanging here in suspense like that? That's cruel."

Millie laughed. "I caught him kissing another woman the night of my bachelorette party."

Esther raised her eyebrows and chuckled, "Just kissing, how lucky could you get? My husband hopped from one bed to the other. More than once he called me by another name when we were making love. Now that is two timing, Millie. What explanation did he give you?"

"That she came on to him, and he admitted to enjoying it for a couple minutes, then he pushed her away, so he says, anyway." Once Millie voiced it out loud to a stranger, she realized just how petty it was. Hell, she'd been grabbed already and kissed by fellow workers.

"Girl, you have a problem, and it's not your ex boyfriend. You just didn't trust him, did you?"

"I guess I'm afraid, I don't want to be rejected. I've got some personal hang-ups, I grew up with lousy parents. It's a long story."

"I've got lots of time, and I'm good at listening. If you want to spill your guts out; be my guest. Maybe you just need an impartial ear, a different opinion to see your folly?"

Millie took Esther up on her offer and told her everything, not sparing herself and giving Esther the entire story of her mixed up life. The kids let them alone, while they were deep in grown-up talk. Terry watched her mother talking to her new friend and guided the children into the kitchen. Maybe, just maybe, this woman could get through to her mom.

When Millie was finished talking, they both sat there quietly, each lost in their own thoughts.

It was Esther who broke the long silence. "Man, I need to take advanced psychology. You are a basket case, beyond my apprehension. I don't know what to say to you. Let me think about it for a while. I'm real good at figuring stuff out, just takes me a while." Esther intended to talk to her professor about Millie. She surely didn't want to say anything wrong and add to Millie's problems. This was really heavy stuff that had been thrown at her. Her own problems with her ex was no mystery, he was a tom cat. Esther's first impression of her Millie's story was that she was the one with problems. Esther had heard enough to know J.B. might have some issues of his own, but he loved Millie. He just couldn't cope with her insecurities. Somehow, he kept accidently screwing up with her. They needed counseling.

A beaming Terry handed them both plates of sizzling pizza, and filled their glasses with more lemonade. For the rest of the day, the conversation was light and fun. When Esther piled her tired kids into the car and left, Millie and Terry were both ready for a shower and bed. Millie slept well. It was the first night that she didn't awake having nightmares about her father and J.B. looking down at her from their mighty plateau, demanding the impossible from her. She'd awake, wondering what it was they wanted, why couldn't they just leave her alone?

*   *   *

J.B.'s plan for the future was in progress. He'd informed his parents of his plans, then packed up what he needed for his new life in California. He shipped the crates to the warehouse at Lyon's Industry, and marked the cartons: personal property of J.B. Cornell. He planned on staying at a hotel until he found a suitable home to buy. It could take months to actually get established there, but he was excited. Not only was he going to be working in a profession that he believed in, but most importantly he'd be closer to Millie and Terry: The two women he loved more than life. He wished he knew just how far along Millie was with her pregnancy. The suspense was driving him wacky. When was he going to become a father? It already seemed like years since he'd heard about it. A five-year-old kid old knows it only takes nine months. Why was it taking Millie so long?

Susan suggested that he find out who her obstetrician was and show up for lamaze classes, as his first introduction back into Millie's life. She wouldn't be able to refuse. He was the father of her unborn child, and he had the right to be there with her.

Susan, Gus and the kids were at the airport to see J.B. off. Since he started this endeavor, his eyes were brighter, hope was shining brightly on his face. That was all Susan and Gus could do, in trying to get them together; the rest depended on fate. If it was meant to happen, it would.

J.B.'s heart thudded as he landed at the airport; he was that much closer to Millie. He took the airport limousine to the hotel with his reservations. As soon as he was settled into his room and had taken a shower, he ate a leisurely lunch, then he called Lyon's business office and asked to speak to the president, Delroy Fredericks. When his call was connected, J.B. explained what he wanted. He asked for his cartons to be delivered to the hotel. "Del, I would appreciate it, if you'd keep this call confidential, I'd just as soon no one knew I was here in town, not yet anyway."

"No problem, J.B. whatever you say." He wondered what was going on, but he didn't ask. So the big honcho was going to live in San Francisco. Was it because of Millie and their child that was yet to be born? He liked both Millie and J.B. and hoped for a reconciliation.

The next thing on J.B.'s agenda was to find out what doctor Millie was going to and when and where the lamaze classes were held. He thought of asking Cheryl, but he wanted confidentially, and he was afraid Cheryl would accidentally confide to Millie that he was in town. His plan of meeting with her for the first time in San Francisco must be circumstantial so Millie had no choice but accept his presence. After twenty phone calls, he found the doctors name and address. He was a little unsure of how he was going to handle this, but first he needed dates. He called the doctors' secretary. He told her he was Mr. Nobles, and he'd been out of town and wanted to surprise his wife by showing up for the next lamaze class.

She gave him the date and where the sessions were to be held: Tomorrow night at the rehabilitation center near the hospital. Good, he'd finally accomplished what he'd been trying to do.

J.B. dressed in casual clothes to go to the class. He stood in the doorway and watched for some sign of Millie. He counted maybe twenty couples stretched out on the floor, and he quickly scanned the room until he found Millie. She was with

Cheryl who was gently massaging her back. His breathing became shallow; his heart pounded. He closed his eyes, made a silent prayer, and walked toward the woman he loved more than life. Millie was concentrating on the gentle massage, her eyes were closed when J.B. stood in front of her. He winked at Cheryl, who recognized him immediately. He motioned for her to step aside and then dropped to the floor and started gently caressing Millie's back.

Millie felt a different sensation, having been accustomed to Cheryl's gentle massage, this was different. Tingles went up her spine, and down her arms. She hadn't felt this sensation since—She quickly opened her eyes and gasped when she saw J.B. sitting behind her administering the back rub. Her breathing stopped, and she gasped for air.

"Sorry, darling, didn't meant to startle you, just doing my job." He laid his big hand on her extended belly. "Time my son and I became acquainted."

The nurse that was conducting the class noticed Millie's distress, went immediately to her side, dropped down on her knees, and instructed Millie. "Millie, take a deep breath and exhale slowly; you're hyperventilating. Calm down."

Millie did as the nurse told her to do and soon her breathing was back to normal. The nurse walked back to the front of the class. Millie stared at J.B., trying not to suck in her breath again. She felt woozy, her head started spinning, and she saw the room grow dark.

When Millie regained consciousness; J.B. was holding her in his arms, whispering softly in her ear. She didn't open her eyes immediately, just laid there in J.B.'s arms, and listened to the soft sound of his voice. "I'm sorry, darling. I shouldn't have startled you like that, but I didn't know how else to approach you. Darling, baby, I've missed you so much. I love you." The feel of his breath on her ear, the smell of his woodsy aftershave lotion, and the smarting sensation of the slight start of a beard, sent tremors down Millie's body. She opened her eyes. J.B. was holding her in his arms. The nurse, Cheryl, and everyone was looking at them. She turned her head toward J.B. to speak, and he dropped his mouth to hers, and placed a whisper of a kiss on her forehead, which caused Millie to quiver again. Then the reality of the situation settled in.

"Let me up. Get away from me." Her eyes sparked vengefully. J.B. released her and stood up, and pulled Millie up to a standing position. Gone was the tender moment; Millie glared at him.

Cheryl had heard the whole story, but this was an eye opening experience. She thought, 'Millie, you fool, you're in love with this man, and he loves you, get real. You're having his baby.'

She didn't say anything, just observed as she watched the man's face change from wonder and joy to a sadness that broke Cheryl's heart. "Millie, I think we'd better get you home, enough excitement for one night." She looked apologetically at J.B. and took Millie's arm.

"I'm J.B. Cornell, ma'am, and I'm sorry I upset Millie. It seems I have a bad habit of doing that. Take care of her." He turned quickly and left the room. Millie's eyes followed him until he was out of sight.

"Let's go, hon, we'd better get you home and in bed; you're as white as a ghost." Millie willingly went with Cheryl. When the nurse observed that Millie was walking okay, and she had a capable companion, she returned to the front of the class.

"Okay everyone, the excitement is over. Let's resume our exercises." The room was still buzzing with speculation and chatter.

Even the nurse had formed her opinion of the recent scenario. The woman did have a problem. The man was drop dead gorgeous and obviously very much in love with her. She wondered what her problem was. She looked around at the class, several single women were here, with girlfriends or relatives as their coach, wishing the man of their dreams would have shown up and made such an obvious display of tenderness and love.

J.B.'s heart was pounding as he went out of the gym and onto the street. It went better than he'd hoped. At least he got to hold Millie in his arms, even though she was unconscious at the time, but her eyes had opened when he'd lightly kissed her. He'd seen the instant response in her eyes before she realized what was going on. For the first time in months he felt hope. He was right in pursuing Millie and winning her back. A love like theirs was a gift that should be treasured, not ignored.

A week later when it was time for the next class, J.B. called Millie at work and asked her if it was all right if he attended with her. Millie knew all along that J.B. would want to be a father to his son. She'd falsely hoped the distance between them geographically would solve that, but obviously J.B. had relocated to California. She'd heard rumors at work. There was nothing she could do, this baby belonged to him too. How was she going to endure his caressing her body when she couldn't control herself around him? She was putty in his hands just like her mother was with her father.

She walked dejectedly into the huge gym where the classes were being held, wearing her bright pink jogging outfit. They were the most comfortable clothes she owned. She spotted J.B. talking to the nurse and several of the mothers; they were looking up at him totally engrossed when he was speaking. One of the other women standing their waiting for her coach said to Millie, "You'll a lucky women, the skunk that got me pregnant is still running. I would need a whole platoon of well-armed soldiers to just get him here, let alone comfort and support me. And your man is so damn good looking. You are one lucky woman." Having voiced her opinion, she walked away and awkwardly lowered herself to the mat. J.B. spotted Millie across the room. He gave her his megawatt smile, his eyes crinkled at the corners. He said something to his companions and walked toward her. Millie's heart automatically started pounding in her chest. I do love him, God, how I love this man.

"Hello, darling, ready for the class tonight? The nurse was telling me we'd be working on breathing exercises tonight; I think I have them down pat now." He leaned over and whispered in her ear. "Short panting breaths like when we'll close to climaxing together, remember?"

She closed her eyes, but she'd obeyed his suggestion and recalled making love to him, they were lucky they didn't die. She never could catch her breath when it became intense. She wouldn't deny to anyone that making love to J.B. was heavenly. He could take her so far and so high, but she shook her head as if to clear her mind and smiled primly at him. He wasn't going to be allowed to rattle her cage anymore. She made an attempt to waylay his sensual assault on her by changing the subject, J.B. was one step ahead of her when he asked, "do you have a name picked out yet?" His question brought them back to earth.

"No, I'm leaving that up to you, if you want him to have your last name, it's your call."

Another megawatt smile, then, "Definitely my last name, but surely you've been running names through your head, just so it isn't James Benjamin, J.B. for short. What names do you like, darling?"

"Bryan, Tracy, David, John, Dalton. Maybe, it'll come to me when I see him for the first time." She put her hand on her big belly, J.B. placed his hand over hers, just then their child moved. J.B.'s eyes got wide with wonder. This time when he smiled, it was a comical grin, like that of a small boy who just got his first puppy.

"I love you, both of you. And Millie, I'm not going anywhere. I'm here for you and our son for anything, for everything." He used all his self-control to keep from taking her into his arms and smothering her face with kisses. He gazed into her eyes, longing for her. He could draw her to him, then she only gave him a blank look. J.B. was determined that he would win her love back, and if it took forty years to do it, he would. He grinned as he visualized the two of them with snow white hair and bodies marked with age. Their grandchildren were gathered close to them. He hoped someday to share that thought with her, but not yet. Susan had instructed him to be patient and somehow he was going to do that. Millie was worth any agony he had to endure.

J.B. took her arm and the pillow she was carrying and found an empty spot on the gym floor. He gently helped lower Millie to the mat and plumped up the pillow behind her. He couldn't resist running his hand up her back and across her shoulders; his hand gliding over her hair. Millie raised her head and blinked. He'd felt the tremor run through her body at the intimate caress. This was why he'd never give up on her and their relationship. He knew Millie's heart was in the right place; it was her emotional baggage that was keeping them apart.

CHAPTER
11

J.B. FOUND THE PERFECT HOME. It was a dream come true for him. He wanted to stay away from Nob Hill, the elite part of the city, and he rather liked the suburbs. He found exactly what he wanted. He looked at it from the road, marveling at the many details that had been tenderly. An old couple was selling it; their only child they'd born had been killed many years ago when he was coming home from college. They had no descendants. They wanted to personally interview this prospective buyer. They'd put their lives blood into the property and they wanted to be sure that whoever bought it, appreciated it and would only add to its beauty: Twenty-five acres of Paradise.

The barn was visible from the road, and a white-railed fence surrounded a good part of the land. Off to the west of the property, were a grove of trees. The sturdy oak trees lined the cobblestoned driveway. It combined very old with modern congenially. His mind wandered to the future and thought he could get Terry a horse, and when his son was big enough, a small pony. He wondered if Millie would like one. J.B.'s mind was filled with future plans for this beautiful, provincial home. It wasn't Victorian, nor was it colonial, maybe a combination of both, he thought as he climbed the stones steps to the small stoop; the bricks were laid in precision. He took hold of an old fashioned knocker, lifted it, and used it to bang on the door.

The door opened and swung wide, then an older woman, whose hair was snow white, appeared and smiled. "You must be J.B. Cornell, we've been expecting you, please come in." Then J.B. was given a complete tour. He had little to say,and just observed every detail. The old couple pointed out the playhouse and the tree fort he'd built for his son many years ago, now badly in need of repair. He mentally put that on his list of changes and alterations. The old man sadly remarked. "All this house ever needed was children, oodles of them, but we weren't fortunate enough to have the big brood we wanted. We only had the one, and we lost him when he was a young man. Do you have children, Mr. Cornell?"

"I have a twelve-year-old stepdaughter, and we are expecting a boy in one month. I'm already thinking about horses, and maybe a pony for the boy."

The old couple laughed with glee. J.B.'s enthusiasm was spilling out, easily detectable. This was the man they wanted to have their beloved home. "It's all yours, Mr. Cornell; it's your home if you want it."

J.B. purchased the home of his dreams, now all he needed was his family to go with it. He'd learned the hard way not to bring Millie here to show her the house. She seemed to have some kind of aversion to his wealth, and she had no idea just how wealthy he was.

The former owners were leaving everything but their personal possessions. They'd already bought a small cottage in Hawaii on the beach. They were keeping their life simple, they'd told him. They only wanted to walk the beach, search for seashells and watch the glorious sunsets for the rest of their days.

J.B. intended to add a built in Olympic sized swimming pool, and extend the back patio. There already was a large hot-tub invitingly hidden in the corner. He'd have an open pit installed for barbecue's and a few more amenities. He wished Millie was here to help with the selections. What if she didn't care for suburban living? The worse case scenario was it would be a wonderful place to bring his son for his visitations with his father.

*   *   *

Esther Mantle conferred with her professor at the college. She told him a condensed tale of Millie's life and what her problem was now. "Doctor Wade, I didn't say anything when she was finished talking to me, it was then I decided to talk to you. What can I say to her? In my opinion, there is nothing wrong with this man of hers, she's the one that is messed up. What do you think of what I've told you and what can I tell her?"

"She came from an extremely dysfunctional family. Good grief, even physical or sexual abuse would be easier to cope with. The victims after many sessions of therapy can accept the fact that they were blameless. You say she visited her parents recently and formed another ill-begotten opinion of their lives. The childhood memory and opinion, could be dealt with, but she's now a mature woman. I don't really think she can make a rational decision anymore. She needs help. Is there anyway, you can persuade her to come in and talk to me?"

"I'll try to persuade her that she needs professional help, and I'm so glad that you're willing to help her. I have all the faith in the world that if anyone could help, you can. I really appreciate this, Doctor Wade. If and when you meet Millie, you'll realize that she is a special kind of person and doesn't need this problem, none of us do. Millie is, well she's just different. I'll call you if she agrees to therapy, and thank you."

At break time that evening after Millie and Esther were finishing eating and relaxing with their tea that Esther still continued adding so much sugar to, Esther broached the subject of Millie's problems. "Millie, how are you making out with J.B. since he's here in San Francisco?

Millie laughed. "I don't have any choice about getting along with him. He comes to all my lamaze classes, and sends flowers, candy and meals to my office all the time. That's J. B. for you. He never does anything in a small way. Right now, I'm concentrating on having my baby and dealing with one day at a time."

"Millie, I talked to my professor about your past problems. I hope you don't mind, but I want to be your friend, and I certainly wouldn't want to ill-advise you. He thinks you should come in and talk to him or a psychiatrist. He said he'd recommend a reputable one for you."

"Esther, did you tell him everything I told you that Saturday afternoon?"

Esther should have felt guilty about betraying Millie's confidence, but she didn't. "Yes, I did, Millie. You need help, and you surely don't need an amateur like me saying the wrong thing to you. I'll tell you my opinion for what it's worth. Millie, you have the problem. J.B. may have some kind of issue concerning his mother and his friends that would explain why he never included you into his social life, but that man loves you and Terry, and I believe what he told you about kissing that stupid blonde the night of your bachelorette dinner. For God's sake, Millie, ask him? Demand an explanation. You have the right to do that."

Millie took in Esther's bold statement. She didn't say anything, but it reminded her of something Susan would say to her. But Millie didn't make waves. It wasn't in her nature to make demands. She didn't feel she had the right. When that last thought went through her mind, Millie knew finally what Esther and Susan had been trying to tell her. She did have the right. Where was it written that Millie Nobles couldn't get angry and demand to be treated fairly and justly?

"Do we have time before the next class to see your professor, and you can introduce us?"

Esther's stood up and offered her hand to Millie. Millie just grinned, then groaned and gratefully accepted the helping hand. She'd go along with Esther's plan. What could it hurt? When they walked into the classroom, there was already a small group of students congregated in the back of the room.

Without hesitation Esther walked up to the desk where an attractive male was shuffling through papers. "Doctor Wade, I'd like you to meet my friend, Millie Nobles."

The over average tall man stood and smiled at Esther, then turned his face toward Millie. With one glance, he took in her physical appearance. She was beautiful, and her full-term pregnancy only enhanced it. He glanced at her sweatshirt with an arrow pointing downward and the words, 'a work in progress' artistically printed on the front. He extended his hand and gazed into Millie's sultry eyes. "I'm happy to meet you, Millie Nobles, and I'm glad you're here to see me. Does this introductory visit mean what I'm hoping it does?" He looked quizzically at Esther.

Esther grinned at him. "She's agreed to talk to you."

"Wonderful. Do you want to come to my office or would you be more comfortable talking in a more comfortable sitting?" Doug Wade looked into Millie's questioning eyes.

"Tonight, or when it's convenient for you, at my home. Come for dinner and please don't expect too much from the menu, my twelve-year-old daughter, Terry is experimenting with cooking. I'd really like for you to meet and talk to her."

"Esther told me about your daughter. Twelve years old, going on twenty. I'd be delighted to come to your home." He took her small hand and gently squeezed it.

Millie gave him her card, smiled at both of them and then glanced at her watch. "I've got three minutes to get to my next class. See you later and thanks, Esther."

The room started filling up with students so Esther didn't have an opportunity to talk further to her mentor. She took her own seat and waited for the class to begin.

Doug Wade was surprised to meet the woman who'd caused this anxiety for his student, Esther. Mentally, he'd expected to see a dowdy looking woman, not this gorgeous one. Something was definitely out of kilter here. Most women he knew with her kind of beauty had no problem with self-esteem and self-confidence. It was like they'd been born to it. He opened the text book, but before starting his class; he momentarily envied the man that loved her and impregnated her. Lucky man.

That evening Doug Wade had no problem locating Millie's house. As he pulled into the driveway, he was impressed with the house and the location. Obviously this man that Millie was involved with had money. He knocked on the door and was pleasantly surprised when a pretty young girl opened the door and giggled. "You must be Doctor Wade. Mom said you were coming for dinner. I made the dinner and would you please be kind? The recipe was easy but it doesn't look at all like the picture in the cookbook. Mom said it tasted all right though. But I've got ice cream for dessert. Come on in."

Immediately, Wade liked this precocious child. He followed her out to the lanai where a round table was set for dinner. Millie was sprawled out on a chaise lounge. Then, as she determinedly struggled to get out of the low chair, Wade stepped forward and gave her a helping hand.

"Now I know exactly how a beached whale feels. They have my deepest sympathy. Thank you for coming to my home. Did you meet my daughter?" Millie wrapped her arm around her daughter who looked so much like her.

"Yes, I did, and we've already reached an understanding." He turned to Terry, winked and asked, "Do you need any help bringing this delicious meal out here? I'm volunteering."

Terry laughed and headed for the kitchen. The prominent Doctor Douglas Wade willingly followed right behind her.

Surprisingly, Terry had been absolutely right about the meal she'd prepared. The look of food was overrated. It was the taste that mattered. Wade leaned over and whispered in her ear. "Terry, I think I have the same cookbook. I did a little experimenting when I tried it. Next time you prepare this, cook the noodles first before adding everything else. Then it'll look better, and I think if I remember right, I added some frozen peas to give it some color and more nutrition. You're welcome, darlin'." Then he grinned at her. The sappy looking tuna fish and noodle casserole was nearly depleted, so Terry didn't feel too badly.

They'd finished eating the promised ice cream for dessert

before Wade subtly started asking questions. Before Millie realized it, she was confiding in him about her childhood and the experience of having a baby at fifteen years old and the struggling years that ensued. Terry had heard about some of it before, but never in such details. Both Terry and Doctor Wade listened intently. When Millie was finished, she picked her glass of water up and nearly drained it.

Doctor Wade leaned back in his chair and pondered for a moment before he spoke. "Millie, I'm sorry.

I'd like to be able to say your mother was this, your father was that, but it's not that easy. I'd have to hear their side of the story to make any kind of judgment about their behavior. For sure, they both had problems. Without knowing them, may I say; Millie, you aren't like them. Terry is living proof that you are a good, loving mother, capable of loving your child. I'll add to that statement that she is wise beyond for her years having experienced your years and raising your niece and nephew for so long without any help is commendable. But you don't want a pat on the back, do you Millie? Your entire life has been to prove what a saint you are, but I'm going to tell you what a bitch you are and how wrong you've been. Ready?"

Millie's eyes widened; she hadn't expected that.

Doctor Wade continued, "In the first place, Millie, that was against the law what your father did to you when you were fifteen and your sister was seventeen. When did she leave home? And why didn't you two sisters join forces and live together then? Why didn't you go to the authorities and report your parents? You had rights, Millie. Your parents were responsible for both of you until reaching eighteen or finishing with high school."

"Susan took off with a boyfriend, and I didn't see her again until she was pregnant with Paul two years later. And that thing about my parents. My father legally emancipated my mother and him from me."

"He could only have done that if you were involved with criminal activities, like pushing dope. Parents sometimes do that to protect their assets. No way, could he have been able to do that just because you were pregnant. He wouldn't have been financially responsible for your child, but he was for you. You should have been placed in a foster home at the very least. What did you tell them at the welfare office?"

"That I was going to be eighteen three months before the baby was due. I was afraid they'd put me in a home for bad kids."

"You obviously had a lousy caseworker. Did she ask for your birth certificate?"

"I showed her Susan's."

"Do you see what I'm getting at Millie. Digging and delving into the details of the past, you have to admit you weren't guileless. You knew you were deceiving the authorities."

Terry stood up and indignantly defended her mother. "Mom was just a kid and scared. She didn't know what else to do."

"You're only twelve, but play this out. What if your mother threw you out of the house and refused to take care of you anymore. What would you do?"

Terry looked angrily at the doctor and vehemently said, "I'd call my Aunt Sue and Uncle Gus or I'd call J.B. He'd never let that happen to me. He loves me." Terry started to cry. Doctor Wade rose from his chair and put his arm around Terry, trying to comfort her. He hadn't meant to upset her.

"Terry, you have someone to turn to. Your mother obviously didn't, and she was scared, and she made poor choices. But she proved her mettle by sticking by and providing for not only you, but your little cousins for almost three years. Terry, the reason why we are digging into this is to find out why your mother felt like she deserved to do everything alone. J.B. immediately changed everything about your lives when he learned of it. Your mother could have done the same thing, but she was too proud to appeal to the welfare office for assistance. Fear played a part in it, but I believe it was mostly your mothers' pride. And Millie, I understand that J.B. loves you and Terry, and he wants to marry you. Why won't you marry him?"

Terry shrugged her shoulders and said, "J.B. kissed some woman and now mom thinks he's a Casanova. A two-timer. I don't believe he is, but mom does."

"No, I don't, Terry. I believe J.B. When he said the woman was coming on to him like gang-busters, and he pushed her away. I have other issues."

"And they are?" Doctor Wade looked intensely into Millie's eyes and saw the confusion, the uncertainty. He was pushing her to break down or get angry. He was forcing her to face the truth. Esther had told him every detail of this woman's story.

"He... he... He never takes me around his friends or his family, and I think he's... he might be ashamed of me." Even to her own ears that sounded ridiculous.

Millie put her hands up to the sides of her face and started rocking in her chair.

Terry, being the astute youngster she was, offered to make coffee and excused herself. When Terry was gone, Doctor Wade reached over and removed Millie's hands from her face and held tightly in his.

"I repeat, Esther told me everything. Why in the world do you now think you're like your mother in the sexual scenario of their marriage? Has J.B. ever bargained for your favors or withheld himself from you so you'd agree with what he wanted?"

"Never. Our relationship is spontaneous. We're perfectly suited to each other."

"Millie, your parents damaged you. You were a frightened child, but intelligent and strong enough to succeed in making a living for you and your child. That was unfortunate that you recently witnessed your parents argument the time you and Susan went to see them. How you got the notion that you were J.B.'s sex slave is unreal? I think you're looking for an excuse for J.B. to be less than he actually is. You don't want to trust him. Esther never met J.B., but she's quite certain he cares deeply for you. A man just doesn't move clear across the country for a mere acquaintance or a one-night-stand."

"It's like I can't allow myself to be happy and accept good things that happen in my life. I made a mistake with that boy years ago and I should be punished. I don't deserve all the wonderful things J.B. has made happen for me."

Terry brought the coffee out just then so the conversation was curtailed. Then, Doctor Wade made a suggestion. "Millie, I believe the delivery of your baby is imminent, so right now is not a good time for you to become emerged in deep therapy. You shouldn't be emotionally upset at this crucial time in your pregnancy. When the baby is around a month old would be a better time, then if you are suffering at all from postnatal blues, we can work on that also. Make an appointment when that time comes, then we'll talk more. You've done real well today and you've made a good start."

Doctor Wade left the mother and daughter in a quiet pensive mood. As he drove off into the night, in spite of years of training and education; he made a silent prayer to God for guidance and a divine intervention that would help this woman and child.

The next day Millie called him and requested another appointment; this time in his office. She explained, "Doctor, I don't want to wait until my baby is born. You've already helped me with one session."

They set up an appointment, and Millie started seeing Doctor Wade on a regular basis. Every time she talked to him, things were made clearer, and she realized she was her worst enemy. Years of false values and conceptions seemed to melt away.

*   *   *

Millie was miserable, and just plain uncomfortable. She didn't remember feeling this bad when she was about to deliver Terry. Maybe it was her age. Less than three weeks to go for the home stretch she kept telling herself as she lumbered down the hall to her office. The just over seven months she'd been here, everyone praised her for the terrific ideas that she had: production was up, sales were booming, and the company had never been this prosperous. Cheryl was at her desk when Millie waddled in. "Less than three more weeks to go, Cheryl, then you won't have to listen to my moaning and groaning all the time."

Cheryl giggled. "No, but I'll hear you beefing about getting no sleep. Babies think they're absolutely adorable at three o'clock in the morning, all smiles and bushy-tailed. Been there and done that three times."

"I remember Terry. I was lucky with her, she was for sure the best baby in the world. Peaches and cream and pure sunshine in my life. I loved every minute of her babyhood, now I'm enjoying a soon-to-be teenaged daughter. She'll be thirteen in a few more weeks."

"A built-in babysitter. Every mother's dream."

"I suppose, she is interested in setting up the nursery and helping to pick out clothes for our baby."

"No name yet, Millie, or is he going to be an 'it'?

"I'll know when I see him, I hope. Right now I'm kinda leaning toward Charles, Chucky for a nickname."

"Wasn't he a monster on that Halloween movie?"

"Hey, you're right, then how about Chip for a nickname?"

"Sissified."

"You're no help." Millie went into her office and shut the door. Maybe, she should just let J.B. name their baby.

*　*　*

After he was born, she noticed a big bouquet of roses on her desk. She didn't have to look at the tag to see who sent them. Seeing J.B. once a week was enough to throw her into a panic, but he kept sending flowers and candy. Sometimes he just sent a meal at lunchtime. He constantly kept himself in her thoughts. Not a day went by when she didn't hear something about him. She just was getting no peace at all. How was she going to forget him when he kept reminding her?

One thing she knew for certain was, J.B. loved her. Anybody that would give up their home, business and friends to move clear across the country to be with her was sincere. Her talks with Doctor Wade and the anti-depressant were helping. She smiled more, was more relaxed and whenever her mind started to drift toward self doubts and unanswerable questions, she could easily dismiss them. She was busy planning a future.

Doctor Wade advised her to stop digging up bones and trying to analyze them. That was his job.

She just didn't know when she was going to tell J.B. that she'd been wrong about many things and ask his forgiveness. She hoped she'd know when the right moment arrived.

Of all things, she actually looked forward to the weekly lamaze class. Looking and feeling like a Goodyear blimp put her at a disadvantage. She wanted to look and feel like herself again when she pronounce her love to J.B. She stared off dreamily out the window and thought about a life with him. Would he want to live in her house with her? Maybe she should invite him for dinner and show him the nursery and the baby clothes, that Terry and she had purchased for the baby's arrival. She bent over and smelled the roses and daydreamed about J.B. She had to smile at that. He was still her dream man from the old days, J.B. used to fulfill every one of her fantasies. Seven o'clock tonight was a lamaze class, maybe she would ask J.B. to come to the house after. It seemed compulsive now for her to start the future again, instead of burying all the dreams she had of J.B. and her together with their family.

She smiled when she recalled Doctor Wade's expression when she told him of her obsession concerning sex with J,B. She told him she couldn't resist J.B. Doctor Wade leaned back in his chair and chuckled. "Lord, Millie, you're perfect. You're what every red-blooded man dreams of having for a woman. Too bad you are taken, I'd be knocking at your door, begging you to marry me. I'm glad that J.B. realizes this, also. That's why he is so persistent and refuses to let go of you. He knows what a treasure you are."

At one time, Millie couldn't have accepted such a flattering compliment. Now she just chuckled and grinned at her young, handsome doctor.

CHAPTER

12

A WEEK AND A HALF LATER, Millie started to get labor pains at work. At first she just thought she was just suffering from a bad backache that was very low on her spine. She put a pillow behind her at work, thinking that would ease the discomfort. Around 11:30 Millie got up from her chair to go to the bathroom, and her water broke. It puddled on the carpet between her legs. She yelled for Cheryl who he came rushing into Millie's office and saw the wet spot on the floor. "Just stand there, Hon, I'll get something for you. She came back in a minute with a package of new undies and a sanitary napkin. They were kept at the first-aid station for women who experienced accidents when they had their period. She helped Millie get dry, then assisted her back in to her chair. "Millie, aren't you supposed to call J.B. when you start labor?"

"If I don't, he'll probably have a bird, won't he? And he is my official coach. Do you have his number?" Cheryl went out to her own office to look at her telephone index and found several numbers for J.B. Cheryl punched in the first number and their was no answer, finally an answering machine kicked in. Cheryl hung up and tried the cell phone number. J.B. answered on the second ring. Cheryl handed the phone to Millie. She heard J.B.'s voice, "hello, hello."

"J.B., this is Millie, my water broke. I'm going to the hospital." She thought, what is going to be worse, having her body ravished with contractions or the agony of having J.B. near her?

"How bad is it Millie? I can be there in twenty minutes. Will you be able to wait that long?"

"I don't have any pains, my water broke, so hurry, come and get me."

J.B.'s heart was pounding, she'd called him. It surprised and thrilled him immensely. He just thought he'd be notified after the baby was born. He ran to his car, ignored a few red lights, and drove well over the speed limit through town. He pulled his car into the visitors slot and rushed into Millie's building. He made it to Millie's floor in record time. He rushed into her office, not knowing what to expect. She was sitting calmly at her desk, when he rushed in, she just raised her eye brows and looked at him. "Why are you so excited, J.B? Chill out. We have plenty of time."

J.B. dropped to the floor in front of her on his knees, hugged her around the legs, and laid his face in her lap. "Millie, you scared the daylights out of me, if anything happened to you, I wouldn't be able to stand it. Give me a couple of minutes to get myself together, and we'll get you to the hospital."

Millie's hand automatically started working through his hair, just a comforting gesture. All the talks she'd had with Doctor Wade made her finally acknowledge that her fears were ungrounded. J.B. loved her and she loved him. J.B. raised his face and gazed into her eyes. "Oh, baby, I love you more than life. I should never have gotten you pregnant, what if you don't make it? What if something goes wrong?"

Millie laughed softly. "Let's go get our son, J.B., I think he's anxious to make an appearance." She paused for a while then confessed. "J.B., you're going to have to pick his name, for some reason, I just can't decide. The only solution for this dilemma is to have four more boys for the names I have picked out."

"God forbid, I could never go through this again." J.B. moaned, not really catching what Millie had just subtly said to him.

J.B. stood up and pulled her up from the chair. "Let's go, love. I don't know how good of a coach I'm going to be, but I'll do my best." He promised.

"I know you will, darling." Her big belly pressed against him, and she leaned further into his body. J.B.'s heart soared, when Millie called him that endearment and showed the first attempt of intimacy since their son was conceived. He kissed her lightly on the lips, savoring the taste of her. His heart pounding.

J.B. couldn't coach Millie. Several times he was asked to leave the room. The nurses were fussing over him more than Millie, who for four hours of intense labor, never let out a peep. J.B. was not in the room when their son was born. When the nurse laid him in Millie's arms, she stared at the small image of J.B./ Millie laughed and told her little son. "What a little memento you are going to be. How could I ever forget your father, with you around to constantly remind me? How about it, little James Benjamin Junior, Jamie for short, that is."

J.B. walked into the room and heard Millie talking to the little bundle, she held in her arms. He gazed down at them, his stomach still heaving. God, he'd been scared. Who ever got the brilliant idea that the fathers should witness their children's births, didn't have J.B. in mind. "So you named our son after all, let me see this little Jamie." He bent over and gazed at his son, suddenly it was all worthwhile, the long nine months, the terror of watching Millie in pain for so long. Millie's eyes were full of love for him and their son. His prayers were being answered. God, he loved them so much his heart actually hurt.

J.B. bent over and kissed the baby's damp forehead, then kissed Millie. His mouth couldn't leave hers, their lips clung to each others, hungrily. It had been so long.

"Hey, you two, knock it off, or you'll be back out here again in ten months, give it a rest." The nurse teased them. J.B. and Millie broke apart, and grinned sheepishly at the nurse.

Three days later J.B. took Millie and the baby home with

Jamie safe in his car seat on the rear seat and Millie beside J.B. on the front seat. J.B. kept looking over at her. He wanted to take them to his—their home—but he didn't know if Millie was ready for that yet.

When they pulled in front of Millie's home, Terry came running out of the house. She kissed her mother, and then threw her arms around J.B.'s neck. He hugged her back, picked her up, and swung her around his waist. "Oh, J.B., I've missed you so much."

Then Terry turned her attention to the back seat. She released the straps and gently lifted the baby up and into her arms. She pulled the blanket from his face and smiled down at him. "Hi little brother, my very own brother. You're beautiful, little man, and I just love you to pieces." She kissed him right on his puckered up little mouth, then she carried him into the house. J.B. and Millie followed them inside.

This was the first time, J.B. had ever seen the house that caused so much controversy. The furniture looked familiar. J.B. still had no regrets for setting Millie and Terry up comfortably. He would learn to cope with this strong-willed independent woman of his, even if it meant giving up his beautiful country estate that he loved.

*   *   *

Susan and Gus were called and told of Jamie's birth shortly after he was born. "Damn, why did she have to move so far away? I probably won't see my nephew for years. I miss them so much." Susan vocally agonized.

"Susan, I've been thinking about this for a long time now. There's nothing really keeping you and I and the kids here in Ohio. My parents are both gone. All I have is you and the kids, and we could live anywhere."

Susan studied Gus's face; he never talked just to hear his own voice. Susan believed him when he said he'd been pondering making a change. "Gus, your trucking business, this house is here. Everything you've worked so hard for, you'd have to leave behind."

"We'd get a good price for the house, a lot more than what I paid for it, and the same with the trucking business. I've been approached several times over the years. The big guys always like to buy up the small independents like mine, too much honest competition."

"Well, I guess they need small trucking outfits in San Francisco, too. But the house, Gus, I love it. You've completely refurbished everything, and I think it's perfect. You did a wonderful job."

Susan could say things like that to Gus and make him feel like he was ten feet tall. He thought, how in the world, had he gotten so lucky, finding this wonderful, beautiful woman? Compared to his short pudgy physique, she was way out of his league. He'd really lucked out, and he'd do anything to make her and the kids happy. "I love you, babe, I'd give you the moon if I could. I don't deserve you."

Susan crawled up on his lap and nestled close to him. "Don't talk like that Gus, ever again. You're everything I ever wanted in a man, you've already fulfilled my every dream. I'm the one that's lucky and I love you so much, Gus."

They were kissing when the phone rang. Susan whispered, "let the machine get it, we're busy." After the four rings, they heard the beep of the answering machine picking up, then Susan heard her Mother's voice. She jumped up and rushed to get the phone. "Mom, I'm here, what do you want?"

"Susan, may I come over and talk to you? Please, dear." Susan couldn't help but hear the desperate plea in her mother's voice.

"Of course Mom, do you know where I live?" Susan looked at Gus and raised her eyebrows.

"Yes, I'll get a taxi. I have the address. Thank you, Susan."

Susan was having second thoughts about her mother ever since Millie and she visited her. Susan saw her mother as a weak woman, and a victim that allowed an overpowering man to dominant her life, and control her with sex. She'd run into that type of man herself. Melody's father wanted Susan to leave her baby on a church doorstep. He'd said, "who needs this baggage? It's bad enough I have to tolerate your stuffy-nose son, but at least we can leave him alone, unlike this damn bawling brat." She'd left him. Give up her children, no way, but she thought about leaving them with Millie for almost three long years. God, she'd been a mixed up piece of shit. It took Doctor Simpson and J.B. to get through to her. But it was Gus who gave her the self-confidence she needed in herself. She actually liked herself now, which was a feat in itself. She wondered, what does my mother want from me?

Twenty minutes later, the taxi pulled up in front of their home. Gus opened the door when Susan's mother knocked. "Mrs. Nobles, I'm Gus Fredericks, Susan's husband. Won't you please come in."

Carrie Nobles walked into Susan and Gus's home. Her eyes quickly swept over the large living room, the fireplace burned invitingly in the corner; the room was pleasant, cozy, warm and lived in. A real home. Carrie smiled and walked toward her beautiful daughter. Her little Susan, her first born baby.

They embraced, both of them crying. Gus went into the kitchen to make a fresh pot of coffee, leaving them alone. "Susan, I don't know where to begin." Carrie began hesitantly.

"Mom, you don't have to tell me. I know my father dominated and controlled you. You should have used a little more back bone and told him a long time ago to go to hell. Even as a kid, I knew you wanted to be different than he was, but every time you made any attempt, there was hell to be paid. Melody's father was like that, it was his way or the highway. I left him. I could make enough mistakes of my own doing. I never wanted to follow in your footsteps."

Carrie studied her daughter for a couple minutes before speaking. She observed that Susan was little on the tough side, and certainly not a genteel lady. Where had it gotten her? Secrets, shame and regret. Maybe it was better to tell it like it was, the way Susan did. How could her daughter have a ladies vocabulary and be demure? She hadn't raised her. Carrie smiled. "I see you've picked up a little street talk along the way, but a person knows right up front what you're thinking. There's nothing presumptuous or pretentious about you. I've heard the young people at school make different slang remarks. You go for it, girl."

Susan laughed and hugged her mother again. Susan thought to herself, if my outlandish speech and vocabulary is offending my mother's genteel nature, I'll have to lighten up a little.

"Don't change, I think I like it, at least I'll get used to it." She grinned at Susan, darn if that didn't remind Susan of Millie. Exactly the same expression. They both relaxed.

"Susan, I'm going to leave your father. We've been arguing practically nonstop, since you and Millie came to see us. He won't budge an inch. He's adamant, he just never wanted children in his life. I've been a slave to his self-centered peculiarities. He's an obsessive neat-freak. Everything has to be in its place. I just can't surrender my own life to please him, not anymore. I probably would have broken it off years ago, but as I told you girls, one thing your father is, is an accomplished lover. When I'd displease him, he would turn his back on me. I don't know if it's because I'm getting smarter in my old age, but it's not worth it anymore. To use one of your quirky quotes, he can stick it."

They were both laughing hard when Gus came into the room carrying a tray with her best cloth napkins, china cups, cut glass creamer and sugar bowl, that she never used and kept in a china closet. Now it was prominently displayed on the tray Gus had brought in. Gus used an old carafe for coffee. Mrs Nobles noticed his effort and remarked about it. "Gus, you didn't have to fuss on my account. I could have gone into the kitchen to finish our conversation. That works for me." God, she'd been hearing the kids talk like this for years. It felt good to lighten up and let it all hang out, as she heard one kid say. Susan laughed again.

Gus joined in. "Whew! That's a relief. I thought we were going to have to put on the dog for you. You're regular, huh?"

Paul and Melody came in the front door, and slammed the door shut behind them. They were arguing and yelling about something. When they saw that their parents were entertaining company, they stopped shouting at each other. They both looked real guilty as they flashed their parents an apologetic look. Gus grinned at them. "Come on in and meet your grandmother, you two little hooligans." He said affectionately.

Melody shyly crawled up on Gus's lap and sneaked a look at this woman, that their dad said was their grandmother. Susan took Paul's grubby hand and pulled him to where her mother stood. "Mother, this is Paul, our son. Paul, this is my mother, your grandmother."

Carrie gazed at the handsome boy. What was he, around nine or ten years' old? Oh, she'd missed so much. She stepped forward and put her arms around him and hugged him tight. "Hello, Paul, I'm so happy to meet you, sit down here with me and tell me all about yourself. How old are you? Just talk to me." Paul grinned, and sat down. He was embarrassed about being so dirty, but even though his face and hands were crumby, this nice lady seemed to like him, right off the bat, like he was special or something.

As Paul was talking to his grandmother, not wanting her brother to get ahead of her, Melody slid off Gus's lap and slowly walked over to her 'grandmother'. Carrie put her arm around her as she crawled up on the other side of her. "Grandmother, this is my sister, Melody, she's only four years old. She doesn't even go to school yet." Then he stood up and announced, "Come on, Mel, lets go get washed up and change our clothes, so we look more 'pectable'.

Carrie smiled lovingly at them as they walked hand and hand towards the bathroom. "They're wonderful, so full of life and so happy. You've done a wonderful job raising them. Oh, they're just so precious. Thank God, I'd made the decision to get to know you all better. I've missed so much, but not anymore I won't.

"Carrie, just before you came here, Susan and I were seriously talking about moving to San Francisco so we'd be nearer to Millie and her family. What do you think about it? I couldn't help but overhear what you said to Susan about leaving your husband. Would you consider moving in with us? We could all be together, and if your husband changed his mind, he could always join us."

"He won't change his mind, he'd never take such a chance. Everything is his life has to be so precise, he'd never risk it. Besides, he won't ever change; he never has."

"That's because he's always gotten his own way. Maybe when he realizes that you really mean business, he'll come around to see your side for a change." Gus quietly said.

"That would be his choice. I've had enough. I want a relationship with my family now, one that I have always wanted, but he wouldn't me to have." This ordinary man that was her son-in-law and was married to Susan possessed more wisdom than Carl did, and he'd earned a doctorate degree in college.

"Gus and Susan, I meant what I said, when I told you that I left my husband. My luggage is on the front porch, but if you don't want me or you don't have room for me, I can go to a hotel." Carrie was mentally crossing her fingers, hoping they would accept her into their family.

Gus grinned and brought her luggage in. "We've got a spare room, Carrie, you are more than welcome to share our home." Susan fell more in love with her wonderful man at that very moment, he always came through for her and the kids, and now he was coming through for her mother too.

Carrie was delighted, she sighed with relief. She'd taken a big step and it was so wonderful that her family wanted her, It was more than she'd hoped for and deserved.

Paul and Melody appeared in their pajamas, squeaky clean and smiling from ear to ear. Carrie held out her arms, and they both rushed to her, to sit on each side of her on the sofa. Paul explained to Melody what a grandmother was while they were getting cleaned up.

"You're the first grandmother, I ever ever had." Melody shared with her.

"And you are the first granddaughter I ever had, and I'm very happy about it."

"You have Terry and a brand new grandson. He's just real teeny, and his name is Jamie. I've never seen him yet." Paul added.

"I'm very lucky, really truly lucky." Carrie grinned, good heavens, now she was mimicking Melody's baby talk. Wouldn't Carl be aghast at her spontaneous behavior?

Carrie was shown to the bedroom she'd use and the children followed her inside. They continued to keep up a constant flow of chatter, which delighted Carrie.

Then Susan came in and insisted the children say good night to everyone and go to their own rooms. She reminded them, "tomorrow is a school day and have to get up early in the morning." They hugged and kissed their grandmother, mom and dad then went to their own rooms. That brought tears to Carrie's eyes. If only she'd been a stronger person and had defied her husband, and abided by her own convictions of right and wrong. Instead she chose to be selfish and fulfilled her own needs. Maybe She would have known the joy of loving children and being loved in return, maybe Carl, if he loved her enough, would have relented, and they would have become a regular, loving family after a while. Maybe. She'd never know. She hadn't had the courage to even try.

How many books had she read that were well written by learned scholars in Psychology? She'd poured over their testaments of wisdom and therapeutic treatments for the mentally and emotionally disturbed. Why couldn't she have used this vital information to heal her own family? Had she tried? Was leaving the man she loved the only answer? She didn't know anymore, but ever since her two daughters visited them, they were back in her life and back in her thoughts like they'd never been before. Two beautiful daughters, and two sons-in-law and four gorgeous grandchildren. She missed Carl desperately as she lay in the double bed alone, but tomorrow her day would be filled with happiness. She was beginning a new life.

If only Carl were different. What made him the way he is, she wondered as she dropped off to sleep. Why hadn't she asked him?

CHAPTER
13

SUSAN PICKED THE PHONE UP that was sitting on the end of the kitchen counter. She looked at the clock; it would be a little late in the evening for Millie, with the time change, but Susan couldn't wait any longer. She punched in Millie's number. Susan was surprised, but pleasantly so when J.B. answered the phone. Had Millie and J.B. gotten back together? "Hello". She admitted to herself how much she missed her family.

"J.B., it's Susan. I want to know all about this wonderful new nephew of mine, and I need to talk to Millie." Susan heard a click, indicating someone picked up another phone.

"You've got it, girl, what's your problem?" Millie's cheerful voice rang out in Susan's ear.

"No problem, are you sitting down, because you're in for a surprise?"

"Shoot for the moon, kid, tell me all." Millie sounded happy and gay.

"We've decided if the mountain can't come to us, we're all coming to the mountain. Gus, Paul, Melody and I are selling out and moving to San Francisco, and that's not all, so is our mother. She's here right now, staying in our guest room. She left our father and she is wonderful. We've got ourselves a mom, girl."

Millie was speechless. She tried to talk but all she could do was try to get her breath. She loved her home, job and now her family was coming here too. She'd been overwhelmed; first J.B. relocated to prove that he was sincere in his love for her and the family, now her beloved sister, her mother; she started crying.

J.B. watched her struggling for words that wouldn't come, then he tenderly watched her start to cry. He wanted to rush to her and hold her tight in his arms, but Susan was waiting for a reply. So he responded to Susan's exciting news. "Hey girl, that's the best news I ever heard. I've missed you all so much, and as soon as Millie gets her breath back, and stops bawling, she'll tell you too. Susan, I sent some pictures of our boy to you; they should be on your computer. Needless to say this little six and a half pound dynamo has taken over our lives. He's wonderful. Right now, his sister is feeding him a bottle. We've been fighting for our turns to do that. We all gave him his bath. I'm sure he's probably thinking, he's a little prince, a shah or maybe even a pharaoh."

J.B.'s happiness and paternal pride was conveyed across the many miles. Susan smiled. All was well with her sister, the stubborn, determined little brat. She'd caused a lot of her own grief. Susan was always sure that J.B. loved Millie. Susan's eyes raised and caught Gus gazing at her with such love and adoration in his eyes, that genuine emotion caught Susan's heart. J.B. And Gus as far as she was concerned was heaven-sent. At last, she and Millie were on the homestretch. Happiness was within their reach. "I can't wait to take my turn. Who does he look like?" For the next five minutes, J.B. described his sons' good looks without a hint of modesty.

Millie, still sniffling, picked up the phone. When J.B. heard her voice, he hung up. They might need some privacy. "Susie, this is the best day of my life. Right now, I'm in shock, but we'll make plans, make sure you have a place here to move right into. Oh Sue, we'll all be together and after the initial shock, I have to wonder, are you sure about mother? Beware, she let us down before, so be forewarned. I'll believe it when I see it happening. You know, when our father comes to get her, he'll try to talk her into coming back. She'll be putty in his hands, or should I say in bed? He'll have his own way. He doesn't want us or our families; he's proved that. Be careful, Sue, don't get your hopes up too high."

"I know Millie. We'll just have to wait and see, but for right now, I don't have a choice. She has to know she has some place else to go to. Someone that does want her."

"I know that feeling, so do you."

Look, J.B. and Millie, I'll ring off now, and we'll keep you posted. It might take awhile to sell out and make the arrangements, but it's definitely what we are going to do, but I'm not sure when it's going to happen."

"I'm so happy about it. You call and keep us posted, especially about mom. Love you guys!"

"Right back at you. You too J.B., love you. Goodnight."

After Susan hung the phone up, Gus took her in his arms. Neither of them spoke; they just drew comfort from each other. Susan knew what her mother went through, to love a man and not be treated right, but to share great chemistry. There would never be another like Melody's father, but Susan wouldn't go back to the passion and rapture she'd shared with Kevin. What she had here with Gus, was 24/7, loyalty trust, and unconditional love, not just interludes in bed. This was something her Mother needed to know.

The next night Susan was not a bit surprised when her father showed up at her front door. His tall lithe physique remained the same. He was wearing casual clothes, and his appearance belied his age. Just one look at his face and she knew the mood he was in. As a child she feared him, now she just glared back at him. "Susan, is your mother here? I'd like to see her."

"Come in, father. Mom is resting, but I'll get her for you." He started to shove her aside so he could pass.

"Where is her bedroom? Your mother and I need privacy to talk." Susan laughed, he was so obvious, all he needed was to get her mother in bed. Not this time, Buster, not anymore.

Susan spun around and asked Paul. "Honey, will you go wake up Gram? Tell her she has a guest, please." Paul stared at this white-haired man, even being the child that he was, he could sense the hostility radiating from the older man.

"Mom, maybe it's not a good idea to bring her down here, he looks angry. He won't hurt Gram, will he?" Before Susan could answer her son, Carl bellowed, "Do as your mother told you to do, young man. I don't tolerate insolence." He glared angrily at the shocked young boy, who never in his life had been spoken to in that tone of voice.

"Don't use that tone of voice on my son, he has a right to his opinion, and you aren't making a very good impression." Susan was seething. How dare he come into her home and think he could berate any one of them. "He's concerned about his grandmother."

Carrie heard the loud confrontation and got up, wondering what was going on. When she started down the stairs, she recognized her husband's angry voice.

As Carrie walked in the livingroom, and saw Susan's arms protectively around her son and Carl's dark scowl on his face; she knew this was going to be a make or break situation. "Carl, you have no right to shout at Susan's son. This is between you and me."

Carl glared at his wife. "You're coming with me. What is this nonsense all about? You and I get along superbly, we've never quarreled."

"Yes, we have Carl, you just didn't listen to my side of the argument, like right now. It's over with us, Carl. This is something I should have done years ago when the girls were little, and I realized that you were never going to become a supportive parent. Oh, you paid the bills, supported them financially, but you were never a father, and you wouldn't allow me to be their Mother. I was wrong to allow you to do that to me, to the girls. No more, Carl. I've had it. It's over between us."

Susan watched as her fathers' expression changed abruptly. Always a handsome man, age had just given him distinguished good looks. He smiled at her mother. Susan thought, well, here goes, she wondered if her mother could resist his obvious intentions. Her mind flashed back to Kevin, how she'd turn to putty when he smiled at her that way, he could take her higher than she'd ever believed possible, but he could also take her lower than a human being should ever go.

"Darling, what has you so upset? You know, all you have to do is talk to me and we always soothe everything over. Darling, I love you so much, I can't bear not having you near me." Susan watched him intently. She now believed that he really did love her mother, but selfishly so. He wanted her all to himself.

Carrie's stomach fell to the bottom of her abdomen. Her legs felt weak. She closed her eyes and prayed she could resist her husband. So, he could take her to paradise, but it was always short lived. Afterwards she would be forced to deal with reality and that was what she couldn't do anymore. It just wasn't worth it. She wasn't a young impressionable, hormonal teenager or a woman in her thirties that had an unquenchable appetite for sex. She was past menopause, a mature woman that wanted more than anything just to be a grandmother.

"Not this time, Carl, nor never again. I told you it was over between us. I want my family, my life." She was able to walk closer to him and lay her hand on his shoulder.

Carl scooped her into his arms and kissed her passionately. Carrie melted, her arms went around his neck and pulled him closer. Susan sadly watched her parents. She empathized with her mother.

When Carl released Carrie and raised his head, just the smug self-satisfied, smirk on his face was enough for Susan to want to bash him over the head with something. Hesitantly she looked at her mother, wondering what she would do. For just a moment, Susan saw the desire on her mother's face, but abruptly it changed to self loathing. "Damn you Carl, it's just not going to work this time. I won't allow it."

Shock registered on Carl's face. "Carl, I love you, and I'll always want you, but now, my desire to have my family is stronger; I can let you go. I'm free, at last." Carrie stepped away from him and put her arms around Paul's young shoulder. "Getting to know and love my grandchildren is more important to me now. I'll have my lawyer notify yours to make the disbursement of our financial affairs. Let's try to be amiable about all this."

Carl hated Susan and this brat that were hovering close by. If he could be alone with Carrie, he was sure he could dissuade her from this silly notion of hers, hadn't he always? "This is not the end, Carrie, my love, I'll give you some time to come to your senses." Carl leaned close and whispered softly in her ear. "Just try and forget me, my sexy little darling, grandchildren won't warm your bed, or make you happy like I can. You know, how it is with us."

"Yes, I know how it is. Please try to understand and believe me, Carl, life with my family around me is better. Carl, maybe for the first time in many years, happiness won't be just a few fleeting moments. My entire day will be filled with happiness." Carrie raised her chin and stared back at Carl. It reminded Susan a lot of Millie. She smiled encouragingly at her mother.

Carl turned around and left the house, but before he went out the door, he turned and stared at Carrie. He couldn't understand what was going on, but for sure, he knew it was those damn kids' fault; they always were nothing but trouble. If only he could get Carrie alone. He got in his car and drove home to the empty house thinking how could she do this to him? To them?

*   *   *

Millie put the phone back in its cradle. She sat quietly trying to absorb everything Susan had said. The news about their mother wasn't good. How could Susan trust her so quickly after all the hurt and anguish their parents always caused them? The good news was, Susan, Gus and the kids were moving out here, and they'd be together again. J.B. came out of the guest room, tying his robe together. She'd never seen him with pajama bottoms on before. She missed not seeing his muscular legs. J.B. had insisted upon staying at her home and helping until Millie was on her feet again.

"It wasn't a good phone call? Something happened? Talk to me, Millie." When he entered the room, Millie was sitting there in a daze.

"Most of it was terrific, I should be doing hand springs or something. Susan, Gus and the kids are selling out and moving out here. We'll going to be together again." J.B. still wondered why she was so glum.

"What else, Millie?"

"Our mother is living with them, she left my father. Why, after all these years?"

J.B. didn't know how to answer that, he could only speculate. "Maybe seeing you and Susan the night you paid them a visit, jarred her memory. Maybe in her older years, she wants more than what your Dad can give her. Who knows? But I think we're going to find out."

"Susan and Gus can handle it. Susan always did have a better perspective of their relationship than I did." She shook her head in puzzlement. "I just can't see my mother ever getting the courage to do such a thing. I've always thought, if it hadn't been for him, she would have tried to become a better, more loving mother to Susan and me. Why now? Susan and I and the kids are doing just great without her in our lives."

"I don't know, maybe she wants to become a grandmother, maybe she wants a second chance to love the kids and be loved back. If what you've told me about your life with them is really true, maybe she finally realizes that having a great sex life isn't everything. You and I have certainly proved that, only it didn't take us thirty some years to figure it out. In order for a marriage to really exceed, it takes it all; love, trust, truthfulness, faith, friendship, and last but not least; great chemistry." J.B was trying to send Millie his own message.

Millie grinned. "With that attitude, you sound like a perfect candidate for marriage, why haven't you hooked up yet?"

"Still waiting for my woman to say the word. She still has her reservations about my intent." J.B.'s heart was pounding, his hands sweaty, and he was concentrating on just breathing.

J.B.'s eyes gleamed with love and desire. "Not anymore, J.B., you've proved to me many times that you're sincere. Are you going to propose to me again or do I have to ask you?"

J.B. laughed, his eyes crinkled in that endearing way. "On your knees, woman."

Both of them wriggled off the sofa and got down on their knees, . Putting their arms around each other, and their faces a mere five inches apart, they both asked, "will you marry me?" Looking deeply and lovingly into each other's eyes, they both answered.

"Yes, yes, yes." J.B. lowered them both to the floor. They sealed their bargain with their first real passionate kiss in months. J.B. wanted to devour her, reminding himself that Millie just gave birth a few weeks ago, but that didn't stop him from savoring the feel of her, and relishing the taste of her in his mouth. It was glorious feeling the splendor of her body close to his own. There was going to be plenty of time, a whole lifetime. He hugged her close, while laying contentedly on the floor with her. She was going to become his wife, at last.

"Millie, I love you, more than life. I promise to make you the happiest woman in the world."

"I could never be any happier than I am right this minute. I'm so sorry I had doubts about you. I never will again. I promise you that I'll never mistrust you again."

J.B. raised his head, his eye brows pulled together. "Just one request, that's all I'll ever ask."

Millie nestled lazily and looked so contented, roused and asked. "What do you want, darling?"

"That we get married as soon as legally possible. I'm not taking any chances of you getting upset with me again and pushing me away. I couldn't live through it again."

"I don't blame you for being paranoid. J.B., but I'd like my family here. I'd also like to feel better and have more vitality, because I want a long wonderful honeymoon with you."

"We could have a civil ceremony, then have a church wedding when your family gets here. We still have a few days left before we have to send Jamie's birth certificate information into the Court House. If we were married, I wouldn't have to legally adopt my own child."

"Deal. If I felt better, we'd fly to Las Vegas tonight, like you wanted to do, when you first proposed. I wish we would have. It would have saved us both a lot of grief."

"We'll go to the courthouse tomorrow and get our marriage license. I don't know, maybe here in California; there is no waiting period, all right with you?"

"Yes dear, whatever you say." Then they both laughed, at her reply. That would be the day, when Millie Nobles acted like a submissive, pious, obedient woman; the very thought was ludicrous.

J.B. had been sleeping on the sofa until Millie recuperated from childbirth. Tonight he wanted to follow her when she went into her bedroom, but he didn't. Maybe he was an old-fashioned guy at heart, either that or he still felt like he was walking on eggshells with Millie.

Soon. Every fiber of his body screamed that truth to him. Another day, maybe three was no problem. He could wait.

CHAPTER
— 14 —

T HE NEXT DAY J.B., MILLY, Terry and Jamie got in the car and headed for downtown San Francisco. J.B. had already made a call to the Court House. Millie would become his wife today. "Are you nervous?" He anxiously grinned at Millie.

"No, are you? You're not getting cold feet are you? Too bad, if you are, especially when they think this is a shotgun wedding." She laughed as she took Terry's arm and exited the elevator. J.B. followed carrying their baby son, who was going to sleep through the whole thing.

Half an hour later, J.B. and Millie were man and wife. No flowers, no music, just a stern looking judge performing a civil ceremony, giving J.B. dirty looks, 'like why not before this child was born.' Terry beamed, thinking the ceremony was the most romantic thing in the world. Now, she was going to have a dad. After he kissed Millie, he wriggled his nose against Terry's and kissed her on the check.

Millie also thought it was wonderful: no stress, no last-minute problems like worrying about caterers, the band showing up on time, or the delivery of the cake. She wanted to shout from the mountain top, then have an airplane carrying a banner through the sky, that proclaimed their marriage and their love. J.B. is my husband, after all their problems, doubts and misunderstandings, they were finally together. Now they could start loving and caring for each other as they were destined to do right from the beginning.

Millie would always remember the love and devotion showing in J.B.'s eyes as he repeated the vows. Maybe, they wouldn't have another service; this was special. Now Millie was Mrs. James Benjamin Cornell.

J.B. started driving out of town. "Darling, have you lost your sense of direction, we live that way." Millie's finger pointed to the opposite direction they were moving.

"Nope, I'm not lost, just wanted to show you something, before we go back home." After driving for a while he pulled off the main highway and started down a private paved road, which converted into an old fashioned cobblestone driveway. Millie started looking around. The trees lined the road and through the trees, she saw three horses galloping across the field and was mesmerized; then she spotted the house. Further back on the property were sheds and barns. From a distance, could see the rocky shore line and the Pacific ocean. The house was beautiful. The white pillars in the front stood out majestically. It reminded her of Tara, the palatial mansion in the movie, Gone With The Wind.

"What a magnificent house, do you know the people that own it? I would love to go see the inside of it."

J.B. grinned at her.

J.B. was snugly smiling to himself as he pulled up to the front door. He left the car parked in the center of the road. Millie noticed it was a very wide circular driveway, much wider than her own driveway. She gazed at the ornate fountain spraying water where several blue jays were trying to get a drink. So many azaleas bushes, it would be gorgeous in the springtime. J.B. got out of the car, went around, opened the doors and unstrapped his sleeping son from his safety seat. Together they walked up the steps. Millie turned and looked at the view. The house was sitting on a knoll, looking out you could see the entire vista, even the ocean from the small front porch. The front door opened and a small Chinese man slightly bowed to J.B. "Welcome home, Mr. Cornell, everything is prepared as you requested, sir." He stepped aside so they could enter the house.

J.B. placed the baby in Millie's arms. "Welcome home, darling." J.B. put his arm around Millie, picked her and the baby up and carried them across the threshold. She looked slightly more than dazed. What was going on?

"Home." She was shocked. J.B. couldn't be this wealthy to own a beautiful estate by the ocean like this, or was he?

Millie tried to look around as they were led to the rear of the house, where a table was decorated. A small wedding cake sat alone on a small table. A maid stood ready to serve the food. "What's this, J.B.? I thought we weren't going to make a big fuss, whose house is this and where are they? I feel like an intruder."

"It's our home, Millie. I bought it several months ago. I've made a few changes, but mostly it's just the way the former owners left it. It's your home now and if you want to change anything, just do it."

Millie walked across the huge veranda. The house was built on a knoll, thus giving the view a bigger scope. She could see the rocky shore of the Pacific Ocean, the green fertile pastures where three horses galloped through the field. The green of the pasture connected to the blue sky toward her right. It seemed to go on into infinity. An artist's paradise. From a distance in her mind she heard her son cry for food. The little guys' appetite was insatiable. She turned to tend to him, but J.B. was handing him over to a woman with a nurses uniform on.

"Come sit down darling, I've had a small wedding luncheon prepared for us. It's ready to be served." J.B. put his arm around her and helped her into a chair. Immediately soup was placed in front of her.

Millie looked at J.B. like she'd never seen him before. "J.B., this place must have cost a fortune, it's taking my breath away. It's so perfect. This has got to be a dream; tell me I'm dreaming."

"No, sweetheart, it's our home. It's fully staffed with servants to clean, cook, clean and whatever else that needs to be done.

You'll be free to devote your time to your career and school. Or just love and taking care of the kids; anything you want to do." He picked up his soup spoon and ate a bite. "Humm, this is good, try it.—One of those horses, the palomino you just watched is yours, Terry." He winked at her. "She's small and gentle, A real good horse for a beginner to learn to ride." He watched as Terry's face lit up with joy and pleasure.

Terry looked at her mother and J.B. and she watched as her mother gasped and delight… "Damn it, J.B., you could have prepared us for all this." Millie thrust her arms out wide.

J.B. laughed. "Hey, I've been trying to, miss little independence. The small amount of assistance I've given you up until now has raised your hackles. I told you I could afford it, that it was no big deal. It's whatever you and Terry want. We can live in the smaller house or we can make our home here."

Terry and Millie looked at each other and simultaneous replied. "Here."

J.B. laughed and was thankful they wanted to live here, now it would surely be paradise. "Lets enjoy our meal, and I'll give you a tour. Would you care for some champagne?" J.B. drew a chilled bottle from the silver ice bucket. "You too, Terry, this is an occasion. Your Mom and I are married, and now you are my daughter. I'd like to shout it from the roof. I've never been happier in my life. Having you two and our son means more to me than anything." He raised his glass to make a toast. "Forever."

They enjoyed the good food and joked around with each other. Millie was still dazed. "Terry, did you know about this house?"

J.B. and Terry giggled. "Yeah, Mom, Aunt Susan and I have been coconspirators, we made a plan to get you and J.B. back together again. I helped pick out the horses and helped plan this meal. Come on, finish your food, I want to take pictures of you and Dad cutting the cake."

"I didn't stand a chance, did I? Susan too? What did she do?" Terry got up and walked to where the serving maid stood and she talked to her quietly.

"Susan was the one who told me to come here, even going to the lamaze classes. I got orders to court you and take you to bed. I've been through hell these last nine months without you. Life just wasn't worth living. Oh God, baby, I want you, need you, I ache for you." Terry walked back to the table, not noticing the sexy come hither glance that her mother gave her new Dad.

J.B. closed his eyes and visualized their wedding night. Just a few hours. Lord, it was still daylight. He hadn't told Millie yet but they were flying to Hawaii for a brief honeymoon in two days. Right now, he was content to watch Millie digest everything that he'd thrust unto her today.

Millie was tempted to smear J.B.'s face with cake, but she refrained, instead she wanted to lick the icing from his lips. It must have been too much of a temptation for J.B. because he did. Millie wanted to say to heck with the tour, lets make that later, much later as she felt J.B.'s tongue glide over her mouth licking the icing away.

Millie forgot her sexual frustrations as J.B. gave them 'the tour'. He used a jeep to take them all around the spacious property. Millie and Terry both wanted to stand on the cliff and watch the ocean. Imagine an ocean in your back yard. Terry wanted to stop and pet her horse that already recognized her. The horse whinnied as it nuzzled his head into her. Millie thought, what a perfect place to raise a family, the horses, the swimming pool, the tennis court. The parties Terry could have here when she was older. She would probably become popular with high school and college kids. Is this what J.B. was thinking too? Why had she so foolishly doubted this man's love and devotion for them for a moment? She watched his strong muscular arms maneuver the jeep. So what if she was so sexually attracted to this man? He wasn't at all like her father. Terry adored him, right from the start, and he loved her.

Later when they returned to the house and were relaxing on the lanai, J.B. heard Millie speak softly, "I'm never leaving here. Wild horses couldn't force me away from here." Millie declared to no one in particular.

"Not even a few days in Hawaii, I guess I'll have to call and cancel our honeymoon trip."

J.B. said very seriously.

Millie's mouth gaped open. "J.B., you do play dirty pool, what person in their sane mind could pass that up. Really and truly, Hawaii?

"A private, secluded beach and all. Don't forget to take a blanket along." He eyed her amorously.

Terry was beginning to feel like a fifth wheel. "Mom, Dad, I'm going to my room. I have homework and I want to e-mail all my friends and tell them the good news. By the time I get all their replies, it'll be noon tomorrow." She gave them each a peck on the check and rushed up to her room. Millie shook her head, where in the world did Terry get her thoughtfulness and consideration from? She turned to J.B. and ran into his arms. He picked her up and carried her up the stairs to their bedroom. The sun was still shining brightly, but they were oblivious to that fact.

When Millie walked into the mammoth bedroom, her eyes quickly scanned it. On one side was a huge, mountain stone fireplace with a marble mantle, with antique fireplace. Antique tools hung down from the marbled mantel. Decorative furniture was placed in front and alongside the cozy corner, including a small table and two overstuffed chairs for cozy, intimate dining. On the table was a silver bucket with a bottle of wine chilling next to tastefully displayed hors d'oeuvres, two long stemmed crystal glasses and silverware for two.

Millie's eyes continued to scan the room. Her eyes rested on an antique vanity table and a long skirted bench in front of it, then she spied the French doors leading outside. She walked toward them as though she was magnetized. She opened the doors and stepped out onto a balcony. A gentle ocean breeze wafted over her. She inhaled deeply and gazed at the magnificent vista. The sun was reflected on the ocean, and the high waves glistened with the vivid colors of the sunset. The green of the pasture and the blue sky with puffy white clouds was breathtakingly beautiful.

She turned to see J.B. standing quietly behind her, observing her delight and happy that she too, was falling in love with their home. "Darling, look out further, I can see a ship moving down the coast. Does it make you think of pirates and more exciting eras in history?" He moved behind Millie and wound his arms around her waist and drew her close to him.

"What is the history of this house? Do you know?" Always a history buff, she was curious.

"The original house was built here in the middle 1840, but it burned. It was rumored that pirates did it, they also say that there is hidden treasure buried around here. There are caves below the cliffs overlooking the sea. This house or part of it was built in 1890. Since then it's been renovated and modernized."

She raised her eyebrows in delight. "Do you think it's haunted by pirates?"

He chortled. "It hasn't been since I've slept here, maybe, I don't know. We'll find out. Don't tell Paul, when they get here, we'll never get any peace. He'd become a dedicated ghost buster and treasure seeker. I can't wait until our son grows and does neat things like Paul does. We have so much to look forward too."

"Well, starting in two months, you can practice your parenting skills on a teenaged daughter. From what Tess and Sally told me, I've got mine coming. You know, paybacks are bitches."

They were laughing as they went back into the bedroom. "Want a glass of champagne, love?"

"Later." Millie murmured as she started to unbutton J.B.'s shirt. She lifted her eyes from the task and looked into her husband's eyes. "I love you, husband, and right now, I don't want to be a parent, I just want you. I've missed you, and dreaming about you just doesn't cut it for me. I want the real thing."

"Your wish is my command, Madam." J.B. bowed his head in a mock salute, then unzipped her dress and pushed it over her shoulders, along with the lacy bra. J.B.'s hands caressed her still enlarged breasts, not fully recovered from childbirth. He sucked his breath in as he dropped his mouth to gently lave her protruding nipples with his tongue. He unlatched his belt and took off his trousers. Then his underwear released from his waist as they dropped to his ankles.

J.B. left the rapture of her touch, just long enough to remove his socks, shoes and clothes. He couldn't remember ever being this hard and needy before in his entire adult life. "Darling, you're right about dreams, nothing could compare to this." Together they hastily removed the rest of Millie's clothes and fell on the bed, pressing their naked bodies to each others. The last time they made love was when Millie conceived their son and that was over ten months ago. They had an eternity of longing and pent-up emotions. With very little foreplay, J.B. plunged into Millie's hot sheathe and expelled his breath. Neither moved, they were just rapturously enthralled with the unity of their bodies. J.B. found her mouth and his tongue encircled hers in a dance as old as time. Millie raised her hips and tightened her muscles around J,B,'s engorged member and instantly climaxed, her body quivered with spasms as they started a rhythm, before J.B. could reach his own climatic finish, Millie started to quake and quiver again and together they went over the brink of ecstasy into oblivion.

Millie was unaware of J.B.'s full weight on her, and gradually her senses returned, as J.B.'s did and he turned to his side, taking her with him. Neither moved, nor spoke. Millie thought they'd already reached the acme of their passion many times in the past, but this time was like no other they'd ever experienced. They drifted off into a dreamless sleep, encased in each others arms and hearts. Their marriage had been consummated with all the passion and love that the two of them possessed.

J.B. woke up just as the sun was rising. He gently nudged Millie awake. It was too beautiful a sight not to enjoy together. Hastily they donned their robes and stepped out onto the balcony. They watched it until the sun had risen above the horizon and brought daylight to the valley. The sea was unusually calm today, not for the first time, J.B. wished he owned a boat. Maybe someday.

Warm champagne was not what they craved this morning. J.B. grinned at his beautiful love-tousled wife, then pressed the button for the intercom and requested coffee. A scant fifteen minutes later, coffee arrived with a tray of fresh fruit, bagels and good old American sticky buns. They feasted on the food and savored the coffee, but were in no hurry to leave the privacy of their bedroom. Maybe, they should just stay there forever, but on the other hand, who could resist Hawaii?

CHAPTER

15

ILLIE AND J.B. DIDN'T LEAVE their bedroom until the afternoon, but before they went downstairs, they went into the nursery. Clara, the newly hired nanny, was feeding Jamie his bottle, and soothing him in the rocking chair. His little hands were trying to grasp the bottle. They didn't disturb his meal, but promised him they'd be back later.

J.B. asked Ho Chun where Terry was. "Young Missy was up early and riding fast as a bullet. A buffet is in warmer for you and Missy. Anything else, you just give holler. Okay."

While they were eating brunch, Millie made a suggestion. "Wouldn't my house be perfect for Susan and her family? There are four bedrooms, so Mom could have one, or she could maybe come here sometimes and stay. I wonder what Mother will do? She's not old enough to retire yet."

"I think you're right, but it'll have to be their decision. It'll be what they want. It'll give them a place to live while making up their minds. Are you excited about your Mother coming out here, Millie?"

"Yes, I am. It's too bad my father is like he is, and she won't be totally happy without him. I will give them that; their love for each other has never faltered. It must have been very difficult for her to break away from him. I could never leave you." They shared a tender look.

"Millie, I have to fly back to Ohio for business in six weeks, maybe I'll call your father and try to talk to him. Do you think it would do any good?"

"Who knows? Mom might have already gone back to him by then. We'll just have to wait and see."

A week later, J.B. and Millie were walking up the tarmac to the entrance of the SFO Airport. As usual the terminal was crowded. J.B. deposited their luggage in the designated area and they sauntered toward the gate where their plane would depart from. It was difficult for Millie to maintain her eagerness. She didn't want to appear like a country bumpkin with her sophisticated husband that had probably traveled all over the world at one time or other. When they boarded the land, Millie could hardly contain herself.

"Excited, Sweetheart? I can feel you trembling. I love it when I can do something that excites you this much. This is all 'old hat' for me, but I'm enjoying this thrill together. Where we are heading for, will surely beat the hell out of Toledo, Ohio. Buckle up, Honey, we're about ready to take off."

Millie couldn't help but remember the last time she'd taken off in a plane. She'd watched J.B. on the ground until her plane disappeared into the sky, and her heart was breaking. Miraculously they'd overcome their problems and were together. The love of her life, her dream man was her husband.

It was a relatively short flight to Hawaii from California. Millie refused the wine the hostess offered. She couldn't help but notice how boldly the attractive girl flirted with J.B. Millie wondered how in the world she had attracted him, when he seemed to have his pick of beautiful women. She recognized the thoughts of her old insecurities raising their ugly heads again. She hastily put the negative thoughts away and grinned at her husband, remembering the passion they'd shared the night before.

Millie felt the plane descending and looked out the window: lush green foliage and the bluish green of the water separated by nearly white sand. Many boats, all sizes were causing the crystal clear water to wave and flap onto the shore. So this was Hawaii, a place she'd never expected to see, not even in her fantasies.

The large plane landed at Honolulu International Airport and taxied them to a deportation area. J.B. and Millie were the first two of the passengers to walk down the steps to the tarmac where locals were waiting to greet them. They had big smiles and personally placed leis around each of their necks. Immediately Millie caught the scent of the local flowers not only from the colorful lei around her neck, but the landscape was abundant with flowing shrubs. Millie recognized the hibiscus, but nothing else. J.B. ushered her to a limo after he'd retrieved their luggage.

It was just a short ride to the Ohana Hotel where they had reservations for the night. Tomorrow they'd rent a car and travel to their cottage and the private beach. That evening they dined at the hotel dining room. Before the trip, J.B. had suggested that Millie bring a gown along. She was grateful that he did when she saw how the majority of women were dressed. What if she hadn't brought along a dress? She was thankful her husband was suave. Millie wondered if she would ever learn these things on her own or would J.B. have to constantly tutor?

After their meal, J.B. suggested taking a limousine tour ride through the city. They'd been told that the area was breathtaking at night. They ended up in a nightclub and danced the night away, it was nearly dawn when they returned to the hotel and collapsed on the bed. For the first day of their honeymoon every second was filled to capacity with happy memories.

Millie was the first to wake up early in the afternoon. They'd both removed their clothes and slept naked. The room looked like a crazy evening of debauchery took place due to the carelessly flung clothes around the room. She giggled and snuggled back in bed as close as she could to the handsome man sleeping naked beside her. J.B. had been awake, but he'd kept his eyes closed faking sleep. When Millie laid back down on the bed and snuggled close to him, he joined her in laughter, just before his mouth found her. They never did leave their room until check-out time at 3:30.

The cottage was perfect and the freezer and refrigerator was fully stocked with pre-cooked entrees from a local caterer. All Millie had to do was make salads and heat up the delicious food. Most of the time they wandered on the beach, took naps and made love under the sun or stars. The third day they took a boat ride around the islands, and blended in with the many tourists.

This was the first time Millie had ever been separated from her daughter, and she was ready to return to the states when the week was up. She also was pleasantly surprised when J.B. confessed that he missed the kids. Millie laughed and admitted to fighting the urge to call several times a day, but successfully fought down the impulse. They made the call together.

Talking to Terry brought back the nostalgia. They both felt and longed to be home with their children. Terry informed them that Jamie was no longer looking cross-eyed at everything and was starting to coo. Millie giggled when Terry described his first smile at a stuffed animal. The last thing Terry said was "Mom, Dad, I miss you guys. Can't you finish your honeymoon here? Come home."

The next day they were on a plane returning to the states. They agreed with Terry. Since they planned on living life like it was one continuous honeymoon, why shouldn't they be home with the kids and in their own new home?

Two weeks after returning from Hawaii, Millie and J.B. were enjoying breakfast in their small alcove, when the phone rang. Before J.B. picked it up, Millie told him she was going to the nursery. J.B. picked up the phone and was slightly nonplussed to hear his father's voice on the other end. This was unusual for him to call. The conversation was brief, but shocking. J.B. headed for the nursery to tell Millie about it. He never expected this to happen. He'd been hearing his father threaten this since he was a boy.

Millie was sitting in the rocker, holding their sleeping son, his little face snuggled close to his mothers' bosom. "Was that an important call, J.B.? You look a bit harried."

J.B. ran his hand through his hair, a sure sign that he was upset. "That was my Dad on the phone. He left my Mother. He said he was going to break up the marriage months ago, years ago but I've heard that before, and I didn't believe him. He actually did it, after all these years. For the first time since I was a kid, I actually feel sorry for my mother. Dad is on a cross-country flight as we speak. His plane will be landing at the airport in another hour, then he's coming here. He wants to meet you and the kids."

"I'm sorry J.B. Maybe it's for the best that your dad left your mother. Why should she change her behavior, when she has no motivation to do otherwise? She was getting away with her bazaar behavior. Now she'll pay the piper, so to speak."

"Just like you're hoping your father will conform and change. I've got my doubts about your father or my mother ever changing their lifestyle patterns. It's been going on for too long." J.B. knelt down and gently kissed his son's cheek, then gazed into his wife's eyes. "Let's pray that we are better parents than the ones we had, darling. I, for one, do not want to mess up Terry and this little guy."

"My psychologist tells me it's mostly communication. Possibly shortly after your mother learned she couldn't cope with the cattiness of so many of the people in society, your dad should have done something, instead of ignoring her strange behavior. She needed help from him, and he failed her. The same with my mother, maybe if she would have demanded a more loving support from him, he'd have given it to her and us girls. We are such cowards sometimes. God, surely has to cope with more than his share of problems with us earthlings, doesn't he?"

J.B. nodded in silent agreement.

*　*　*

J.B. and Terry were just returning to the barn after an invigorating ride on their horses. They dismounted and handed the reins to the high school student working part-time during the summer vacation. "Give them a good rub-down, Tom. We put them through the paces today."

Tom smiled as he took the reins. "Good, they've both been chomping at the bit for days now. They needed a good run." He patted J.B.'s stallion on the neck and led the two horses into the barn. As J.B. and Terry jumped in the jeep to go back home, they noticed a strange car driving toward the house. When they pulled into the driveway, Craig Cornell was just getting out of his car. J.B. shook his hand and put his arm around Terry's shoulders and drew her into the circle. "Dad, I want to introduce you to my daughter, Terry. Terry, this is my father, Craig Cornell.

"Happy to meet you, Terry. I've heard all about you and welcome to the family."

"Thank you, Mr. Cornell. I'm happy to meet you too."

"None of that formal Mr. Cornell, Terry, my girl. Please either call me Craig or Pap, whatever is comfortable for you." He flashed her a smile that was very familiar, the enigmatic smile of J.B.'s and the same one little Jamie was starting to give everyone. Terry smiled back at him and instantly accepted this stranger as her grandfather.

Together they walked into the house and found Millie ensconced on a chaise lounge out on the lanai. She was holding a sleeping baby. Jamie's little mouth was doing the suckling motion in his sleep and nestled close to his mothers' breast. Craig gazed down at the beautiful picture before him and gazed joyfully down at his sleeping grandson. J.B. made the unnecessary introduction. "Dad, this is my wife, Millie and our son Jamie."

Craig squatted beside Millie's chair and gently caressed Jamie's little hand. Obviously feeling his grandfather's gentle caress, Jamie opened his eyes, and stared questioningly at the strange face, then smiled. Craig laughed when he recognized the familiar smile. His eyes met Millie's questions eyes and knew that he eventually would have to answer the muddling query in her eyes. He picked Jamie up and snuggled him close to his chest. A grandson, a precious child to love.

On sight, Craig knew he was going to like his daughter-in-law. Craig couldn't help but notice how devoted J.B. and she with each other. In the days that followed, Millie casually mentioned Marsha's name in conversation, maybe it was time to try to explain his marital state to Millie. J.B. seemed to have no curiosity or opinion one way or the other. He simply accepted the estrangement between Marsha and himself without any questions.

One evening several days after he'd been there, Millie and Craig were left alone. J.B. was making urgent phone calls and Terry excused herself and went up to her room.

Now it was up to him to ensure a better understanding between them right from the beginning. It was like Millie's multi-colored eyes had looked into his soul and found it lacking. How was he going to explain his marriage?

"Millie, I'm going to save you the trouble of asking where J.B.'s mother is. This isn't the way I'd planned or wanted this reunion, but I don't seem to have any control of the situation. I'm sure J.B. has told you about my marital problems, so ask away. I'll try to answer your questions to your satisfaction."

"Craig, I don't have any questions, but I think you do. We've all got our problems; Lord knows, J.B. and I have had our share, but I got some help to deal with it, maybe you should too."

"I'm not the one with the problem, Millie. My wife has the problem, and I just can't deal with her any longer." Craig looked into her eyes and silently begged for understanding.

"J.B. and Mary told me how your wife changed when you came into money and how she had trouble dealing with the new status in society. All I want to know is where were you then?"

"There. I've always been there for her and J.B."

"Obviously, she needed more than you just being there, she needed your help then, instead of being thrown to the wolves, so to speak. Craig, I started messing my life up when I was fifteen. I blamed my parents, who weren't supportive of me. Hell, they weren't even interested in my life. I was on my own. That's young to make decisions, but I was intelligent enough to know there was help out there for me. I should have gone to the school counselor, that's all it would have taken, instead of doing everything on my own. I made a martyr out of myself, because I felt I had to prove my worth to my parents and they didn't even care. I'm lucky my daughter is well balanced and not paying the piper for my foolish pride."

"Millie, what could I have done differently?"

"Craig, I wasn't there, so I can't answer that question. Mary told me the entire story. J.B. has never mentioned it except to say that he didn't know how you stood it as long as you did. Mary told me she liked Marsha a lot when she first starting working for the family, but then Marsha started changing and nobody seemed to question it. Mary said she tried, but Marsha shut her out. Where were you, Craig?"

"I was very busy at that time. Business demanded all my time and energy. I was just a salesman before my stock took off and left us wealthy. I had to make a lot of personal adjustments myself. I just presumed Marsha was doing the same thing. You're right. It was communication. I needed her to handle our influx into society. I thought she handled it rather well."

"From what Mary told me about Marsha before she changed, she was out-going and funny. She had a good sense of humor and was very witty. Mary said sometimes her jokes were somewhat odd, but that was who Marsha was. I have a friend like that. Trying to make a lady out of Tess would be like trying to make a silk purse from a pig's ear. Marsha more than likely humiliated herself in front of the elite members of our society. That was when she changed, trying to act like she supposedly should be. This left her with no alterative, but to become false. She'd lost her own identity."

"That's why Marsha acted so differently when we were alone. She could just be herself. I feel so stupid that I didn't realize that before, but the difference in her personalities was like day and night. I tried to tell her that we didn't need those people to be successful. Our wealth assumed us of our status. But, Millie, I did talk to her. I explained all this. It was like she'd been locked into this behavior and couldn't stop."

"She must have been terribly embarrassed by them in the beginning. It's a cycle now. She'd need professional help to break it, just like I did. I still see my therapist frequently. I think you should talk to him yourself. J.B. often goes with me now, Terry too. I nearly screwed her life up, but thankfully we're all on the right tract now. Doctor Wade has finally gotten through to me that dysfunctional is a word, not a way of life."

"Next time you call him for an appointment, please include me. My father used to say, it's never too late to learn. You've just made me realize deserting my wife is not the solution to our problem. Healing and getting back in sync must be done together, not thousands of miles apart."

Millie just smiled, then patted his hand reassuringly. He'd gotten the message loud and clear.

Susan let out a shriek, when she read the e-mail from Terry. Gus and the kids came running into the room. Susan was holding her hands up to her mouth.

"Mom, did you see a mouse or something?" Paul asked.

"No, this is so good, wonderful, wonderful, it's so—. J.B. and Aunt Millie are married and J.B. took her to his fabulous country estate. Aunt Millie loves it and they are so happy and in love. They went to Hawaii for a short honeymoon. It's just awesome. Terry's and my plan worked. How about that?" She gave her son a high five.

"Don't you just love it, when a plan comes together?" Gus actually giggled. Susan looked lovingly at her man, he'd changed so much since they'd married. No more hesitant, careful remarks. He was getting as mouthy as she was. She looked at him and wondered how she'd ever thought he wasn't a handsome man. The gray in his hair gave him a distinguished look, his dark eyes flashed with pleasure. He'd even changed in the love making department: he was more aggressive, more demanding. She'd long since forgotten she'd ever even known Kevin. Gus could take her to the top of the world. All the unhappy struggling years, she remembered, how did she ever get so lucky? What did she ever do to deserve this happiness?

"What's going on in here, I heard all this screaming and laughing. What happened?" Carrie appeared in the doorway.

Gus put his arm around her and pulled her into the room. "J.B. and Millie got married, by a judge, not much of a wedding as far as weddings go, but from what Terry writes in her e-mail, the brief ceremony was beautiful. They are very happy."

"A civil ceremony performed by a judge. Really. Susan told me Millie had made all the gowns and her wedding dress was gorgeous. Why didn't they wait until we got out there? I would have loved to see her get married."

"Idea! I just had a flash. When we get out there, we'll get them married again, the whole enchilada. Gowns, flowers, church or maybe right in their backyard, from what Terry has been telling me, the place is awesome. Could we do it?"

Carrie laughed. "I haven't a doubt in my mind that you could do anything, Susan, my love." Carrie's mind wondered back to the lonely unhappy years without her children. She'd missed so much. She never was this happy in her life. This carefree family she lived with now proved to her again that she'd been wrong, terribly wrong to live with Carl and meet his demands. She should have left him when she became pregnant with Susan, and he detested her swollen body. She would have been personally unhappy without Carl, but she would have been able to become a good mother and just maybe Carl would have missed her too, and come around to thinking right. No—she wasn't going there with what could have been. She was in the here and now. Just where she wanted to be.

She quietly observed Susan and Gus's marriage. She could always tell when they'd made love the night before. Their joy exulted and affected everyone around them; it wasn't just a momentary pleasure that made them closer, more loving, and happier all day long. She was so thankful that her daughters knew the joy of a happy marriage. She looked at little Melody, she was going to grow up beautiful, maybe she could be there for her, candidly guiding her into making the right decisions. Paul was a handsome lad now, but she saw some of those familiar selfish tendencies. She could gently point out a better way. Could consideration for others be taught or was it a personality trait? She silently prayed that none of her grandchildren inherited Carl's genes. Certainly their daughters hadn't. They were both loving, compassionate, human beings. Daughters that she was so proud of that it actually made her heart hurt. Her daughters were wonderful. She smiled at that thought. Now instead of being indifferent toward her children, she was over-indulgent and wanted to tell everyone she ever knew how wonderful they were. She presumed this new emotion was called 'pride'

*   *   *

Everything happened so fast. One day Gus got a splendid offer for his trucking business and two days later their house was sold. Paul was disappointed that they weren't going by way of a stagecoach or wagon train. What a wild imagination that boy possessed: A truly adventurous spirit, not staid and predictable like Carl. Carrie was watching their behavior closely without saying a word.

When Gus sold his business, he made the deal that the one large moving van wouldn't be sold. They'd need that to transport their personal belongings and keepsakes.

Millie made the offer of her home and the furnishings if they wanted them, but Susan was in love with the many antique pieces that Gus accumulated over the years. Carrie wanted to take some of her family keepsakes with her, things that had been her mothers. They could fill a van easily.

Carrie called her lawyer and asked him to make the arrangements for what she wanted out of the house that Carl and she had shared for so many years. When she walked through the house, the cold meticulous atmosphere still hovered; a house without love and joy. She kept her thoughts and her memories to herself as she went through the house and labeled the possessions she wanted. The two men with her packaged or boxed the items with care and then took them out to the awaiting truck. She'd asked that Carl not be there, but she couldn't force it. She suspected there would be at least one more confrontation. This time she was stronger. She'd grown and learned a great deal about herself and what it took to make her happy.

Carl walked in the front door, just as she was going to go upstairs. She wanted the quilts and crocheted doilies that her mother had been famous for creating. They were family heirlooms. The only things she wanted that was jointly owned and possessed by Carl, were their two children. He could have his precious artwork that would have paid for college for both the girls. She tried not to think of the life they could have given their daughters. How could she have allowed Carl to throw Millie out on the street when their daughter was fifteen years old and pregnant. When the girls were forced out of their home, she should have gone with them, then. She'd not only missed her first chance at being a good mother, but her second chance, as well.

Carrie knew that Carl was following her upstairs, she deliberately went into their bedroom. This was going to be her severest test, resisting his offer of lovemaking. How strong was she? The two men doing the packing nodded to her sending a silent message that they wouldn't follow her upstairs.

Carl followed her into the room, then shut and locked the door behind him. He walked briskly to where she was going through bureau drawers. She'd left the house with only the barest of essentials, now she would take all her personal belongings.

Carl took her arms and swung her around, not gently and lovingly like she'd seen Gus do with Susan. His mouth came down hard against hers, and she felt his hardened manhood and felt repulsed by it. No apologies, nor tenderness, just lust. Well maybe he did love her, but it was selfishly. She remembered telling Susan he could stick it. She pulled away from him and could have laughed in his face. When she didn't respond to his advances, he became angry. "You bitch, you've found someone else, haven't you?"

"No, Carl. I just came to my senses, at last." She looked him straight in the eyes, and remembered the rapture they'd shared, now it seemed a hollow fake reproduction of the real thing. "I'd try to explain it to you, but you wouldn't be able to comprehend the meaning. I feel sorry for you, Carl, I really do. I love you, Carl, I always have, but it's not strong enough to live your kind of life anymore. I want my freedom. I want to enjoy the rest of my life with my family. I want to laugh, be silly and even do a little cussing if something pisses me off." Carl's eyebrows shot up in shock. Carrie never talked this way before; she had always bee the perfect sedate, genteel lady. She'd been his perfect match, what he'd always wanted in his woman.

It was those damn kids again, changing her into trash like them. He studied her for a minute and quickly changed his tactics.

"Carrie, my love, please, don't leave me. Darling, come back home to me. We'll take a nice cruise, like a second honeymoon, I want you, I need you." He ran his hands over her slim figure, lingered on her breasts; his mere touch always inflamed her. He didn't feel the familiar tremor and see the desire in her eyes. My God, he'd lost her. The realization hit him. He couldn't make it without her; she'd turned into a woman just like his mother. Cold and frigid, that was why his father always ran around with other women and wasn't home much. Leaving him alone with a hateful bitter shrew. His life as a child was unbearable. Carrie always gave all her love to him, him alone. He was the sole recipient of all her love and devotion. "Baby, don't leave me, please, don't leave me," he dropped to the floor on his knees, running his hands down her body, as he dropped to the floor, he put his arms around her legs and held her close to him, sobbing quietly.

Carrie was shocked. This was so out of character for him to lower his dignity, to actually beg and cry. How many times had she cried and begged him, and he never once relented. "Carl,

I'm sorry, I don't want to hurt you, but I just can't live this way anymore. I've changed and maybe you can to. It's up to you. I'm moving to California. Susan and her family are moving there, too. Millie just gave birth to a son and married the love of her life. I need to be with them now. I need to, Carl. Please be happy for me, and I'll pray that you can change too. Come to me, my love if you can do that, if you can't, I'll understand."

She pulled away from him and continued laying out what she wanted packed. She watched as he slowly stood up, then walked to the door, unlocked it, and went out. His shoulders stooped and walked wearily away. When she was finished choosing the things she wanted to take, she took one last look at the house that she'd called home for so long. She shut the door behind her and drove to Susan's home. The memory of Carl looking so dejected was like a nightmare. She'd tried too often to draw out of him what really troubled him, and what had made him into the man he was. This had caused Carl to only love her, but he had often left her feeling lonely, sad and unhappy. No longer was she going to pretend she was happy. She was going to be.

For real.

She was going to love her family, resume her career and enjoy whatever time she had here on this earth feeling loved and needed. She drove the miles to her daughter's home feeling a sense of expectation and also a hollow feeling of loss.

When she pulled up in front of her daughter's house, she watched as they stood on the sidewalk and waited for her to join them. Susan knew where she'd been. She walked up and put her arm around her shoulder. "Mom, it gets better. Believe me, it does. Welcome home."

Gus traded in both their vehicles and bought a new mini van for the trip. Susan was going to drive it. He would follow with the moving van. One fully packed vehicle. He hoped it wasn't overweight, it seemed no one wanted to leave anything behind. He indulgently kept packing and squeezing until the truck was jammed full. He'd strapped the kid's bicycles to the roof. Bikes he'd bought them for Christmas.

Paul was ecstatic as he studied road maps and campgrounds. Gus smiled to himself. If Paul had his own way, with his plans, it would take them six month to make the trip. It was so hard to refuse the exuberant boy that was likening the trip to the early settlers. This was going to be a real adventure for all of them. He smiled to himself as he tried to picture Carrie out camping. No longer was she acting like the snooty, high brow person, he'd first met. She'd come down off it, a completely different person from what she was at first. Now, she was just as rowdy as the rest of his precious family. When they were making their departure, Gus looked back at the home he'd created, praying every moment of hard tedious working hours and remodeling it, and he knew that was lucky to have found a woman like Susan to share it with. The house meant nothing without her and the children that were now his adopted children. They'd make a new life out west, just like the pioneers did, only they would have a few more amenities.

They were bringing air mattresses to sleep on and an easily assembled tent to keep He remembered the chill of the night air off them, a small generator to provide electric, and an electric burner to cook on. He knew Paul would want to build a fire. He'd try to persuade him that they could take lots of camping trips in California: guy fishing and hunting trips. He planned on taking eight days to make the trip. Susan wasn't used to long haul driving like he was and Melody was little, there would be lots of bathroom stops, and fast food would get them through lunches. If it was raining at night when it was time to pull over and camp, he planned on staying at motels. That would be difficult for Paul. He'd have to deal with the boy's chagrin with the necessary change of plans. With every mile he planned a future, one filled with Susan and the kids. His family.

CHAPTER

—— 16 ——

J.B. AND MILLIE RETURNED TO their home after a successful meeting with several agencies and went upstairs.

"Hi little guy, I missed you." He beamed again at J.B., then spit up, soiling his mother's blouse.

"This is what I've been missing, perpetual sour clothing. I guess we juggled you about too much, didn't we? Sorry love." She wiped his face and kissed him. He snuggled close to her. Millie dropped into the rocking chair and held him tenderly. How different it was from when Terry was a baby. She was so scared, so alone and there was no one to share the worries or the joys of parenthood. She looked into J.B.'s face and saw so much love and tenderness, it made her heart hurt.

"I'll go downstairs and try to find Terry. I'll lay odds she's out riding like the wind on her horse. I hope she has picked a name; it doesn't seem right just calling him horse." He dropped a kiss on his wife and son and went to find his teenager. She was going to be thirteen soon. He would have to crowd a lot of loving into the few years they was left before she starting her own life away from them. Maybe he could talk Millie into having a couple more babies. He smiled at that prospect as he grabbed a cold beer from the fridge and started his search for his big girl. His daughter.

At the dinner table that evening Terry was full of information. There was a lot to tell them. Susan and the family were on their way, they figured on eight days, and planned on camping instead of getting motel rooms. She told them how excited Paul was about roughing it like the pioneers did coming west.

"Hey, that sounds like fun. God, I'll be glad when they are here; they light up the world whereever they are. That camping idea is great, and I'll bet Paul suggested it. I'll be glad when Jamie is old enough to go camping, sounds like a lot of fun." J.B. was deep in thought planning adventures with his son when he got just a little older.

"What do you mean, father, you don't think I'd like camping? We'd have a blast! I wasn't even a girl scout, but I would love to tour old mother nature with you."

"What a girl! You are a girl, aren't you?" He mocked her merrily.

Terry laughed with glee and threw her napkin at him and then stuck her tongue out in protest. "Mommy, he's picking on me again."

Millie laughed and shook her head. "Don't get me in the middle of your battles; I've got enough of my own to fight."

"Aw, lets have a pity party for Mom." Maybe becoming a smart ass was part of becoming a teenager. Something she was never able to be. It was going to be a learning experience. Maybe that was when mothers starting getting gray hair. Lady Clairal, here I come, Millie thought to herself.

All Terry and Millie's personal belongings were moved to their new home. The smaller house, they'd lived in was cleaned thoroughly for its new tenants. Millie was grateful for this house but somehow it'd never became a home. She'd missed J.B. more than she would ever admit. Her pride was a curse sometimes. Nowadays everything was different. She adored her new home, and never tired of roaming through all eighteen rooms. She could start an orphanage, and still have rooms to spare. Maybe she'd better have a talk with her husband about filling some of those lonely empty bedrooms. She was only twenty-seven, lots of child bearing years yet left. Maybe she could match the Kennedy brood. No, not really, but a couple more would be great.

One night, J.B. and Millie were just lulling about in their bedroom. J.B. was reading briefs for his work at the office, and Millie was contemplating what she was going to do with the rest of her life. She wondered if being a wife and a mother were enough.

J.B. must have read her mind. "Hon, are you going back to school and getting your degree?"

"Yes, but I'm sticking to the night classes. I want to finish, but I don't know about going back to my old job; you are making a bum out of me. I've lost my drive, and Cheryl should have gotten my job anyway. I hate to take a job from someone who really needs it. She'd earned it the hard way. Do you need any help in any of your organizations?"

J.B. put down his papers and grinned. "Millie, you've been there and done that. You could be such an inspiration for these single mothers, and newly divorced women on their own for the first time. You know first hand all about their lives and their problems. You'd be a real asset. I could keep you busy seven days a week, God, you would be great."

Millie beamed at his praise. Was he right? Could she help and comfort downtrodden women? "I'd certainly have a lot to choose from. Anything from unwed teenagers to drug and alcohol dependent mothers to God, you name it, I've been there, or Susan has. My advice to all of them would be to capture their dream man and hang on for dear life, or did I just luck out, with you?" She flirted with him.

J.B. watched his wife's beautiful face as she speculated on a career change. Maybe she would get the same satisfaction he always got by helping to make these women's lives a little better. They could work as a team. She could provide the savvy of her story about becoming strong and succeeding emotionally, and he could arrange to make their living standards better.

Providing education, housing, support groups were his specialty. Plus his usual personal gifts that gave him so much pleasure and so much satisfaction.

"Actually you might benefit more and people influence many by speaking to groups. Not every girl that has a baby alone when they're fifteen becoming a bum AND marrying a millionaire. Think of the good inspiration you've become for these down-trodden, hopeless women."

Millie grinned impishly at him, there would have been a time when she would have gotten insulted by his last remark. Now, thanks to her sister, she could take it, and she could give it right back. She stuck her tongue out at him, then grinned, "hey Dude, you want to make another baby in a couple more months?"

Millie watched J.B.'s eyes come alive with a fire that blazed in his heart.

"Are you serious?"

"Yeah, you want to start practicing tonight, we've got to get it right, and you have to admit we made one beautiful perfect son together. Terry will be out of here before Jamie even starts school, then he'll be all alone."

J.B. grinned and winked at her. "You talked me into it." It pleased him to know that Millie's thoughts were parallel with his. Philosophically, he conceded that maybe Millie and he were destined to go through the fire and brimstone of their courtship in order to reach this peaceful plateau in their relationship.

"You're so easy." They tried to seal their bargain with a kiss, but both of them were laughing too hard.

*　　*　　*

Carl Nobles watched as the small caravan started for the west coast. He'd park his car discreetly so they wouldn't see him watching them. He couldn't believe Carrie had actually left him after thirty-five years of marriage. The house was a tomb without Carrie's sweet personality to warm and liven the place up. She breathed life into the gloomy house. Why did he stay in the place that he grew up in so unhappily? The walls seemed to talk to him: The violent arguments he'd heard, the bitter accusations his parents often shouted and hurled at each other. Then afterwards when his Dad slammed angrily out of the house, he was left alone with frustrated woman. Maybe if he hadn't looked so much like his father, or if he'd been a girl, his mother would have treated him differently. He often wondered.

Carrie was right, when she told him, he closed his mind and his heart to their daughters. He'd decided when he started college and was living with other happy, well adjusted young men at the dorm, that he wasn't normal, that he'd most likely be just like his parents. He declared silently to himself then, that he'd never be a parent who would put a child through what he went through.

But, Carl!!! You did become a father, maybe you didn't treat your daughters like you were treated, you did worse. You totally denied and forsook them. Somehow, your daughters survived and became strong, well-adjusted women, but the rejection, the pain they must have endured during their childhood lay at your feet. You were worse than your own parents.

The voice in Carl's head, the one he always ignored as weak and shallow wouldn't meekly disappear anymore. Day and night, these thoughts haunted him.

Maybe you are a smart man, Carl. You're a professor, a mathematician, an expert in your field. But you're dumber than dumb when it comes to human emotions. You've got a problem. The pain and anguish you've caused your family is unforgivable. Do something about it, you dufus, your life isn't over, all you have to do is get with the program. If you can't figure it out in your head, get help.

Get help! Get help! As if from a distance, he heard his voice speaking the two words. Maybe he was going insane, losing his mind. The voice was so persistent. It kept getting louder and louder. He buried his head in his hands, put his elbows on his knees, and rocked back and forth, and pleaded for these unwanted thoughts to go away.

Carl had never made close relationships with his fellow professors. He kept his distance but was always polite. He never formed any kind of friendship with anyone but Carrie. He flicked through his little black phone book he kept in the desk. His associate, Doctor Joshua Hamilton was supposed to be one of the best in his field of psychology. He dialed the number, and held his breath until he heard the phone pick up. Joshua's wife answered the phone. "Beth, this is Carl Nobles, is Joshua there?"

"Just a moment, Carl, he'll be with you shortly."

When Carl heard Joshua's voice, he hesitated for just a second. He didn't really have a choice. Either he confided in someone about his problems, or he'd go stark staring mad. "Joshua, Carl Nobles. I need, I really need to talk to you. I know, I probably should have called your office and made an appointment, but I think I'm going crazy. Man, I need help."

"Carl, are you all right to drive? If you are, meet me in my office. If you feel you shouldn't drive, I'll come to your home."

"I'll meet you in your office, but when?"

"Right away, it only takes me twenty minutes to get there. You can meet me there." Joshua was stunned; he always sensed that Carl Nobles was carrying around a heavy burden, but the patient has to make the first move. It's the first step toward recovery. Joshua informed his wife, he'd be gone for a while, then he slipped on a jacket and headed out the door.

Both men pulled into the parking lot at the same time. Joshua was surprised at Carl's appearance, always a neat freak, his clothes looked like he'd slept in them, his hair was tousled, and he needed a shave. His eyes told the real story though; they looked haunted. They nodded and Carl followed him into the building. Once inside, Joshua removed his jacket, and told Carl to get comfortable, too. He walked to the fridge and got two bottles of water, then gave one to Carl.

As he sat down, he took a leisurely drink from the bottle. "Carl, this is how it works. You need to talk. I want to hear everything about you, from your first memory right up until today. The truth, exactly as it happened, no sugar coating, no excuses, no versions of what you thought. I need the truth, or I won't be able to help. Understand?

Carl took in a big breath and slowly exhaled. Whatever it took. He started talking. After a while the memories poured out. Some he'd forgotten or buried deep. He'd take a break once in a while, then would take a drink and stay quiet, then he'd start in again. Joshua listened to him for two hours, occasionally taking notes. Joshua heard rumors years ago about the Noble's wayward daughters and empathized with the family. It was hushed up, no one ever got any details. Now, Joshua was hearing the whole story. He silently prayed that he could handle this. He delved in his mind for similar cases he'd worked with, but nothing came forth. He was on his own with this one.

Finally Joshua spoke when Carl completed his tale of wrongful acts and felt the guilt exulting from the man. Half the battle was won. Carl was feeling remorse and he'd asked for help.

"Carl, what do you think? I've listened to your story. I don't want you to be embarrassed; I've heard worse; believe me. Tell me, since you've actually voiced it out loud to another person, you tell me what's wrong."

"My parents screwed me up big time. I should have gotten some counseling when I was in college and realized how the rest of the world lived. My childhood wasn't normal. It was not me, or my actions, that was wrong; it was them. There was nothing wrong except I was scarred by my parents. I actually thought it was automatically a proven fact that I'd be just like them, and I was."

"Go on, Carl. What can be done about it now? For sure, nothing with your parents. They're both dead, and your daughters are grown, so you can't go back there and fix anything in their childhoods. What do you plan for the future?"

Carl resumed his favorite position: Head in hands, elbows on knees. He even rocked slightly. "My wife and children would never forgive me. I can't forgive my own parents. Why would they forgive me?"

"There's no way of knowing what your parents' problems were, perhaps your mother was a frigid, cold woman, and your father was a hot blooded normal man who went elsewhere for comfort. You can run through several scenarios, but you'll never know the truth. Maybe your mother was molested, even raped when she was a child we'll never know, will we?"

"No, we won't."

"Carl, behavior is not inherited, it is a learned thing. There is nothing in your genes that says you are like your parents. You only mimicked their behavior. Your daughters, however, left their environment at an early age and were on their own, out of necessity. Susan, with her drug and alcohol problems was always getting hooked up with the wrong type of man. She did have more principals than you're giving her credit for. At least she knew when a relationship wasn't right, she'd get out of it, thus so many men. Millie raising a baby alone at fifteen; she had to mature quickly at such a young age. She was unable to accept love or any kind of help. She became too proud, and too independent. I'm glad to hear that they are both doing well now."

"Just telling them, I'm sorry, wouldn't cut it, would it?"

"I'll be honest with you Carl, even Carrie wouldn't believe you."

"Do you have any suggestions, Josh?"

Joshua laughed. "Carl, you are starting to get the idea now. Don't go near your family until you've really got it all figured out. They'll know and then they will believe you when you say you're sorry."

"What did you mean when you said I'm was just starting?"

"Lose some, no a lot of this attitude, you've been carrying around for years. Make friends, laugh, get human. You called me Josh, not my formal name; it's just a beginning, and in the meantime, we are going to spend a lot of time together. If you start getting a half baked idea in your head, I'll let you know. I would also send flowers to Carrie, buy small inexpensive gifts, but something that she'd like and maybe even smile about.

You'll have to court your wife all over again and show her you're an older, wiser man. It'll take time, but it's all you've got left."

"I'm fifty five years old, Josh, a lifetime of rigid behavior. Is it possible to change?"

"Carl, don't think of it as changing, think of it as becoming your own person, the one you've buried all your life. Like my teenaged son is always saying, 'let it all hang out'. Another thing, my advice for you today is. To go home and take a shower for gripes sake. Change your clothes and come to my home for dinner tonight. There will be other people there that you will know. That way I can observe you, and see if you are getting the hang of it. Oops, that is another one of my son's favorite quotes. It's too bad, you didn't enjoy your children, Carl, you missed out on something really wonderful, but you've got four grandchildren. You get another chance."

"Thanks, Josh."

"No problem." Carl laughed at that.

"Another of your son's quotes?"

Together they walked back to their respective cars. The sun was shining bright. It was like a new day beckoning for Carl. Carl thought, I was always good at basketball, maybe I could help coach a team. These young kids sound pretty smart, more together than I am. He started making plans for a different life. His own intelligence told him this was going to take time. He'd really have to change and get a totally different attitude before he could expect his family to accept the person he intended to become. First he had to learn with strangers, develop friendships and alter his image with his colleagues whom he'd shunned for years.

He went back to his empty house and felt the loss, not only his wife, whom he'd loved so selfishly, but the children who should have been precious to him, but weren't.

He looked into the portrait of his parents. He stood quietly and studied their faces and asked the unresponsive picture. "What was your story, Mom and Dad? What made you the way you were?"

The silence and unspoken responses in the room were becoming deafening.

Carl knew he'd get no answers from them, and he wasn't going to waste the mental effort to try and figure his parents out. The real answers were buried with them. Josh told him to concentrate on the future. A future without Carrie was just too depressing to even consider. He thought about Susan and Millie. They were both a part of him. He really was a bastard. How was he going to convince them that he was different. Spots on a dog never changed.

CHAPTER

17

A FTER A TIRING, EXHAUSTING TRIP, Susan and her family arrived in San Francisco. Millie, Jamie and Terry were waiting at the house when they pulled in the driveway. Susan stopped and turned off the car then ran towards them. "Oh let me see that baby. I could hardly wait to get my hands on him." She picked the bundle of joy from Millie's arms, uncovered his face and stared at a little replica of J.B. She immediately noticed the same winning smile, minus the teeth.

"Hi, big guy, I'm your Auntie Sue." She kissed Millie and Terry then quickly went back to admiring the baby. "You just look good enough to eat." Susan buried her face into his neck and he giggled.

Carrie walked hesitantly toward them. She leaned over Susan's shoulder just as Jamie cooed. "Oh Millie, he's precious."

Susan handed the baby to her mother. She was taking short glances at Millie, and Terry, then back to the smiling baby.

Millie was smiling but her thoughts were confusing.

I wish I could feel love for you, Mother, but there is nothing there, not yet anyway. Susan is glowing with love and happiness, maybe she knows the secret of letting go. She's better at forgiving and forgetting than I am. Lord, please show me the way.

Millie leaned over and kissed her mother. "Welcome home, Mom. We have a lot of catching up to do, but I'm willing if you are." Carrie leaned into her, squeezing the baby, who instantly protested. They all laughed as Susan took Jamie back and comforted him. Jamie gave Carrie the lower lip. That made the tears come. Through smiles and tears, Terry ran into Carrie's arms.

"Oh, Grandmother, I'm so happy to meet you at last. Tell me, do you bake cookies and knit booties?"

Carrie laughed. "Sorry, none of that, but I'm a real good listener and teacher. If you ever need help with your homework and I'm your 'man'."

"Cool." Then Terry ran to hug Melody and Paul. Gus then appeared to greet everyone. Susan took his hand and they walked into the house together; the kids whooped and hollered as they followed.

Millie took that quiet opportunity to really welcome her mother. "Mom, I know your heart must hurt leaving your husband, but I'm awfully glad you're here; welcome to my family. J.B. can't wait to meet you." Millie wished she were able to put her arms around her mother like Susan did, but the wall was still there.

"Thanks, Millie." They walked into the house together. The rest of the family was nowhere in sight. Millie and Carrie found them in the back yard. When Paul spotted the pool, he laughed for joy, then he jumped in clothes and all; he did, however, take the time to remove his sneakers. Susan giggled, kicked her shoes off, and dove into tepid water. She let out a big war whoop, when she surfaced.

Laughing, Gus walked over to Millie and Carrie. "How am I going to teach the kids anything when their own mother is the ringleader?"

Carrie laughed and replied. "Don't fight it, join them."

Millie's eyes flew open, that didn't come out of her mother, did it?

Laughing about what she heard, Millie and Terry went out

to their car and carried the food out to the picnic area. Terry spread the tablecloth and set the food out. Instead of grilling hotdogs or hamburgers, Millie asked the cook to make a crock pot of meatballs. Everyone was starved; they commenced eating and talking. Paul told them about the big adventures they saw while coming across the country, and Melody would butt in and say, "Yeah, that's right." Looking to her big brother with pride and admiration.

Carrie listened and watched her family, enjoying every second, but she secretly wished she was sharing this joy with Carl. She'd write him again, and send him the pictures she'd been taking. She'd tell him about the wonderful experiences she was having. Oh how, she wanted to share this bliss with the man she loved. She was still hoping for a miracle. And that's what it would be if Carl changed.

*   *   *

J.B. was pleasantly surprised when he arrived at the house. He'd called Toledo home all his life. J,B, was surprised to see his father back in residence, and his parents seemed to have made a truce of some kind with each other.

When J.B. had moved to California, he'd stripped the house of many antiques and pieces of furniture that were given to him by his grandparents, but the house didn't look empty by any means. J.B. had a lot to tell them, conversing by telephone is not the same. He'd showed his mother pictures of his wife and children, of the house he'd bought and was so proud of.

"Son, I believe you're really happy and I really and truly enjoyed my time spent at your home."

His mother gave out with a loud 'harrumph'.

J.B. studied her, trying to figure her out, surely there was nobody here to impress, just her husband and son. Why couldn't she relax and just become herself again, whoever that was? He wasn't sure anymore.

"Mom, Dad, would you mind if I invited a guest for dinner, say tomorrow night? Millie's parents are separated; Millie's mother lives in California, but her father still lives here. I'd like to get acquainted with him, and if it's okay with you, to bring him here."

His dad laughed. "Good heavens, Son, you don't need to ask, this is your home too."

"Craig, don't be so hasty about inviting that riffraff into our home."

"Mother, I never met the man, but he's a professor of mathematics at the university. I'm sure he's not a riffraff as you so pleasantly put it."

"But they're separated, for heavens sake, what kind of trash are you involved with?"

"Dad, how do you stand it? I'm afraid I couldn't; I'd bust out of here." He glared at his mother.

"Believe me, I've been tempted many times, but I know deep down she's not like this. It's those damnable high faluting airs she believes she has to put on."

"Stop talking about me like I wasn't here. Craig, how can you be so mean?"

"Lighten up, Marsha, like you do when we're not here in this town or around society people. You know I've just about had all I can take of this, I've warned you. I won't stand for it anymore. I'm giving you your last chance. That's why I came back this time.

"Invite your prestigious father-in-law. You don't care about what I think anyway." Marsha got up and rushed from the room.

Craig held his head down. "J.B., I missed out on so much of the good things in life because of your mother, but she's like a different person when she's not here, or around high-class people. I really enjoyed being there, and your mother would too, but I can't get through to her. I've tried to remember all the things Doctor Wade said to me, but nothing seems to apply to your mother. She's got it in her head that your Millie is no good, and that she tricked you into marriage because of the baby."

J.B. didn't answer his father. Let them think what they wanted to. They never gave a rats ass what he thought anyway.

J.B. picked up the phone and called Carl Nobles, he wanted to walk up to him and punch him in the mouth for treating Millie and Susan like he did, but he would bite his tongue and be proper. Millie told him on the phone that her mother was there, and she couldn't believe how much she'd changed. J.B was about ready to hang up when he heard a man's voice.

"Mr. Nobles, this is J.B. Cornell, your son-in-law, I'm married to Millie. I'd like to meet you. Would you come to dinner at my parents home tomorrow night around seven?"

Carl replied with a yes and J.B. gave him the directions and the address. Done deal, he'd soon find out what Millie and Susan dealt with when they were kids. Damn, he hated this polite society, he wouldn't give the man the time of day otherwise.

Ten minutes before seven the next evening, the doorbell rang. His mother went all out, even wore a gown. J.B. told her it wasn't necessary, that it was just a casual dinner, and she didn't need to impress anyone. He didn't know how and why his dad put up with it. When J.B. opened the door, he immediately saw the family resemblances—especially with Susan. "Come in, Mr. Nobles. I'm J.B. Glad to meet you." He extended his hand. Carl took his hand and shook it, looking J.B. straight in the eye, knowing he'd probably heard all the horror stories of him as a father.

"Good to meet you, J.B. How's the family, do you hear from them?" He wondered why J.B. was here.

"I'm just here on business, I'm flying back tomorrow. Three days is my limit to be away from them. Come in and meet my folks."

J.B. introduced them. As always, his father was warm and friendly, but his mother was cool, with that snooty expression. She had that look down to a science. Damn, he wanted to go back home to California and put her out of his mind.

Dinner was served immediately, and they went into the dining room. After they were seated, Craig asked J.B. "Son, what happened to Mary, it's just not the same around here now?"

"I gave her the money to go to Ireland to visit her relatives. She met a man and she's married, happy as a lark. I talk to her on the phone quite frequently."

"You don't call me and talk to me, your own mother." His mother whined.

"I haven't much to say to you, Mother. I don't abide your behavior. As a matter of fact, I don't know how in hell Dad has stood it all these years." Maybe, now wasn't a good time to air the dirty linen in the family, but Carl was certainly no stranger to it, just maybe if the fur flew for a while here in the confines of their own dining room, his mother would see the light.

Carl listened and decided to butt in, he thought he might be able to help the feeling since he acquired new skills. He could read this woman like a book, but her husband, J.B.'s father was a regular person, and he liked him. Didn't she know she was making her family miserable? The last four weeks, and Josh held true to his promise: either change, become the person you should be, or else. Josh, always cut right to the chase and set Carl straight. Now he believed that behavior could become a habit after a long time. He thought, I don't know these people. Chances are, I'll never see them again and so somebody ought to set this old dame straight.

"I suppose you know, Mrs Cornell, that my wife and I are separated after thirty-five years together. For thirty-five years my wife was a saint, how she endured me that long is surely a miracle." Marsha's eyes flew open, no body in society aired their dirty linen in public like this. First her son and now this man. Her mouth was open in shock. "I feel I can speak frankly, since J.B. and I are related and we're more like family now, so don't look shocked. Your reputation is well merited, Mrs. Nobles. You're not the only one to inquire about backgrounds; I made a few myself about this family. It just so happens that we share a baby grandson, and a twelve-year-old granddaughter, that probably neither of us will ever meet, because of our damn shenanigans."

"What are you talking about, sir?" Marsha indignantly asked.

"I'm talking about making your family's life a living hell just because you're screwed up. I've done it for years. It took losing my wife for me to want to do something about it. You can do the same thing, Marsha. I'm seeing a real good psychologist. I never admitted I had a problem until I lost my wife. You're heading in the same path. If you don't knock it off you'll be sitting alone with no family left, just like me."

"Craig, throw this, this... this gentleman out of our home, you can't just sit there and let him talk to me that way."

"Yes, I can Marsha. If you want the truth, you're getting it. That's why I brought you back home here. I've made plans to leave you, only this time it's permanent. I want a divorce. I've already talked to my lawyer. I've had enough."

Marsha gasped in horror. "Craig!"

J.B. turned the so-called conversation toward Carl. Boy, would Susan love to hear this. It looked like the was going to hit the fan.

"Carl, I'm glad you're getting help, who is this man that is helping you?"

"Doctor Joshua Hamilton, he's an associate professor at the University, and he has his own practice. I recommend him highly. He knows what he's doing. I'm sorry J.B., I'd heard about your mother's reputation. I wish to God someone would have socked it to me before I ruined my daughters and my wife's lives. I was wrong. I was also screwed up by my parents, but I'm told that isn't a good excuse. People can change, bad behavior is not inherited, it's just a habit, a cop out."

"Craig, you aren't serious, are you?" Marsha looked pleadingly at her husband. So many times he'd made this threat, but never in front of anyone else. Well maybe J.B. a few times. How could he embarrass her like this?

"Yes, I am, I've tried to warm you, I've been telling you for years that you had to knock this damn uppity behavior. It sucks, Marsha. I want the woman I married forty years ago, my little girl that was sweet and loving to everyone. We had more friends than we knew what to do with, and they loved being around you. I thought you were wonderful, that I was the luckiest man in the world. I've regretted getting this damn money for years. It's brought nothing but trouble and unhappiness to us. Thank God, J.B. had Mary growing up; she was his mother. I've tried to tell you, not to cater to this ignorant bunch of people you think are so damn hot. How about trying to impress our son and me for a change?" Craig got up from the table and poured a half glass of bourbon, then gulped it down.

J.B. wondered if this was called a round table discussion. Everyone was on a roll. He always admired people that he did business with that were up front. He looked at all of them, they were Jamie's grandparents, and with the exception of his father, he didn't want to expose his son to the other two. He wanted to go pack his bag and leave, but he'd hear out all the ugliness in these dysfunctional families.

"Look J.B, I guess I've said enough. I'm so damn glad that Millie has you and you have it together. You went through a lot to get her feet on the ground, thank you. I'm trying to get my act together. If I know deep in my heart that I've changed; I'll be out in California in a flash. I'd also like to make it my permanent residence, but not until I'm sure. I'll never hurt anyone again. I could be in therapy for a long time. One thing you can do for me, if you will, is tell them all I love them when you return home."

Carl and J.B. shook hands, then Carl turned to Marsha and Craig. "Look, perhaps I should apologize, but I'm not going to." He shook hands with Craig and put his hands on Marsha's shoulders. "Go to Doctor Hamilton, Marsha, what I did was a hell of a lot worse than what you did. I'm learning to accept it and understand it. Maybe we'll both get cured, and we can become good grandparents. If that ever happens, I'll see you both in California."

J.B. watched Carl leave, then he started for his bedroom. He felt it best to leave his parents alone. He didn't dare hope, no, he wasn't going there. Too many times he'd been disillusioned about his parents, even his father threatening to leave, he wouldn't. When he visited them in California, he only stayed six days, then rushed back home to his wife. How many times had he heard that familiar threat from his father before?

*　*　*

After two weeks of living in California, Susan and Gus settled comfortably in the house. They decided they liked the house and told Millie they wanted to buy it from her. When they mentioned it, her hand flew up to her mouth. She'd forgotten all about the debt she owed the credit union at work. She must surely be overdue for a payment. Since having the baby and getting married, she had totally forgotten about it. She placed a call to them intending to apologize for being tardy. Millie shouldn't have been surprised, but she was, when the loan officer assured her that the loan was satisfied. J.B. himself took care of the matter. The debt was paid in full.

A mere few weeks ago, Millie would have gotten angry or upset about this latest development, but this time she just laughed and shook her head. This was so typical of J.B. to intercede and take care of winding up her affairs as a single woman. Why had she ever fought it? Right from the beginning, she hadn't stood a chance. J.B. truly loved her and intended to make her his wife and take care of her.

Carrie hinted to Millie that she would like to visit her for a while before she registered at the local colleges for a position. She wasn't in a big hurry; she'd never even taken one Sabbatical leave. She could actually retire, she already had her tenure in, but what would she do with herself? She enjoyed teaching and being around the young people. She was only fifty-five years old, too young to do, just nothing.

She'd leased a car, so she'd have her own transportation. She missed her own Camry, but to have it shipped here was out of the question. She'd consulted with her lawyer and asked that it be sold. As the time passed, she felt better about leaving Carl. Now she was certain she'd done the right thing, especially when J.B. returned from his trip and told Millie about the melee at his parents home. It seemed so out of character for Carl to make a scene like that. He sent his love to her and the girls, when J.B. repeated that, Carrie knew that he was playing some kind of mind game. Maybe he was going insane. This kind of behavior was so out of character. No way would Carl Nobles speak like that to strangers.

Carrie was on the cell phone to Millie and she was directing her to her home. When Carrie started in the driveway, she slowed down to a crawl so she could look at her surroundings. Susan and Gus had told her about J.B. and Millie's property, but mere words couldn't describe this. She sat and quietly observed the entire area. She thought, it is too bad I can't paint. You could spend months right here describing the scenes on canvas.

After parking her car, she stood on the front porch. She could see for miles; it was clear and sunny today. She saw Terry riding a horse in the distance, what a wonderful place to raise a child. She smiled when she took her hand and raised the old-fashioned knocker, someone had gone in for a lot of detail, the whole property looked like it received a lot of TLC. Now her daughter and her family were reaping the benefits of their effort.

J.B. opened the door, and smiled broadly. "Good morning, Carrie. So good to have you here. Give me your car keys, and I'll get your luggage out of the car. You just go on in and check the pad out. Millie is up in the nursery. She's going to bring Jamie down when he wakes and take him outside for a while. What a gorgeous day."

Carrie explored the massive home, and she wondered why they'd bought one so big. She didn't go upstairs, but she spotted the terrace from the kitchen patio door and went outside. No wonder Millie had said she could stay there forever, and never leave. Carrie was sitting on a chaise, just gazing at the perfect picture of the green pasture and the blue sky. She didn't even hear Millie until she was right on top of her.

"Makes you wish you were a painter, doesn't it? I can't draw a glass of water, but I take a lot of pictures, and try to capture it on film. Good to have you here, Mom. Is Susan all settled in?"

Carrie nodded as she heard her cell phone ring. She opened her purse and answered it. It was Carl. This was the first, he'd called her. "Hello Carl, good to hear your voice, how are you?" she asked.

There was a long silence on the other end, she wondered if he'd hung up, then she heard his voice. After all this time, it could still send shivers up her spine. She closed her eyes, and hoped Millie hadn't noticed the reaction she was getting.

"Carrie, you sound wonderful, darling, I miss you so much, and I have a lot to tell you and plenty for you to relay to J.B. I presume he told you of the scene I created at his parents home. Well, I've gotten acquainted with both of them. Marsha, J.B.'s mother called me the following day and invited me back. You know the old saying, misery loves company. Well, I went and I took my now good friend, Joshua Hamilton with me. We've created a small group session. Marsha and I both talked and shared until our voices were hoarse. Enough about me, what are you doing with your time out there?"

"I helped get Susan settled in her home, and I've spend a lot of time with Melody and Paul. I'm so in love with my family, that I could float away. They are the most amazing children, now I'm sounding like a biased grandmother, aren't I?" Carrie laughed. She then began to brag about Paul. "I had a blast traveling with them. We camped at night, and Paul pretended ending we were old-time pioneers, we sat around the campfire and swapped stories. He has a wonderful sense of humor. I've never been happier. Now I'm at Millie and J.B.'s home, and soon as I hang up the phone, I'm going to hold little Jamie. He's so precious, such a delightful baby, all smiles, but he can sure let you know if he is displeased about something, that kinda reminds me of you." She laughed again and listened for a long time. Millie saw the tears forming in Carrie's eyes and knew that her father must be talking lovingly to her.

Millie thoughts closed in on her as she shut her eyes and recalled.

Even as a child, I knew there was love in our home, but there was none for Susan and me. It was a good thing, they had two of us, or, I would have never reached adulthood. If it is possible to die of loneliness and unhappiness. I can't imagine J.B. not loving Jamie and Terry as much as I do. How did Mom do it? How could she turn her back on Susan and me?

Carrie closed her cell phone and laid it on the nearby table. She leaned back, and closed her eyes, like she was concentrating real hard. "Millie, your father tells me he is in counseling. He just told me, it's no quick fix, and he could be in therapy for years. He'd like to move out here. Josh, his therapist told him, that leaving the home he grew up in could help. This would provide him with new surroundings away from the constant memories that the silent voices must edict for him. You know, I always thought it was a depressing house. I tried to brighten it with different, brighter furniture, and your Dad bought all those beautiful paintings, but nothing ever altered it."

"Would you go back with him, if he comes out here, Mother?"

"Millie, I'd be lying if I told you I didn't miss him, but surprisingly not nearly as much as I thought I would. My days are filling up with beautiful experiences with my family. I'm just sad that Carl and I couldn't enjoy them together. He sounds different, Millie, but I do know he's a good actor. I may never trust him again."

"A little family tradition, it took me forever before I trusted J.B. with my heart and my children."

"But, you do now. How did J.B. prove himself?"

"Not any one thing, a series of things, really it was the consistency. He never wavered, after he came out here."

Carrie laughed, her voice carrying across the expanse of the veranda. "Maybe, it's this California air here in the mountain, the ocean breeze and warm climate that seems to relax your very soul. I'm so tired of conflict; I just want peace and serenity. Is that asking too much. You have it all with J.B. I miss your father, the love of my life, so no matter how happy I am, there is always sadness in my heart when I'm without him. You and Susan are lucky. You're both happy with your mates and living a normal life."

"Now."

Just the one word told Carrie of the long unhappy years her daughter had endured because she didn't have a real family to support her. That was the closest thing to a reproach that Carrie ever heard since she'd been with her girls. She remembered the old cliche, everything worthwhile is not worth having if not paid for by sweat and tears. Perhaps they had paid the price.

She thought about Carl. Could he possibly get the help he needed from a therapist, and what was wrong with J.B.'s family? Had J.B. endured an unhappy childhood too? It was small comfort to know that Carl and she weren't the only parents that had screwed up their children's lives. She didn't want to ask Millie about it. Maybe the truth would come out someday. She smiled when she saw Terry walking toward her carrying the small baby in her arms. She loved that child with total abandonment, as it was the most natural feeling a mother could have. Oh how she'd loved her babies, but obviously not enough to fight for that God-given right to keep them. She would be forever grateful that her daughters forgave her enough to allow her into their lives now, even though she didn't deserve it.

Terry placed little Jamie in her arms, and he immediately smiled at her with recognition. At least she'd been given a chance to become a good grandmother. She was grateful for that.

Carrie smiled warmly at her beautiful grandchild and talked softly to him. He snuggled in her arms, giving her a taste of the love and warmth a small child can bestow on a family.

She'd send more pictures to Carl of their wonderful grandchildren. It would be all they'd ever have. Carl wouldn't change. It was impossible. People there age were set. Molded for life. It would take more then California sunshine and four lovely grandchildren to change the pattern of Carl's stoic life. She would find a lovely little cottage and resume her teaching career and spend as much time as she could with her family. Thirty-five years of loving a man wasn't something easily forgotten. But the joy of having her families love and understanding was beginning to outweigh the longing she still felt for her husband, who was incapable of loving anyone but her. She'd hurt her daughters because of her selfishness. She'd made her own desire more important than the love she felt for her baby daughters. Then, as the years flew by, it became a way of life. It was small wonder that she could have a loving relationship now. Maybe by doing all the reading she did on the subject, she'd healed herself. She'd always carry the guilt. It had been wrong. Did her daughters really love her and had they truly forgiven her? Or was she just disillusioning herself again?

CHAPTER
18

CARRIE MADE AN APPOINTMENT AT one of the Universities. She'd already mailed in her resume. This appointment was either a position or a denial. When she arrived and told the secretary who she was, Carrie felt like they were rolling the red carpet out for her. She was offered a splendid position with remarkable benefits. The groundwork for her new life was laid. California was going to be her new home. She accepted the position. Now all she had to do was find a suitable house to buy. She'd canvassed the area several times, thinking perhaps she should just hire a realtor and be done with it. But roaming the neighborhood for new homes provided her with the opportunity to explore. She was beginning to love California.

Actually she was thinking a lot of J.B.'s work. She intended to make an offer to attend some of the seminars and speak personally to people about the problems she'd experienced in her married life. Millie started several weeks ago with him, speaking to high school girls and young mothers at the clinic. She spoke about childcare, preservation, and living alone with a child. Millie certainly knew all the pitfalls and the daily struggles.

Carrie heard Millie say more than one time. "Don't be too proud to accept help that is willingly and graciously offered, join support groups, never isolate yourself, and it's natural for you to desire a man. Just be sure your next relationship has depth. Tell yourself, once is enough, somewhere out there is the right man for you. Make sure you keep your morals and reputation fairly decent, so a decent, self-respecting man would be able to accept you. Loving and sex is great, but so is respect." She could talk endlessly to these young frightened faces. Carrie attended several of her seminars. She was so proud of her daughter when she honestly shared her own experiences with these young impressionable women.

Several weeks later Carrie was driving back to Millie's home, after a rewarding day teaching school. This was just too far to drive every day. Carrie wondered what the hold-up was. Why wasn't she getting her divorce settlement? She'd signed all the necessary papers and Carl was not contesting anything she'd asked for. It was time she made her own home. She only wanted a cottage type, maybe a cape cod; something homey. A nice yard to plant flowers and flowering shrubs was a must in her mind. She visualized it, the walls painted a cheerful pastel shade, and flowered furniture and drapes. She wanted a house different than Carl's parent's home. Nothing splendidly formal and formidable, although she could afford it, she preferred just a simple dwelling.

Carrie finally reached Millie's home after a fruitless house hunt, but was delighted with her new teaching position and the prospect of working with Millie and J.B.

If only—. But wishful thinking was as futile as her house hunting had been. Carrie had noticed the strange car in the driveway, and she just presumed, her daughter or son-in-law had guests. She intended not to intrude, to allow them privacy as she walked toward the stairwell to go quietly and unseen up to her room. She barely reached the second step when she heard her name being called. The voice was excruciatingly familiar. Before she turned to face the speaker, she felt her heart thumping in her chest, and her knees going weak. Carl! What was he doing in her new world, her new life? Carrie turned and faced him. She gasped as she saw the relic of the man Carl had been. He'd lost a considerable amount of weight and his handsome face looked haggard and drawn. She stepped back down to the foyer and walked toward him, as if in a daze. The compulsion to touch him overrode all her good intentions of keeping her distance from her husband.

Carrie walked into his out-stretched arms and her body molded to his. Neither of them moved as they hungrily absorbed the emotion evoked by this tender reunion.

"Oh baby, baby, I'm lost without you." Carl murmured in her ear. He pulled his head back and gently encased her face in his hands and gazed lovingly and tenderly into her face. "Carrie, I love you more than life." He lowered his face and gently kissed her. His mouth barely touching hers.

It was Carrie that deepened the kiss when she put her arms around his neck and drew him close. She'd been as starved for this as Carl was. How could she have turned her back on the man she'd loved most of her life?

Millie saw her parents embracing and quietly returned to the kitchen, then prevented Terry from going into the foyer. Her parents needed some privacy. Millie was confident that her mother had been happy with her sisters and her families, but she also knew all about the heartache that her mother had been secretly enduring. She'd never forget the months when J.B. and her were estranged.

Millie heard the front door open and close, then she went into the hallway to see where her parents were. She looking out the window alongside the front door and saw them walking hand and hand toward the ocean. Millie said a silent prayer that somehow all their family problems could be resolved. Wouldn't it be wonderful to have both parents? For the first time in her life, just maybe she'd have their enduring love and support, not only for each other but for the entire family. Foolish dream. It would never happen, not here in the real world, Millie thought as she walked up the steps to retrieve her son from a very efficient nanny. One that she was starting to resent. She missed not taking care of her baby son.

The sun had set, the evening was cool, and still her parents were sitting on the bench by the sea that had been installed there by the former owners of the house. Millie said to J.B., "Maybe you should drive over there with the jeep and bring them back to the house. They'll both catch their death. It's getting quite cold tonight."

"I know, but I hate to disturb them. Maybe we should have Terry ride her horse over there and take them a couple of blankets nonchalantly. What do you think?"

Terry overheard the conversation and asked J.B. to call down to the stable and tell them to saddle her horse. She rushed to the utility room off the kitchen and returned carrying two sleeping bags a sack containing food, and a thermos of coffee. Millie and J.B. laughed when they saw what their daughter intended to take to her grandparents. J.B. drove her down to the stable and promised to wait for her and return her to the house. He watched as she skillfully rode her horse in the direction of the ocean.

Terry smiled when she reached them, dismounted then carried the sleeping bags and food to them. Carrie and Carl had been so absorbed in talking, they hadn't realized it was getting late. Carl jumped up and said, "Good heavens, I feel like a fool. I didn't realize it was getting so late. Is that coffee in that thermos? Wonderful. Tell your Mom and Dad we'll be back to the house shortly. We enjoyed watching the sunset."

Terry giggled and said, "no problem, but until you do come back to the house, I hope you will now be more comfortable. I hope you both like the roast beef sandwiches. It was either that or peanut butter and jelly, enjoy!" Terry jumped back on her prancing horse and galloped back to the barn. They watched her until she was out of sight, then they checked out what their granddaughter had brought them, besides coffee and roast beef sandwiches.

Carl realized that for the first time, he was actually being the recipient of his family's warmth. Tears welled up in his eyes.

God, he'd been so stupid. So much love could have been enjoyed by all four of them while Millie and Susan were growing up. He had been too stupid to realize that he was acting worse than an ass. "Carrie, how can you even consider forgiving me. I don't deserve it. God, I was so wrong, so stupid and I've missed so much and made you endure the same loss. You should have belted me or packed up, then taken the girls and left me. I'm so sorry, my darling."

"What is that old adage, 'never cry over spilt milk'. I believe that saying applies here. It's all in the past. We have to concentrate on doing the rest of our lives the right way."

"Oh Carrie, does that mean that you will give me another chance? Darling, I'll not let you down again. I promise that from the bottom of my heart." When Terry turned to look back at her grandparents, she watched as they tenderly embraced.

Carl zipped the two sleeping bags together, and they made themselves comfortable on the bench. Carrie poured them coffee and Carl unwrapped the sandwiches. Also in the bag were homemade chocolate chip cookies. Cookies, Carrie had made for her granddaughter, who'd been slightly disappointed when Carrie told her she didn't make cookies, as grandmothers were noted for doing. Not only did they enjoy the warmth of the sleeping bags, but the loving gesture of their family. It was a good beginning. Carl could hardly swallow because of the lump in his throat.

Two hours later Carrie and Carl walked back to the house by the light of the full moon. Both of them were emotionally full of the new resolutions. Carl thought back and could recall all the sessions he'd had with Josh repeatedly telling him that it wouldn't be easy, and he would backslide occasionally. He prayed that he didn't backslide to the extent that ever hurt his family again.

Carl stayed with Millie and J.B. and quietly observed J,B,'s behavior with his children. Carrie had told him, that that was what she did in the beginning—until she felt confident as a grandmother. Paul was the only one of the grandchildren that Carl was having a problem with until Gus, J.B., Paul and he went camping up in the mountains. It was on the camping trip that he began to get along with his eldest grandson. Sitting and listening to the campfire stories enlightened Carl on what he'd missed as a kid with his own father. It was like filling in the missing pieces of a puzzle. He realized he had a talent for telling the wildest stories around the campfire. He didn't know where they came from, but Paul's face was the mirror of his success as a storyteller. From then on, he became Paul's hero. Carl could have cried just for the shill joy of it.

Carrie, Susan and Millie consoled Terry by taking her shopping. She'd wanted to go on the camping trip, but she'd been told it was just going to be a man-thing this time. She got over her disappointment when she found the perfect clothes to buy and Millie allowed her to get her ears pierced, which led to more shopping for just the right earrings.

When returning home, it was Terry who spied the darling little house that her grandmother had been searching for in vain. "Aunt Susan, slow down and go around the block. I think I just found Gram and Pap's house. I'm sure of it. It looked sooooo neat."

Susan maneuvered the car back to the street where the mystery house was located. She pulled into the driveway and all of the women let out a big 'Ahhh'. It had a 'For Sale' sign in front, so they all got out of the car. Before they reached the front door, an elderly lady stepped out on the porch. Carrie told her she'd like to see the house, that it was exactly what she'd been looking for. The woman introduced herself then used her cane as she led them to the backyard instead the house. At first sight, they all knew why. There were beautifully designed flowerbeds and an alluring gazebo. The misty water into the pond full of lily pads. It was perfect, no other word could possibly describe it.

Smiling smugly, the old woman led them through the back door and into the house. Carrie noted that the kitchen and bathroom needed to be updated, but other than that it was light, sunny and all the rooms were already painted in soft pastel shades, exactly as Carrie wanted her new home to look like. Besides the kitchen, diningroom and livingroom, it had a library downstairs, that Carl would love. It had been paneled in knotty pine and finished off naturally. This showed off the luscious wood. A cozy fireplace was in the corner.

The old woman smiled as Carrie turned to look at her and inform her that she needed this very house. "I'm glad you like the house. It hasn't been up for sale long. I hate to leave my home, but my daughter and son-in-law want me to come live with them. It's probably for the best. This is Saturday and I'll probably be vacating this coming week, so if you want to do any remodeling, you are welcome to get it started before the closing."

Carrie didn't even ask the price of the house. Regardless she was going to have this house. She'd told Carl what she was looking for. He'd scowled at first, but quickly remembered what Josh had told him. A happy woman has choices and preferences. He could learn to live in this humble little cottage that Carrie had her heart set on. If she was happy. It was really quite simple pleasing his family once he got the hang of it.

Surprisingly Carl was delighted with the house that made Carrie so happy. He never saw her so enthused about the changes she was planning. It dawned on Carl, the reason he liked this house was because Carrie was so happy with it. He hadn't realized she wasn't happy in the beautiful old homestead back in Ohio. Of course, he hadn't realized a lot of things then. They'd be able to move into the house in two weeks, in the meanwhile, they shopped for just the right furniture. Carl recalled the expensive pieces of furniture they'd owned before, but what made Carrie face light up now was totally different.

Carl had applied at the same college where his wife taught and was hired as a substitute for a professor who was retiring at the end of the school term. Then Carl would then he would be the head of the Mathematics Department. He couldn't believe his good fortune.

All the family members helped with moving and organizing the house, except Melody and Jamie. They were left in the nanny's care. Susan had prepared a picnic luncheon for them and they enjoyed the gazebo for the first time. Later Susan and Carrie were washing the new dishes in the new kitchen, while Millie helped and directed the men where to place the furniture. Then Millie opened the box containing the crocheted dollies that her grandmother had made. She knew they would be perfect with this flowery, pastel decor. When she'd completed the livingroom, she interrupted Susan and her mother and asked if they would please come see the room. Millie hoped it was the way her mother had planned it. It was.

"It's perfect, just the way I'd pictured it. I love it." Carl stuck his head around the corner, thought it was a little too feminine, but seeing Carrie's beaming face, he knew he could live with it. Where the sudden devilish streak came from, he'd never know. He made a sickening looking face, just to get a rise out of his now feisty wife. She tossed a pillow at him but missed.

"I didn't mean it, darling, I love it. I love you." He laughed as he grabbed the end of a box Gus was struggling with. He looked up at Gus and said, "that came from page twenty seven from the book on how to make your wife happy. I thought it was a crock when I read it, but my God, it really works." They all laughed, another happy memory was made. Carl thought to himself, and it was so damn easy.

Life settled down for Carl and Carrie Nobles. They were happy with their home, the milder climate, their teaching positions, and most of all, their family who visited often. Carl would place a call to Josh and talk over a crisis or a situation with him, but the calls were getting further and further apart as Carl adapted to this new way of life. He'd never been happier and Carrie literally glowed with contentment.

J.B. was delighted that Millie's family had resolved their problems and were no longer dysfunctional however his own parents were still struggling with irreconcilable differences. Josh was not the magic bullet for Marsha. Surprisingly it was Millie's old work buddies, Tess and Sally that seemed to produce subtle changes in Marsha's attitude. It came to Millie one night when they'd returned from visiting her parents home and she noticed how quiet J.B. got. She knew his parents' problems, concerned him, even though he denied it. She e-mailed Tess and made a suggestion. The three of them, Tess, Sally and Marsha definitely didn't travel in the same circles, but if anyone could connect to Marsha, maybe it would be those two. Marsha could never go back to the happy care-free girl she'd been, but perhaps she could reach a happy medium.

Tess was the first to contact Marsha. Having known J.B. and Millie for years gave them a common link. When Tess called, she told Marsha who she was and how Sally and she had introduced Millie to him because they thought the two of them would click. Marsha was about to end the strange call when Tess said something that rang a bell with her. Tess said that Sally and her were concerned about Millie and J.B., and wondered if they'd worked their problems out. They hoped everything was all right. Tess said that more than likely Millie, since she'd married a wealthy man like J.B., wouldn't have anything to do with them, since they were still working girls. Marsha quickly digested this information and saw a parallel with her own life. Did Millie change? "Tess, I'm glad you called, and if you and Sally care to come to the house, maybe we can both reassure one another. I'd like to know more about Millie anyway."

Tess could have jumped up and down for joy. Millie had told her what a snob she thought she was, but J.B. believed they were just false airs she'd perpetuated through the years. Maybe she just needed to see herself through someone's eyes. Tess and Sally went to Marsha's home wearing jeans and t-shirts that they had worn to work. They apologized, but told Marsha they were just too anxious to hear about J.B. and Millie to bother taking the time to go home and change their clothes. Marsha immediately felt comfortable with them. They gushed over her home, and told her how lucky she was to be living in such a grand place. Marsha asked them if they cared to stay for dinner. Sally hesitated, then said, "Mrs. Cornell, we aren't dressed very proper; we're just wearing jeans. We wouldn't want to embarrass you in front of your other guests." Tess laid it on real thick. As if in reality, she gave a rat's ass what people thought.

"There is just going to be my husband and I and he won't mind." Marsha assured them.

"You didn't answer me when I, asked you how Millie and J.B. are doing. Are they happy?"

"As far as I know they are. I don't talk to them much, but my husband talks to J.B. frequently." Marsha wasn't about to reveal what her personal relationship was like with her own son, let alone her new daughter-in-law.

"Don't tell me Millie changed, and she's acting snobbish and not treating you right. I can't believe it. Millie was always so kind-hearted and pleasant to be around. I never thought this would happen, not to Millie."

Just then Craig came into the room. Marsha introduced the two women to him and said she'd invited them for dinner. Mealtime had been going so horrible lately that Marsha would have invited the garbage collector in for dinner. Josh had told her she'd have to change her attitude and entire perspective on her lifestyle or her marriage was going to fail. Craig surely didn't care for her 'status quo' social friends, maybe he'd like Millie's friends. As it turned out, he did. Very much. And so did she.

After the introductions were over. Sally looked Craig over, then laughed and said, "for sure the apple didn't fall too far from the tree, J.B. looks just like you." Then heartily laughed.

Craig, burst out laughing and so did Marsha. The laughter relaxed everyone and soon Sally was telling Craig and Marsha how they'd schemed to get Millie and J.B. together and how J.B. had messed up with Millie and was miserable for months without her. "After all we went through getting those two together and keeping them that way, we didn't even get invited to their wedding. We told Marsha here that probably Millie is getting high-hat now that she's married to a rich man like J.B. But we're still concerned for her. We loved her like a daughter, and I don't mind telling you; I'd been proud if J.B. had been my son. He's something else. Never thought I'd see the day he'd settle down with one woman and get married. He was really against getting married for some reason or other. How are they doing, anyway?"

"I was out to California a few months ago and stayed with them; they seem to be very happy. They have a wonderful little baby boy. He's the chip right off the old block, if I ever saw one."

Marsha laughed, then turned to Craig and said, "I miss our old buddies; these girls remind me of them. I haven't enjoyed myself this much in ages." She turned back to Sally and Tess and continued, "I'm so glad you called me and we got together like this."

Sally winked at Tess. "You're sure that Millie isn't getting hifalutin? Damn shame if she is, because she was the greatest. J.B. is a lucky man. This food is delicious, wait until we tell the other girls at work that we dined in style. La te da." Marsha laughed at the remark, she was catching on to what they were up to, she wondered who'd sicced them on to her, J.B. or Millie. Nothing Josh said had affected her the way these two ordinary women did, who probably could really kick up their heels, given the right opportunity and the occasion. They were more than likely on very good behavior tonight. She missed these kind of people. Her old friends. Her old life.

After, Tess and Sally left and promised to come back again, especially if they didn't hear from Millie and J.B. "I'm really glad J.B. has regular people like you for parents, because whatever you did you certainly raised a swell guy." Tess added just before they went out the door.

Marsha turned to Craig and laughed. "Well, did you invite them here, Craig? Or maybe J.B. did, it's something he would do, but whoever did, I'm glad. I enjoyed myself tonight like I haven't in years. Darling, I think we are going to change friends. I wonder if the old gang still goes to the Jail House Pub on Saturday night. Wouldn't it be nice to see all our old friends again and have fun, really have fun for a change, instead of pretending we are?"

"I doubt our old friends are still carousing around on Saturday night anymore, more than likely their sons and daughters are. Marsha, tell me the God's truth. Is there anyone in the crowd we've been associating with that really mean anything to you? Did you make any close friends among them?"

Marsha thought for a time, then answered, "No, Craig, not really. You don't really get to know these people intimately. Half the time I don't believe what they say and the rest of the time, I'd rather not even be with them. You know, J.B. shunned society, per si. Why couldn't we, except for your business dinners and business associates. We don't have to be in the society clique, do we?"

"I've been trying to tell you that for years, Marsha. Has it finally started sinking in?"

"Craig, You know what Tess said tonight about Millie changing. Do you think she has?"

"Millie, no, she isn't. From what J.B. tells me, since he's working in a different type of law, she's been doing a lot of public speaking. After all she was a teenage mother and was single for a long time. She would be able to help these struggling women if they incurred the same problems she did. J.B. tells me she wants to have more children just as soon as her doctor tells her it's okay physically. With the vast differences between Terry and Jamie's ages, she'll be going to college by the time Jamie starts kindergarten. Marsha, why this sudden worry and concern about Millie? Did Tess or Sally say something?"

"I'd like to go to California and meet her and get to know my grandchildren. I'd also like to and try to make some much needed amends, if I can, with my son."

"You mean you're ready to accept Millie and be decent to her?" Craig raised his eyebrows at her.

"Craig, you make me sound like such a bitch."

He just looked up at her over his glasses and didn't say a word. He wondered how long this pleasant behavior was going to last. He wouldn't hold his breath; that was for sure. She'd let him down too many times before. He knew it would take more than just a casual dinner with two normal people to change her way of thinking. Old habits die hard.

CHAPTER 19

CRAIG WAS MORE THAN surprised when Marsha's marvelously different attitude remained. She no longer went for the luncheon dates with her old friends, instead, she surprised him when she said she applied at the hospital, personnel office, and signed up to do volunteer work. The changes in Marsha were subtle at first, then became more obvious. She seemed to laugh a lot more then she started wearing jeans around the house. Sometimes she even went to the store with them on.

Craig asked her one time why her fashion changed. She surprised him when she said, "Craig, what do I care what people think as long as you keep admiring my shapely little buns in jeans, I'll keep wearing them." She giggled like a teenager, then wriggled her butt when she walked in front of him. That was so like his girl he'd married.

Craig was still leery. He wasn't about to take her out to California and have her make J.B.'s and Millie's life miserable. That evening they were entertaining business clients at the Country Club for dinner and then dancing. Len and Cindy Sterling, although extremely wealthy, were fun-loving, down-to-earth people. Their conversation was usually a bit on the brusque side. He'd never taken Marsha along with him when he'd entertained the couple before. He was anxious to see her reaction to them, now. It was a sneaky test of sorts, but he had to be sure that Marsha was really reverting back to her own disposition and personality. One that could mingle with the best or the worst of people. He'd already told his lawyer to put the divorce proceedings on hold until further notice.

God, he didn't want to end this marriage. He still loved the woman, but he just couldn't abide this false facade she put up.

That night when they entered the Club and they checked their coats with the hat-check girl, they headed to the bar where Craig told his associates he'd meet with them. Craig turned and studied Marsha's face; it was noncommittal. She nodded her head and spoke to several acquaintances, but in a normal tone of voice. Then he saw Mel Sterling at the end of the bar; he took Marsha's arm and headed toward them. He felt as nervous as a Freshman taking a Senior to the prom.

The introductions were barely finished and Mel voiced his first personal insult. "How in hell did an old fart like you get to hook up with a good looking woman like this, probably lied your ass off to impress her." He lasciviously leered at Marsha, who merely raised her eyebrows.

Craig had to admit that Marsha was still a darn attractive woman for fifty-four-years old. He knew she'd had several surgeries to maintain her look of youth. He knew she'd spent a fortune on different beauty treatments. Her figure was still slender, not like it had been when she was twenty, but yes, she could certainly pass for a woman at least fifteen years younger than she was.

Craig thought she was just going to let the remark pass as crude behavior, or possible give the man a brutal sit-down like he'd seen her do many times, but she winked at Len and coyly retorted, "he just got lucky." Len laughed loudly and boisterously, then Len and Cindy seemed to be satisfied that Marsha was just a regular gal and a good sport. The evening they spent with them was quite enjoyable. A lot of jokes were told, but nothing ribald, as sometimes he'd heard from the couple. It seemed they respected Marsha as a lady.

Marsha carried on several conversations with women that stopped at their table. All of them asked where she'd been lately, but Marsha just pleasantly smiled and informed them she'd been busy. Marsha herself realized her folly of thinking. She had to mimic these people in order to fit in. Now she realized she didn't need to do that. She could call the shots with these people, probably could have done so for years, but she'd allowed them to intimidate her. Besides, most important of all, she liked the way her husband was looking at her and the way he held her on the dance floor.

Craig was delighted with their evening out. Not only with his business associates, but many of Marsha's acquaintances. She'd been proper but not stymied by anyone. She acted like she was her own woman. Was it something Josh had said to her or just the brief time spent with two women like Tess and Sally? Had she found herself, at last? Could it be that he'd gotten his girl back?

Craig officially dropped the divorce proceedings. Much to Craig's delight. For the first time in many years, he was truly happy with his marriage. Two of their best friends were Tess and Sally. They often went to the club where the old gals hung out. Marsha saw her society friends occasionally, but she acted lady-like, but didn't put on airs. She even found several of them quite likable and formed closer relationships with them. It was like they too, were weary of the false protocol and airs. They all relaxed and enjoyed their activities much more. Marsha contemplated this and even discussed it with Craig. She paraphrased it this way, "Craig, it was like starting out with a snowball and ending up in an avalanche, It just kept escalating until it got a lot bigger and worse all the time."

Craig kept J.B. informed of his new, wonderful life with his wife, but it was close to six months before he agreed to take Marsha to meet her new family in California. He tried hard to put the past behind them, but Marsha was still suspect. Would he ever just be able to relax without this dread of her changing back to the despicable way she was?

When they landed at the SPO Airport, they retrieved their luggage and rented a car. It was getting late. Neither one of them wanted to disturb the family at night, so they got hotel room and dined at the hotel restaurant. Craig was well known, and he met two acquaintances of his, that he'd done business with several years ago. They had a few drinks with them and again Marsha was a delight. She was ladylike, friendly and allowed the men to openly discuss business, though he knew she was bored to tears. When they were walking back to their table, he apologized to her. "Sorry, Darling. I know that must have been boring for you, but it couldn't be helped. Sorry."

Marsha just grinned at him. "I've always liked to watch and listen when you are wheeling and dealing. You're good at it. Is J.B. good at it too?"

Craig threw his head back and laughed, "Darling, I've learned a lot from him. Our son is incredible. People naturally like and respect him. The kid amazes me." Pride was in his voice as he talked about their son. She had even been aware of how successful J.B. had become. Before, she had been so involved in her small little world, she hadn't given it much thought. She had a lot to make up for, besides being the wife Craig wanted and expected. She had to mend a lot of bridges with her son and his family.

Craig called J.B. and told him when they would arrive at his home. J.B. told him he was going to cancel his appointments and be there waiting for them. When Marsha saw where they lived, she couldn't keep her mouth shut. She was so awestruck. "Craig, I can't wait to see the inside of this spectacular home. The outside perimeter is like a movie set. It's perfection. Look at the horses. Is that J.B. riding?"

"No, J.B. rides a big black stallion. That is Terry. She is riding a lot better now. You'll like her. She's a great kid."

When they pulled into the driveway, J.B. walked out of the front door and greeted them. First he hugged his father, then he turned to his mother, slightly hesitant to make a move. Marsha thought, 'was I that bad?' She was the one that threw her arms around him and embraced him. He reciprocated with a hug. It had been a long time. She brushed the tears away. "J.B., I want to meet your wonderful family and I want to apologize to Millie for the horrible way I talked to her on the telephone. I was wrong. I only hope both of you can forgive me."

"No problem, mother." That wasn't the answer Marsha wanted, but she knew she'd have to pay the piper, until they saw that she was a more lovable person again.

They all went into the house. Millie was coming down the steps carrying the baby. They all met in the vestibule. One thing Marsha had overcome was shyness. She didn't hesitate walking toward Millie. She was half crying, half smiling when she reached them. "Oh Millie, you are beautiful. J.B. why didn't you tell me Millie was so lovely. And this small replica has got to be Jamie. He looks just like his father. It's almost uncanny, the resemblance is astonishing." Little Jamie smiled at this strange woman and stretched his arms out to her. "May I?" She asked Millie

Millie handed the baby to his grandmother who by this time was crying unabashedly. Jamie took his small hand and wiped at her tears and puckered up to cry too. "Sorry Jamie, I'm really happy to see you. Don't cry, Sweetheart. Your Grammy is just a silly sentimental old lady." Marsha smiled through her tears, thus reassuring Jamie.

Craig put his arm around her and they both looked adoringly at their grandson.

J.B. and Millie's eyes locked. His dad had been telling him that his mother had changed, but he'd never believed it. He still didn't.

Craig and Marsha walked further into the house and as most of their guests did, they headed for the lanai. Craig took Jamie from Marsha's arms and lifted him high up into the air like he'd done to his Daddy years ago. Jamie screamed with glee.

Marsha took that opportunity to talk to Millie. "Millie, I'm sorry I talked to you that way on the phone. I was at the time acting like a genuine, certified asshole. Pardon the language. I've mended my ways. Will you forgive me?" She gave Millie that endearing smile that had captured Craig's heart many years ago. It still hadn't lost its effectiveness as Millie opened her arms and the two women embraced.

Still J.B. had his reservations. Tom, the stable boy dropped Terry off and she came running up through the back yard, Her long hair flying wild. She was out of breath when she reached the family, but immediately ran over and hugged her grandfather. Then she kissed Jamie on the mouth, "Hi squirt, love you." She turned to Marsha, grinned at her and Marsha opened her arms to this beautiful young woman who looked so much like her mother.

In the days that followed, J.B. became convinced. There couldn't have been anybody happier to see his parents together, and his mother, whom he could barely remember before she changed, was normal and wonderful. He hadn't known his mother had been a horsewoman and J.B. and she often took long rides together and talked. At one of their favorite spots: a was the bench overlooking the ocean.

That Saturday night, Millie invited Carl and Carrie to dinner so they could get acquainted with each other again. Carrie had never met them, but Carl had a bad memory of Marsha. The dinner was a success and the two sets of grandparents talked incessantly of Jamie and Terry.

It was at the dinner table, when J.B. announced to them that they were going to be grandparents again in a little over five months, and it was suspected that Millie was carrying twins this time, a boy and a girl. They were ecstatic. Carl and Carrie planned on staying the night and making a weekend visit out of it. The two couples got along well and it made J.B. ponder as he observed his own happy parents and marveled at the difference in Millie's parents.

Why in hell hadn't they got this kind of help years ago? Before they caused all this heartache for their families. He made a mental list to listen to the young people he was involved with that had dysfunctional families. They should get help before they wreaked so much havoc on their loved ones. There was such a need. Maybe he could get both sets of parents to help like Millie was, doing. The endless suffering could have been avoided if they had gone into counseling years ago. It was a comfort to know that Susan, Gus, Millie and he had reached their impasse. They might make mistakes rearing their children, but would never damage them emotionally.

J.B. leaned into Millie and asked, "It's hard to believe, isn't it? After the hell they put us through, now everything is hunky-dory. Why couldn't this have happened years ago.

"Do you think it's all over? Hell it's only been a matter of months after years of that behavior. They can't be 'cured', can they?" J.B. raised his eyebrows in total disbelief.

"From what I've read on it, actually it's not over. They'll probably suffer many relapses. New behavior has to become habitual. They've just got a real good start."

"Look at your Mother, Millie, what do you think? You only have to look at the two of them together. I'm surprised they were separated as long as they were. When she left Carl, he was motivated to change. Now that she's back with him, will it start all over again?"

"Wait until I check my tarot cards, or have my next revelation. Reading minds and predicting peoples' behavior is out of my league, hon." Millie laughed. "I'm just going to enjoy today, remember, life gives no guarantees."

Smiling and holding hands, Millie and J.B. joined their parents. Millie whispered an aside. "Maybe we can give them enough grandchildren, so that it'll keep them occupied and won't get into any more mischief."

J.B. hugged her close. "It's really tough bringing up parents, isn't it, Love."

"You got that right. Just ask Terry, she knows."